Another

MARGARET

other Ravenstone mysteries by Janice MacDonald

Sticks and Stones
The Monitor
Hang Down Your Head
Condemned to Repeat
The Roar of the Crowd

Another
MARGARET

A Randy Craig Mystery

By

Janice MacDonald

Another Margaret

Published by Ravenstone
an imprint of Turnstone Press
Artspace Building
206-100 Arthur Street
Winnipeg, MB
R3B 1H3 Canada
www.TurnstonePress.com

Turnstone Press gratefully acknowledges the assistance of the Canada Council for the Arts, the Manitoba Arts Council, the Government of Canada through the Canada Book Fund, and the Province of Manitoba through the Book Publishing Tax Credit and the Book Publisher Marketing Assistance Program.

Printed and bound in Canada by Friesens for Turnstone Press.

Library and Archives Canada Cataloguing in Publication

MacDonald, Janice E. (Janice Elva), 1959-, author

Another Margaret / Janice MacDonald.

(A Randy Craig mystery)

ISBN 978-0-88801-551-8 (pbk.)

I. Title. II. Series: MacDonald, Janice E. (Janice Elva), 1959- . Randy Craig mystery.

PS8575.D6325A66 2015 C813'.54 C2015-903094-3

Not a day goes by when I don't think of and wish for my mom.
Like so much of what I do, this is for her.

Joyce Elizabeth Jaque MacDonald
June 12, 1922 – June 1, 2000

PREFACE

In 1987, several monumental things happened in my life.

I got my Masters of Arts in English, having written a thesis on "Parody and Detective Fiction," which made me eligible to become the mystery reviewer for the *Edmonton Journal* for several years. Writing the monthly column "If Words Could Kill" allowed me to read widely across the genre and develop strong feelings and favourites in contemporary writing just as my research into my thesis had grounded me in the classics of the genre.

That was also the year I became a mother, an occupation which has delighted me twice over, and consistently ever since.

1987 was notable to me also as that was the year I moved from writing non-fiction for sustenance and radio plays for love into working on my first mystery novel—a work that became *The Next Margaret.* The novelty and exhaustion of motherhood took its toll, along with the arduousness of finding a publisher, so the first Randy Craig mystery didn't appear until 1993. It launched well, got good reviews, and went out of print shortly after that, all of the copies presumably being bought up by friends of my mother. It was the story of Randy Craig coming to grad school as a mature student to work on a new Canadian writer, Margaret Ahlers, a writer Randy was sure would carry on the great tradition of Canadian female writers named Margaret (Margaret

Laurence, Margaret Atwood…). Hence the title that I thought was so clever, and everyone else seemed to stumble over.

By the time Randy reappeared in *Sticks and Stones*, she was happily housed at Ravenstone Books, the genre imprint of Turnstone Press. A lot of people assume this is the first Randy Craig adventure, and by rights it ought to be. Randy, a sessional lecturer at the University of Alberta, is clearly aware of her place in the world in this book. And it is also the book in which she meets Steve Browning, her handsome police officer. And, if you pick up any of the books, you note that Ravenstone lists it as first, which is only fitting. No publishing house worth their salt advertises for another's backlist, after all.

The thing is, I was getting tired of people asking me which was the first book, or better yet, what number the one I was working on was. It always got complicated. And on top of that, more and more people were discovering Randy Craig, and proportionally fewer and fewer of them would ever know how it all began. Since *The Next Margare*t had always been what my husband considers such a "zippy little mystery," I began to wonder about finding a way to bring the book back into accessibility.

My publisher floated the idea of turning it into a print-on-demand e-book, so I went back to the original to check it out. It was still a fun story, but I realized that as the years had gone on, my style had expanded. (I think that I used to write so sparingly for two reasons: training in playwriting and a terrific fear of boring readers. Obviously, I have gotten over the latter.) Elements of the plot were contingent on out-of-date technologies, and might need explaining. Turning it as-is into an e-book would be unfair. I countered with the idea of a revisiting of the novel, incorporating the original into a brand new adventure.

And that's how this book came to be. It's again a dyed-in-the-wool academic mystery, in that reunions and homecomings are what universities are made of—mostly, of course, to make rich alumni cough up funds for their alma maters, but also to allow us to indulge in the "best years of our lives." The Alumni Association of the University of Alberta turns 100 the same year as this novel's publication, 2015, which was a delightful coincidence. They also, happily for me, handed out lovely green-and-gold scarves as part of their festivities, which I had blithely created for Leo, anyhow.

The Next Margaret has been trimmed and tightened and in places commented on from the present, and embedded into the fabric of Another Margaret, the book you are about to read. Randy's twenty-year reunion is dredging up memories and incidents from her past—a past she thought dead and buried.

Welcome to the official sixth Randy Craig mystery. I hope those of you who read the long-gone original will enjoy the revisiting and reimagining. If you are coming to this part of Randy's life for the first time, the look back ought to deepen your understanding of her.

Enjoy. And please, buy another copy for any of your friends named Margaret. Wouldn't that be a nice gesture?

Janice

It is the blight man was born for,
It is Margaret you mourn for.

—"Spring and Fall"
Gerard Manley Hopkins

Another
MARGARET

1.

Whoever said "when things get rough, you can always fall back on teaching" probably had not considered the rigours of pedagogy. Of course, they probably had no idea what the word *pedagogy* meant in the first place.

What it had meant for me was, after being out of the sessional world for more than a couple of years, I had to do quite a bit of catch-up on the expectations placed on first-year English students, in order to craft a syllabus that would pass muster with the 100-level overseer. There was far more focus on theory in the first-year courses than there had been when I was a student, or even when I'd been teaching for the few years I had found regular work after defending my thesis.

Then, it was a combination of offering a survey of literary types, examining them with an eye to writing about them in a skilled manner, and determining what literature could tell us about a time period, a culture, or the human condition in general. Mostly, it was about teaching first-year students how to shore up their opinions with reasoning, in order to craft a sensible and legible essay.

I hadn't even grasped literary theory till I was well into the third year of my BA, and I had been immersed in English courses. I wasn't totally persuaded that the youth of today were somehow more sophisticated thinkers. Half the eighteen-year-olds I'd met were pretty sure a "meme" meant "Internet cat picture."

I didn't complain too much, though. If theory, rhetoric, and literature, in that order, was what they wanted, that is what they would get. And I knuckled under and tossed in a little Derrida, Foucault, and Saussure with my punctuation tips. I must have done something right, because I'd been offered a full roster of courses for this, my second year at Grant MacEwan University.

I was just so happy to have courses to teach, I probably would have smiled and nodded and agreed to put in two weeks of Russian grammar. My stress nightmare around exam time had always been that I had somehow enrolled in Russian 100 and yet neglected to attend the course, but still had to write the final. Once I began teaching, the nightmares had shifted to me having to teach Russian 100, with no facility for the language beyond the ability to say "thank you" and a vague grasp of the Cyrillic alphabet. In my dreams, I had not taught the class or indeed even found the classroom till the last week of term (somehow it was always situated behind the boiler room in the Biological Sciences Building) and I had to bring a very placid group of students, who had apparently continued to attend hopefully each day, up to speed in time for the final.

Nightmares where I was beholden to people always made me more anxious than ones where I was being chased down long hallways by a knife-wielding maniac, and the Russian 100 dream never failed to wake me up sweating and shaking. There hadn't been too much to cause nightmares otherwise. My friend Valerie was two doors down the hall, the Grant MacEwan English Department held full-scale meetings every second month, and the secretaries and the chair, Katherine West, were always very helpful.

I taught three classes that first term and two the second. I was pretty sure that my schedule had been made up of the courses no one else wanted, since I had two 8 a.m. classes, and a 3:30-till-5 p.m. class on Tuesdays and Thursdays. That meant that my break between classes on those two days was six hours long, which was way more office-hour-timing than anyone required, but I was just so happy to get a foot back into the teaching door that I had agreed to the pickings. It seemed as if I had proved myself worthy, since I wound up with a nicer schedule this fall.

Denise had been annoyed on my behalf, anyway. "What horrible times for classes. But you know, those kids who do sign up for the 8 a.m. classes will be the lucky ones."

She could smile. She had tenure and an office in the Humanities Building at the University of Alberta overlooking the glorious North Saskatchewan River Valley. As far as academe went, Denise was in the catbird seat. Her book on Shakespeare's fools was being published by Routledge in the fall and she had been awarded a medal of distinction for her teaching earlier in the year. I didn't begrudge her any of it; she was my best friend, and besides, she'd had a hell of summer the year before.

I was probably dredging up these memories from last year because we were sitting at the exact same table on the patio of the Highlevel Diner as Denise and I had occupied a short twelve months ago. I checked my watch. As nice as it was to sit in the warm August sun and discuss guaranteed paying work, it would be best to drink my iced tea and head home to get the rest of this year's syllabi done. Denise waved away my offer to pay.

"We're celebrating. Oh, oh, oh, I just about forgot! I have news for you that's really going to make you want to celebrate!" She rummaged in her elegant green-and-hibiscus-flowers canvas bag, and pulled out a piece of printer paper. "Look what I found in *Quill and Quire*'s 'Omni' this morning! The minute I read it I knew you were going to be thrilled."

She pushed the page to me.

"Undiscovered manuscript found" read the headline and the first line of the article sent a chill up my spine. "*Seven Bird Saga* marks a fifth book for Margaret Ahlers, the elusive writer who died prior to the release of what was assumed to be her final work, *Feathers of Treasure*. The new title is being published by Scrimshaw Scripts, an imprint of McKendricks."

It was impossible for there to be a fifth book, and I knew it. What the hell was going on?

"She died when you were doing your thesis, right? How crazy is it that they'd find another posthumous manuscript?" Denise didn't seem to notice my shock, or was just attributing it to happiness that I would soon have another Ahlers book to read and revel in. After all, I had done my thesis on the woman.

"What's more, I just heard that Leo is thinking of coming

to town for Homecoming, to celebrate our landmark reunion from grad days. This is going to be a great year, Randy. Just like old times!"

Just like old times, right. Of course, old times to most folks held no memories of death. Sometimes memories weren't all they were cracked up to be. I had been leery about agreeing to help Denise with her Twenty Year Class Reunion for Homecoming Week in the first place, since, evidence to the contrary, from all the this-time-last-year reverie I'd just been indulging in, drowning in nostalgia was not something I delighted in.

Denise had often tried to get me to join her on her treks to antique malls, which were really just zones for organized boomer hoarders, filled as they were with *Partridge Family* lunchboxes and Etch-a-Sketches. She would flip eagerly through bins of old vinyl and lovingly haul home old Pyrex loaf pans, because they reminded her of ones her grandmother had used. I ended up needing to stop at the pharmacy on the way home for antihistamines from all the dust kicked up on our sojourns down memory lane.

And now she wanted to invite everyone from our grad years back to revel in the fact that we were all old, but not yet dead. Denise, of course, looked great, but I was pretty sure most of us were going to look a lot more pear-shaped and a little less golden than the last time we had seen each other. After all, we were self-selected readers and researchers, activities mostly done in a sedentary position.

Some of my past research, that involving the works of Margaret Ahlers, had involved a whole lot more than just sitting around reading, it was true. But all of that, like the author, was long dead and buried, I had assumed.

But now there was a fifth book? Maybe my research, as unconventional as it had seemed at the time, hadn't been thorough enough. It had, however, been thorough enough to get someone killed.

Part of me wanted to delight in the thought of another novel by my favourite writer. After all, everything she had ever written had thrilled me, and the work I had done on my thesis was some of my best effort and achievement ever.

A new Ahlers was like stumbling across a new Salinger, or another Hammett, or an undiscovered Josephine Tey I had somehow missed reading when I had obsessed about her in high school. It was understandable why Denise was so pleased to bring me this news.

Only this was a new Margaret Ahlers, and I found myself channeling Han Solo as I thought: "I've got a bad feeling about this."

2.

Homecoming, officially titled "Alumni Weekend," was the University of Alberta's biggest splash of the year. It was more than merely an attempt to lure rich alumni back to their old stomping grounds, though there were elements of that. Alumni Weekend, which often stretched from the Tuesday prior to the Wednesday after the designated weekend, took place annually at the end of September. There were guest lectures from notable alumni, tours of new centres of excellence in research and additions to the rare books collection, and games, readings, and tea galore in a big tent in the quad. This had been going on for one hundred years now, and this year the Alumni Association was celebrating its own longevity as well as reunions of any special classes.

As usual, they had sent out feelers to people who had graduated ten, twenty, twenty-five, or thirty years ago, and presumably even longer in five-year increments. The ploy was to engage someone who might like to organize a special reunion under the auspices of the Alumni Association, specifically targeting their own class. Dentistry Students of 1952; Agronomists of 1979; that sort of thing. While it was up to any specific group to arrange their own class reunions, if your graduation year fell on a particular decade marker, the Alumni Office usually tried to help out.

We were at the twenty-year marker, give or take. Grad school was funny that way, since your cohort wasn't necessarily starting or finishing at the same time you did. You bonded with PhD students who weren't going to see parchment for another four years while you were defending your thesis the next month. Your officemate could be there for another year, or maybe six if she didn't time out. Seminars you attended held brand new MA students and seasoned PhD candidates. So, we were approximating on the date, mostly on the connection to a very tight group of us who'd all shared office space in the House, a condemned building across the street from the Humanities Building, in our write-up years. Denise and Leo had got their PhDs, and I my MA, but several other people we were inviting had finished the following year, as well. One of my constant companions in grad school days had been a fellow named Guy Larmour, who had received his PhD the year before I finished. He and I had kept in touch for a few years, and then he had fallen off the grid. I wondered if he was in touch with anyone else, and whether he was planning to attend the English Grad Students' party.

Denise, of course, was in charge as the Class Organizer. To my knowledge, it is only ever the prettiest people who think reunions are a good idea to begin with. She had conscripted me to write to people and invite them to come back for a September vacation in Edmonton, a football game, Tuck Shop cinnamon buns and the chance to reunite with people we hadn't spoken to in over a decade. I had tried to demur, citing the fact that I was up to my elbows in preparing for my new classes, but Denise wasn't going to allow any of that. And after all, since I had involved her in all sorts of unsavoury projects over the years, the least I could do was help out with hers. Of course, the "least I could do" were my watchwords. I was hoping to have the flu that weekend, and not have to rehash a lot of forced banter and bonhomie. Most of my grad days had been filled with worry that I wasn't going to snare an advisor, and then when I found one, the fear that she was going to kill me.

Denise was one of those golden scholars who had written up with lightning speed, defended early, snagged the one tenure-track job offered that year, published her dissertation, which then went on to become a minor bestseller in academic circles, and settled into becoming a respected Shakespeare professor. No wonder she wanted to host a twenty-year reunion; she was the poster child for a successful academic career.

I, on the other hand, had come back to grad school in my thirties to do an MA, with the concept of teaching at the introductory or college level, and ended up becoming a gypsy sessional, forever scraping out a living from three classes a term. When that dried up from time to time, I had found work in other niches of the university—online teaching, the Centre for Ethnomusicology, the Rutherford House Historic Site, the summer programming tied to the Drama Department—anything to pay the rent while using my skills. And what were my skills, anyhow? I was trained to research and read for hidden meaning; I could determine and show clouded thinkers what they needed to do to communicate more clearly; and I could stay the course until I had closure. It was as if the maxims of Thomas King's *Dead Dog Café Comedy Hour* had been written for me: "Stay calm. Be brave. Wait for the signs."

While I wasn't begrudging my friend her golden life, and on the whole was pretty satisfied with my own, there was absolutely nothing I felt like showing off to a crowd of people whose names I was having trouble recalling. My involvement in this reunion was strictly for Denise's sake. She was appreciative, even though she couldn't quite grasp my diffidence about finding out what everyone was doing these days.

The thing was, unless I was directly involved in something, I didn't honestly think it pertained to me. Really, my need to know what people were doing usually limited itself to fictional characters. Of course, now that there was rumour of a new book by Margaret Ahlers, the past might be something I wasn't going to be able to ignore.

It had been the first Ahlers book that had lured me into the whole concept of going back to grad school and ensnared me into a secret I hadn't shared with another living soul. That secrecy, which had eaten at me for a few years, had ceased to bother me after a while. However, with Denise and Homecoming and now this *Seven Bird Saga*, the past was looming up to swallow me whole.

I don't think I regretted my choices, but while a lot of good had come from my decision to return to school, such as bringing me back to Edmonton from Toronto and forging my friendship with Denise and eventually meeting Steve, it had been a lot to deal with. That's what you get for chasing dreams. In fact, it had been around this time of year that I'd just arrived and was busy getting my sense of balance.

No wonder they schedule Alumni Weekend for the fall; there is something hazy in the air, the sun moves subtly to the south with each passing day. It must approximate the fuzzy lens that moviemakers employ as they begin flashback sequences, because the capacity to fall into nostalgic reverie was looming everywhere I looked. Even with all the changes being wrought in post-double-boom Edmonton, you didn't have to squint too hard to recall what had been where a couple of decades earlier, when I had returned to Edmonton as an adult.

My first apartment in Edmonton had been a basement suite in South Garneau. Dingy but affordable, I had tried to make it seem cozy with some bright cushions, a couple of prints on the walls and a multicoloured throw rug over the old broadloom. At the same time, the blissful, golden fall had turned into an early pre-winter, and I recalled wondering if I was doing the right thing after all.

I'd bought a down-filled coat at the Army and Navy. I looked about as fashionable as any well-dressed member of a polar expedition. It did nothing for my appearance, but it warmed my bones. And all this for an MA in English Literature.

When asked why I was embarking on this degree by old friends and colleagues, it was hard to respond. I hadn't been doing too badly as a freelance writer, times being what they were. When the jobs came along, they usually paid pretty well, and I had been getting a decent share of the ever-decreasing pie. The trouble was, I was getting tired; tired of the grubbing around producers and editors for work, tired of never feeling financially secure enough to refuse a job. I had just wanted to come in out of the cold for a while.

I had also loved the idea of going back to university, this time on my own terms. I've always been a nut for research; I count libraries and archives among my favourite places. I'm the sort of person who reads whole pages from the dictionary on the pretext of finding out where to hyphenate "reification."

Besides, I finally had a thesis topic.

I'd been doing a stint of book reviewing when I'd run across Margaret Ahlers' first novel. By the time the weekly paper ran my rave, my opinions had been both pre-empted and confirmed by the *Globe and Mail* and the *New York Times Book Review*. The confirmation almost made up for my "also-ran" status.

> *One for Sorrow,* a first novel by Margaret Ahlers, is a work to treasure by a writer to be reckoned with. The playfulness with which she handles the shifting sands of a seemingly transparent relationship is matched by her artful and deceptively simple use of language. To say that Canada has found its Iris Murdoch would be reductive. Ahlers is a new voice, a fresh voice, and a welcome voice.

I couldn't have said it any better myself, and if I could have, it would be me who was writing for the *New Republic* and not Anne Tyler. All I knew was that I wanted to write about this author. I wanted to immerse myself in her style and delve into the intricacies of her imagination. And, although I knew it wasn't fashionable academic practice any more, I wanted to find out everything I could about her as a person.

Immersing and delving were no problem. Finding out anything about Margaret Ahlers was a different matter. All the dust jacket provided was, "*One for Sorrow* is Margaret Ahlers' first novel. She is presently at work on her second." There was no chatty bio and no picture-with-a-pipe-and-typewriter on the back cover. There wasn't even a dedication.

Little things like this do not deter the truly dedicated snoop. On the ground that I was planning a feature story, I called the publishers, McKendricks and Sons. They were unctuous and available, since free publicity is never frowned on, until I mentioned the author I was interested in. The voice on the other end of the line had then become distinctly chilly. Any more frostiness and she was in danger of falling into cryonic suspension. Telling me they couldn't divulge personal information about their authors, she had suggested I write to Ms. Ahlers care of their address.

I wasn't quite sure what to do after that. While my bluff had seemed fine over the phone, I wasn't so confident about committing in writing to the idea of a mythical feature. While I was mulling over my next move, the phone at my elbow rang. This was apparently my day for talking to book companies. My friend Garth Johnson, whom I sometimes referred to as "my publisher" when I was trying to impress people, had a job for me. The next thing I knew, I was up to my armpits in memories, ghosting the autobiography of a fellow named Jimmie Cardinal, one of the last riverboat pilots to ply the waters of the Athabasca.

In the six months that followed, my curiosity about Margaret Ahlers was relegated to the dustiest corner of my mind. I was busy embellishing the rather meagre facts and sifting through the outrageous fictions it had taken Jimmie Cardinal seventy-two years to weave, too busy to fixate on a mysterious Canadian author. Most of Jimmie's stories involved buxom lady bartenders. The bits about the bars admittedly had a certain ring of truth to them. Maybe it had something to do with the background ambience of the tapes onto which Jimmie had dictated his wild tales. I could almost smell the spilled beer emanating from the terrycloth table coverings as he rambled through my headphones. I'm not a real fan of taverns, so it surprised me that I was growing rather fond of the silly old codger. As a token of my affection, I left in the yarns about Lucy of McMurray and Jennie from Fort Chip. Sometimes the story is the ambience, after all.

3.

I'd cut my ties with the *Gazette* by the time *Two for Joy* came out, so I'd had to shell out the $22.95 from my own pocket. While I have no compunctions about buying books, I can usually resist the urge until they appear in paperback. Not that time. My need to read Ahlers' second novel was substantially greater than my desire to retrieve my suede jacket from the cleaners or my compulsion to renew my subscription to *The Malahat Review*. Besides, I had to absolve myself of the sin of covetousness, and the only surefire way to do that was to just break down and buy the book.

If only I had never read it so I could read it for the first time all over again. It was stunning. She'd made good on all the promises of her first book and then some. Where her first novel had been dazzling, this one was strong and commanding. The voice was sure and powerful. She played with the reader—coaxing and teasing, sometimes infuriating but always alluring. *Two for Joy* was like Pynchon and Thurber and Stoppard and Calvino all rolled into one and at the same time it was a plot-driven narrative. Ahlers was amazing.

I knew what I had to do. I phoned a friend of mine, Sharon Tindle, who is now the chair of her department. At the time, Sharon taught seven to nine courses a year at three different universities in the greater Toronto area, published her requisite articles, and was kind enough to lend me her university library card from time to time. Also, as the only person I kept in touch with from my undergrad days, she was my only remaining contact within academe. I made an appointment to "do that lunch thing" with her on the following Tuesday. She knew I wanted to pick her brains about something, but she didn't mind. After all, I had offered to pick up the bill.

"We should do this more often," Sharon said, forking down her shrimp cocktail. "I haven't seen you since you needed all that history about the Great Lakes."

She was referring to a radio project I'd been hired to write a year or two earlier. It wasn't that I was such a history buff, but it seemed to be where all the freelance money was in those days, especially if you hoped to squeeze any grant money whatsoever out of the government.

"Actually, I want to talk to you about universities, Sharon."

"Really? Is this an exposé, or are you doing another government study?"

"Neither. It's absolutely personal. I want to go back to school, and I thought you might have some ideas about where I should apply."

"You've got to be kidding! You, back at school? I thought you couldn't wait to get out the last time?"

"It's different now," I insisted. "There's a project I want to work on, and—'"

"Don't tell me, I know. I heard all about the budget cutbacks at the CBC."

I remember being annoyed with her superciliousness about my nebulous freelancing career. What right did she have to look at me with such pity; she was only on an eight-month contract herself at the time. I had to resist the urge to point out that fact, though, because I needed her, and antagonizing her was not the best way to ask for a favour. I tried to muster a grin.

"Well, yeah, that's part of it. But the main thing is, there's this writer I want to work on. She's new, so there's bound to still be plenty of scope for thesis material and I thought, why not?" I was treading on dangerous ground; in Sharon's field, it was hard to squeak out another article on *The Beaux' Stratagem*. Luckily, she didn't seem to notice my potential gaffe; I guess she was too caught up in imagining me in a schoolgirl's plaid skirts and knee socks.

"Randy Craig, MA," she mused. "Who'd have thunk it?" She quickly swallowed her last bite of shrimp, roused herself from her state of disbelief, and prepared to give me her full attention. "And who's this wonderful writer?"

"Margaret Ahlers," I said. Just hearing myself speak the name out loud gave me a tingle. I knew I was on the right track.

"Ah, the next Margaret, the Great Canadian Hope," Sharon nodded, a little too smugly for my satisfaction.

"Have you read her stuff?" I demanded.

"Really, Randy—if Bakhtin can get away with stopping at Dostoevsky, I see no reason to justify myself for curtailing my own literary studies with John Gay." Sharon sniffed. "I've heard she's quite spectacular, though."

"From whom? Is anyone working on her already?" I felt like I was fourteen again, lusting after Duncan Winston and hearing that he'd asked Kathy Menzies to the Valentine's dance.

Sharon noted my proprietary jealousy with a smile. "I have seen a couple of articles on her, I think. From a woman out west. Quill, I think, or Quinn. Recently. Well, I suppose they'd have to be, wouldn't they? She is fairly new on the scene."

I was getting confused. "Who's new? Ahlers or this 'Q' woman?"

"Ahlers. No, this woman—I'm pretty sure it's Quinn—has been around quite a while. I'm almost certain I've met her, or heard her give a paper at any rate." Sharon peered at me over her wine glass. "You know, Randy, if you're so het up about working on this Ahlers woman, maybe you should look into working under Dr. Quinn."

This was precisely the sort of information I'd wanted, I knew I could count on Sharon. She promised to find out where Dr. Quinn was on faculty, and to look up the articles she'd written on Ahlers. I could have hugged her. Instead, I cheerfully sprang for dessert and picked up the tab.

Sharon called me a week after our expensive lunch.

"I've photocopied those articles and popped them in the mail to you." Sharon is egotistic enough to never identify herself on the phone. "I've also located Dr. Hilary Quinn, associate professor of English, acknowledged expert to date on the works of that great Canadian novelist, Margaret Ahlers. Seems this Ahlers coming along has done her career a world of good. The only other submissions I can find by her are various *Notes and Queries*. If you ask me, her criticism's a bit stolid; still, it's sound." It must be all those years of lecturing; Sharon's capacity to hold forth without taking a breath was truly impressive.

I finally managed to get in a word. "That's great, Sharon. Thanks so much. I owe you. So, where do I go to study with this woman?"

"I had a feeling you were going to ask that," she chuckled with a condescending tone.

Now that I have lived in Edmonton twenty years, I can see that this is just one of the common slurs people toss at Edmonton—and it's usually people who have never even visited. Having chosen to live in Edmonton rather than just end up here by birth or chance, I found myself being a booster of my city.

Maybe I should look Sharon up online and give her a piece of my mind. Or thank her. Or perhaps it is just enough to think of her as that footnote in my history that got me back into academe and firmly ensconced in Edmonton. Cheaper, too; man, that girl could eat.

4.

There's a standard joke about preparing yourself for an Edmonton winter. You're told to stick your head in a deep freeze and repeat to yourself: "Yes, but it's a dry cold!" At least, I'd thought this was a joke when I'd first heard it, in the middle of September. A few weeks later, I wasn't too sure.

Being a Forces brat, I'd done a longish stint in Lancaster Park as an adolescent, and I had figured I was on speaking terms with Edmonton as a city. The university was brand new to me, though. All I remembered was the Jubilee Auditorium next to the residence towers, and a really boring piano recital I'd been taken to in Convocation Hall. My date had been Howard Davies, a pretentious Grade Niner with illusions of adequacy. The place had been full of Italians who yelled "*Bis! Bis!*" after every number. As I recall, the rest of the known world had been at a now-legendary Three Dog Night concert. That's what you get for being Ms. Nice Guy.

Anyhow, I was unprepared for the campus when I arrived

on the scene. For one thing, it would be hard to tell where the university officially started if it weren't for the "welcome" signs posted along the perimeters. None of the buildings matched. Low-slung, older structures hunched alongside sandstone towers; brick façades gave way to plate glass. It seemed as if the central principle of design had been lifted from one of my grandmother's crazy quilts.

Assorted science buildings sprawled anywhere they liked: Biological Sciences, Agricultural Sciences, Medical Sciences, Clinical Sciences, Earth Sciences, Dentistry, Pharmacy, Forestry. Physical Education had staked out its territory in the western corner of the campus, virtuously distancing itself from the carcinogenic fast-food outlets. One of their buildings was shaped to represent a huge pat of butter. Perhaps they hadn't yet heard about cholesterol.

Maybe it was just my imagination, but the social sciences, humanities and fine arts all seemed huddled together, as if for support, along the eastern front. All the buildings here were attached by enclosed walkways to a long structure named HUB. It was a residence-cum-shopping-centre-cum-universe unto itself that stretched for three city blocks down the eastern edge of the campus, from the central transit stop to the edge of the North Saskatchewan River. Stairwells placed at regular intervals on either side led to a bubble-roofed, enclosed pedestrian mall. HUB boasted a grocery store, a drug store, a laundromat, a bar, several restaurants and food kiosks, a secondhand bookstore, some clothing boutiques, bank machines, knick-knack shops, a video arcade, and several coffee lounges. Student apartments looked out over the mall via colourful cupboard-door shutters. It reminded me of a high-tech medieval street at the time. Since then, of course, the leaking skylight roof has been changed out to a conventional top with high side windows, the flooring has been tiled and most of the idiosyncratic shops have been replaced with chains and franchises. Still, it continues to be a warm way to get from class to class.

The décor wasn't the real draw when it came to HUB mall, though. The daily kaleidoscope of human activity was amazing. At ten minutes to the hour, every hour, a swarm of colour whirled through the corridors, down the sidewalks and across the covered walkways. HUB felt like the Piccadilly Circus of the U of A, if not the New World. You could probably run into everyone you knew—if you could bear to sit there long enough.

There was something disheartening about seeing someone half your age wearing half your yearly budget on her back, though. I took to slinking back to my office with my coffee, at least until I'd had a chance to upgrade my cords and cottons to flannels and cashmeres.

My office was a refuge and haven in all possible senses of the words. I was lucky to be assigned to an office, since I wouldn't actually be teaching till the new year, but since I had a research assistanceship and some essay-marking work to tide me over, I was entitled to workspace. Not that it was a palace. It was furnished with two desks, two bookcases, two garbage cans, one filing cabinet, and a door that locked. At first sight, the second desk scared me; I've never been particularly good at sharing anything, let alone air space. After meeting Maureen, however,

I realized that there wouldn't be any problem. She spent all of two hours a week in the office, during which time she counselled bewildered students. The rest of the time she spent in the library or at home, beavering her way through a massive reading list for her candidacy exams. I never did quite figure out what she was studying, and her dissertation title—"Architectonics in *The Wasteland*"—didn't provide many clues. To tell the truth, I didn't spend many sleepless nights wondering about Maureen. She was pleasant enough when I saw her, but most of all I loved her for her absences. The office quickly became my fortress.

I have always been a big fan of the Second Law of Thermodynamics. Entropy, which most people equate with chaos, denotes to me the contrary. Anywhere you look, you're bound to find at least part of what you're looking for. Perhaps I've only adopted this philosophy as a defence for my sloppy habits. It could be a chicken-and-egg question. Whatever the case, my office soon took on outward manifestations of the organized turmoil that was my mind.

For the turmoil of my mind, there was no solution, but there were plenty of reasons: three graduate seminars a week, a bibliography course which met one hour a week, and a "teaching university English" course that took up another hour a week, and a contract to mark papers and do minor research for two professors in the department. During the breaks, I was trying to fit in a little eating and sleeping. Selfish of me, I know, but then I'm like that. I stopped trying to count sheep. Instead, at the end of a long day, I'd try to recall the reasons why I'd thought university would be less stressful than the real world. I'd usually drop off to sleep after Reason One: Not having any money means not having to balance your chequebook. Welcome to grad student life, Randy Craig.

On top of which, I was still trying desperately to track down and waylay Dr. Hilary Quinn.

5.

Almost the very first thing I'd done after arriving at the Department of English was to sit down and write a letter to Dr. Hilary Quinn, in which I explained my fascination with Margaret Ahlers, made flattering remarks about Dr. Quinn's articles on the subject, and expressed a desire to meet with her—and, perhaps, to work under her. I had contemplated writing to her before applying to the program, but at the master's level, that just seemed too presumptuous. After all, she couldn't very well invite me to come work with her if the school hadn't approved my application first.

The whole rush to get enrolled had been a blur, with deadlines to meet, transcripts to be applied for and sent on, a chesterfield and table to sell, and move to be made—I had received the Department Blue Book, listing all the courses, professors, their specialties and who was teaching what, and Quinn was in there, and it didn't seem as if her schedule was so punishing that she couldn't take on a grad student.

That now seems like such a thin amount of knowledge to base a cross-country move on, but back then I had friends who, on a whim, would drive to Vancouver for a cup of coffee. Being young and stupid has its benefits.

Still, I remember it beginning to scare me when I didn't hear from her right away. It took me three weeks to convince myself that my finely crafted epistle hadn't been inadvertently buried under departmental newsletters. Dr. Quinn wasn't taking the bait.

I wrote another letter. This one was more humble; I was an MA candidate searching for a thesis advisor. Could I make an appointment to see her?

Still no answer. I was beginning to wonder if I'd somehow managed to offend her without knowing who she was. Had I bumped into her shopping cart at the Safeway? Had I barged into line in front of her at the Student Union Bookstore? Was she the woman who had glared at me when I collapsed, exhausted, onto the last free bench space in HUB? If I'd had time to really put my mind to it, I probably could have worked myself into a serious complex.

Luckily, I didn't have time to worry about my own sense of self-worth. I'd just finished marking a set of first-year essays and was starting to organize my thoughts for a presentation in my Canadian Lit seminar. It was tough slogging. Everyone in the seminar seemed to be taking a different critical stance, and as far as I could tell, none of the tacks had anything to do with whether or not you "liked" the story. I was desperately trying to sort out New Criticism (which was considered passé) from narratology (which had little to do with "what" and an awful lot to do with "how"), how to separate deconstruction from structuralism (a stance I had previously thought peculiar to engineers and architects), and how to tell a Leavisite from a Marxist. Some of my fellow students watched my flounderings with contemptuous sympathy, but it didn't honestly bother me all that much. When you come back to school as a mature student, you kind of get a kick out of being called "naïve."

I'd begun to get my sea legs around the department, so I felt comfortable enough to sit in a corner of the Graduate Lounge with a cup of coffee from the drip machine in the corner. Maureen was offering grammatical advice and Kleenex to the under-50% crowd from her class, so it was impossible to get any work done in the office, anyway. Snivelling might be good background music for Chekhov, but it did nothing for my appreciation of Susannah Moodie.

I was immersed in Upper Canada conundrums when a voice broke through the soundscape: "You're Randy, aren't you?"

I bit off my stock reply—"Maybe? What did you have in mind?"—and looked up, nodding, into the biggest pair of green eyes on the planet.

Still nodding, I took in the rest of him. He had dark blond, curly hair arranged in a style someone's mother would call a mop. His long, angular body was covered in a faded plaid shirt, a brown jersey that looked like it had seen better days in 1962, and a pair of blue jeans. His scuffed hiking boots gave the impression he wore them for the right reason. The only thing wrong with the picture was that a knapsack hung from the hand where his guitar case should have been. I twitched my head to clear it; this was the U of A, not the Mariposa Folk Festival. I've always had a thing for musicians, and even for reasonable facsimiles thereof.

"I'm Guy Larmour," the dream spoke. "May I sit down?"

As I slid over on the couch to make room, I realized I was still nodding like a bobblehead. I stopped, feeling heat start to move outward from behind my ears. Guy didn't seem to notice; he was too busy folding himself onto the couch. He stuck one leg up on the coffee table and grinned.

I needed an original gambit.

"I haven't seen you around before," I blurted and kicked myself internally. Even to me, that sounded pretty flat. I think that explains why I became a writer in the first place—I always seem to need the safety net of a second draft.

"No, I just came in to get my mail," Guy said without missing a beat. "I'm working at home this year." Working from home in grad school is code for "I got a big wonking scholarship and don't have to juggle teaching or marking while I am adding to the body of human knowledge, sucker." He then went on to tell me all about his scholarship, his study of wordplay and game theory, and his work schedule, as if he were the most fascinating topic anyone could hope to come across. The trouble was, given the options, he was beating C. Parr Trail's chatty sister all to hell.

"What about you?" The green eyes turned on me like headlights on a rabbit. The tips of my ears immediately began to get hot again.

"Oh, the usual. Seminars, marking for profs, and struggling to find a supervisor."

"What's your area?"

It was as if Ali Baba had just hummed the first few bars of "Open Sesame." Out poured everything: my interest in Ahlers, my attempts to get hold of Quinn, my frustrating inability to catch her in her office.

"Well, she's not around till Christmas, is she?" Guy inserted at the end of end of my diatribe.

"What do you mean?"

"She's on some sort of half-leave, I think. Hold on a sec, I'll check it out."

He unwound himself from the contortions of sitting in a human-sized chair and loped out the lounge door.

He was back in a matter of minutes.

"I've just asked in the office. Quinn is on a half-term, unpaid leave until January. They're collecting her mail for her because she didn't want it forwarded. Her teaching schedule next term is Tuesdays and Thursdays, with an evening class on Wednesday nights. Must make for nice long weekends, don't you think?"

I was amazed. I was about to ask how he'd found out all that information in so little time when I caught sight of those green eyes again and connected the dots: the office staff are all female.

"Thank you for taking the time—" I managed to stammer, before I was silenced by the shaking of his head.

"Oh, no you don't. 'Thanks' does not cut it as a reward."

"What does?" I found myself smiling.

"How about pizza? There's a great place a couple of blocks

away called Tony's. Draft beer, thick crusts, gingham tablecloths, candles dripping over basketed bottles. What do you say to seven o'clock?"

I felt more like a cork on a wave than an immoveable object, but there was no doubt at all about Guy being an irresistible force. I felt myself nodding again.

"Great. I'll see you then."

He was halfway out the door when I asked him, "By the way, how did you know my name?"

He turned and flashed a grin. "Oh, I make a point of being well-informed."

I had no trouble believing him. Taking a gulp of ice-cold coffee, I managed to bring down the blush he'd left behind.

Even thinking about that meeting now still makes me feel hot behind the ears. I wondered again if Guy was going to be coming to our reunion, and how I was going to be able to ask Denise without her making a big deal of it. If he wasn't going to be there, I probably wouldn't have to bother telling Steve about him at all. Of course, Steve Browning could likely suss out what I was thinking from just looking at me. I called it his cop sensibilities. He called it my inability to maintain a poker face.

Not that Guy would be any threat to our relationship, of course. Not now. But back then was another matter. Guy had something about him, a charisma that made girls and women want to drop their books and plans and follow. He was a pirate right in the middle of the safety zone. It was as if good girls who had studied hard and toed the line and headed straight to the cloister of higher education were suddenly face to face with a rock star, and they turned into camp followers and groupies as he walked by.

He was constantly trailed by several girls he had taught in introductory English classes. They would fawn and offer to buy him a cup of coffee or a beer. He had the grace to treat them with kindly distraction, flicking them off the way a stallion twitches horseflies with his tail. They drove me crazy, though, mostly because any time I was with him, I could feel their feral hatred aimed at me, as if I was somehow stealing something that didn't belong to me.

Yes, then Guy would have been a threat to any relationship, no doubt. I too had been quite smitten with Guy Larmour, to the point of being dithery and distracted. That first date was a case in point.

You'd think I was dressing for my senior prom for the amount of time it took me to decide which sweater to pull over my cleanest jeans. I was still feeling uncertain as I pushed open the door that had "Tony's" woodburnt in script across it. Guy was already there and waved to me from a table in the back corner of the nicely dim restaurant. As I approached the table, he smiled with a look of approval that made me thankful I'd chosen the rainbow pullover that looked like it was knit out of pipe cleaners. It had cost a whole fifteen-minute radio segment (first draft) at ACTRA rates, but it had clearly been worth every penny. I wear my clothes like armour, and in that sweater I always felt invincible.

"Isn't this place great?" Guy poured me a glass of beer from the pitcher on the table. "I found it the second week I was here, and it's been my hole in the wall ever since."

Tony's was a nice place. I abdicated to Guy's decision about dinner once I'd made sure he hated anchovies, and I took in the place as he ordered for us. There were enough patrons scattered around the room to put some trust in the food, but nobody close enough to intrude on our dinner. Music was playing softly on a stereo; I couldn't quite put a name to it—Telemann or Mozart, I thought. The waitress left the table, and I felt Guy's attention turn back on me. There was something unnerving about the way he looked at a person, as if he was calculating checkmate six moves ahead.

"So, why grad school?" he shot at me suddenly.

"I thought I'd explained. I want to write a thesis on Margaret Ahlers, and this seemed like the best place." I felt my voice fading as he shook his head slowly.

"No, I don't think that's it," he said. "There's something about you that doesn't jibe with the whole student set-up."

There was a moment where I wasn't clear on whether I should feel flattered by his interest and focused insight into my character after the fifteen minutes he'd known me, or irritated. "What am I then, a spy?" I wasn't sure whether it was his omniscient attitude that was nettling me, or the fact he'd seen right through my pose. I wasn't all that sure I belonged in academe, but I didn't think it shone like some neon mark of Cain.

Guy seemed to think it was funny. "I can see it now—Comrade Randy reports that they use an obscure nine-point grading system at U of A! No, I didn't mean that you're here for some ulterior motive. It's just that I sense you're on some sort of mission, rather than just jumping through hoops to get a few extra letters to put at the end of your name on a business card. Missions aren't all that common in the English Department, in case you hadn't noticed."

"I'm surprised you're not in the Psychology department, putting your interpersonal skills to better use." My words sounded archer than I'd meant, and I immediately regretted them as I saw Guy's smiling face take on a mask-like quality.

"Sorry," he muttered. "I wasn't meaning to pry."

"Of course you weren't," I said, treading water and trying to get back to the comfortable island of conversation we'd been on just moments before. "It's not that I mind, either. Actually, it's quite flattering to be the focus of attention. It's just that no one likes to feel absolutely transparent to total strangers."

"I wouldn't call us total strangers," Guy interjected. "Total strangers do not share Tony's Bacon, Cheddar Cheese and Green Pepper Specials."

"Forgive me, I was wrong," I chuckled. "You belong in Law, not Psychology." I gave him a mock salute with my beer glass. "I suppose that makes us kindred spirits of a sort. You're an attorney in scholar's clothing, and I'm some sort of Moonie in search of a degree."

"This isn't fair," Guy pouted. "Where I come from, I'm usually allowed to be the life of the party." He gave me another quick, penetrating glance. "I was serious before. You're after more than an MA, aren't you? You can tell me—I won't let on to the rest of the flock."

"Would they even listen to the black sheep?"

"Who's the psychologist now? I guess you're right, though.

I've never been sure whether I chose the role or adapted to it once it was thrust upon me." He reached across the table and gave my hand a quick squeeze. "I'm glad you turned up, Comrade. It's been lonely here at the top."

The pizza arrived just in time to keep me from making a stupid remark. As I chewed through the mass of molten cheese, I was glad I hadn't spoken up. It struck me that Guy had been speaking the truth about himself. I'd sneaked a peek at his dissertation proposal in the file in the mailroom earlier in the afternoon. On first read-through it had seemed very scholarly, with references to Huizinga and Nabokov and Barthes. There was something about the tone, however, that made me give it a second read. I couldn't be certain, but I had a growing suspicion that Guy Larmour was making a game out of game theory. Anyone who could pull that off, in what struck me as a rather conservative department, had every right to preen a bit. Guy's words broke into my thoughts, and I realized that I hadn't been the only one doing some clandestine research that afternoon.

"I picked up *One for Sorrow* at Audreys today," he was saying, "but *Two for Joy* isn't in paperback yet, so I checked it out of Rutherford Library. I assume you won't be needing the library copy?"

Startled, I assured him that I had my own copy.

"Why so surprised?" Guy laughed.

"I just didn't think you'd be so interested in a relatively new Canadian author."

"Well, to tell you the truth, as far as I'm concerned, Ahlers can go hang. What I am interested in is a relatively new Canadian grad student, and the way to any student's heart is through her research."

"What about her stomach?"

"Pizza was my backup strategy," Guy admitted.

"Is everything a game to you?" I asked, with more curiosity than condemnation.

"Pretty much. In the long run, it makes it easier to stay clear-headed if you keep the rules in mind."

"I sense that you take play pretty seriously."

"Indubitably," he remarked. "In fact, as you get to know me better, you'll find that I take everything pretty seriously."

"Ha. Well, as far as the research goes, I appreciate the gesture. But I have to warn you that I'm rather jealous of my work."

"Point taken. I'll just read the novels so I can follow what you're saying. I promise not to butt in." Guy crossed his heart.

I laughed at his little-boy seriousness. "I mean it, Guy. Stick to the pizza gambit. I have never felt a need to discuss my work, and I'm not about to start now."

Oh gosh, as I think about it now, I shake my head in assuming at the time that Guy was the arrogant one at that table, thinking I could do everything on my own. If it hadn't been for him, I don't know what I'd have done that year.

I was praying he wasn't going to show up for the reunion. If just thinking about him dredged up all these memories, what would come of seeing him face-to-face? We had lost touch over a decade ago. Either I had stopped sending him Christmas cards, or he'd stopped responding. I couldn't quite remember how the ties had unravelled, but I was okay that they had.

Memories of him were so tied to my thesis time and all that entailed that I wasn't sorry to cease to be reminded of him. Regardless of Denise's present absorption with reunions, the past wasn't somewhere I liked to dwell.

I doubted Guy wasted even a second thinking of me. He had likely just moved on to another set of acolytes. Guy studied game theory for a reason; it was all a game to him, with people as the pawns, not the players. I had amused him for a year or so, so it was worth his while to read a new Canadian author to make me happy. I wondered if Guy still read Ahlers, and if he knew about the new book? And if so, what did he know? Or would he even care? I wondered briefly just where Guy was nowadays and what he was up to.

All of a sudden, I was thankful I had agreed to help Denise with her Homecoming class reunion, after all. I could satisfy my curiosity without appearing to be opening old wounds.

6.

Recalling that first term, it was just as well Dr. Quinn hadn't been on campus to greet me with open arms in September. I was barely keeping my head above water with all the work I had to churn out for the grad courses. In the materials they handed out, it is said the expected time for completing an MA is one calendar year. I'd heard of two people who'd actually managed it, and that was probably because their seminars dovetailed into their thesis topic so nicely that papers for classes could do double duty as chapters for their thesis. In reality, I'd come across about thirty frantic individuals that first year, juggling writing for courses with reading for courses with teaching or marking for first-year courses with trying to come up with a thesis topic and advisor, all looking forward to at least one more year of research and writing, to bring it in under two years. In this instance, I had the jump on them. I'd already drafted three different thesis proposals. Once I could get out from under my seminar commitments, I was raring to get started.

At the moment, I was leaning toward a study of regionalism and the land in Ahlers' novels. I'd once heard Robertson Davies talk about the fact that Canadian writers were sitting in the oldest land in the world, geographically speaking, and that—being such sensitive types—it had to make a difference to their writing. I suppose he was talking about the Canadian Shield, but I figured it might hold true for western writers too, the way the topsoil had been blowing away that year.

A study of the regional quality in Ahlers' work made sense as a project for two reasons. First of all, I hadn't really noticed a particular regional flavour to the novels on first reading, although they were deliberately set in the northwest. Secondly, no one had written about Ahlers and regionalism yet. There were a couple of articles about the two novels appearing here and there, but so far the mysterious Dr. Quinn was still the so-called expert on the topic. I'd tried to winkle an address for her out of the secretaries, but it seemed that not even Guy's abundant charms could work miracles. Quinn hadn't left an address. I determined that hounding her was probably not the best way to begin a working relationship anyway. While she continued to hover in the ether, I devoured books on regionalism whenever I wasn't cramming for Canadian Lit or Narrative Studies, or skimming through the Twentieth Century Novel, or marking sixty-two essays on *Pride and Prejudice*.

In fact, I'd almost completely forgotten about Hilary Quinn until two things arrived in my pigeonhole to remind me. One was a memo informing us that we had two weeks to submit our approved thesis proposals. The other was a copy of Margaret Ahlers' third novel—*The Children of Magpie*.

I rushed through the paperwork for my thesis proposal with a codicil attached, explaining how I hadn't been able to contact Dr. Quinn. I had checked with the Grad Chairman about this; he was understanding and said it would be approved conditionally. *The Children of Magpie* was burning a hole on the edge of my desk, but I'd promised myself I wouldn't touch it until I had my research paper in for one seminar, and the final exams marked for the profs I was assigned to. It was December 16 before I could relax enough to enjoy the yuletide season.

Christmas spirit on campus had, however, dribbled away to nothing by that time. The department party had wisely been held on the final day of classes, because exam time was characterized by excess activity in the photocopying room and dwindling presence in the halls. By the time my papers were turned in, most everyone had faded away to sunny shores or family hearths. I lugged my notes and Ahlers' new novel back to my basement suite, bought a mickey of rum and a litre of store-brand eggnog, and settled into my cocoon.

Guy had left a message on my phone machine, something about skiing in Whistler. Since my idea of winter sports is to burrow into woolen underwear and hibernate, I wasn't even sure of which direction he'd gone. The pang of realizing I wouldn't be able to give him his present on the actual 25th was lessened by the thought of the new novel on my lap. I snuggled under an afghan and cracked the spine the way they'd taught us in Grade

Six, just to prolong the anticipation. In matter of pages, I too was on holiday.

Magpie felt like a throwback to the style of the first novel. Whereas *Two for Joy* had been the exploration of the weird symbiotic relationship of two women, the new book was again a one-hander. The character, Isabel, would often share the role of narrator, mostly when looking back on her life or forward into her dreams. The present of the novel unfolded in a limited omniscient. Ahlers seemed to be playing with the concept of actions of the past informing and shaping the present. It was hard to grasp at first, sort of like watching Harold Pinter's *Betrayal* and then fusing it with its mirror image running forwards again—except that the characters all knew what would happen this time. I wasn't up on the contemporary writers well enough to know whether anyone else was writing like this, but whatever the case, I was certainly glad that Ahlers was.

I closed the covers reluctantly when I reached the end. It had taken me two days to read the novel. I set the book on the side table, made myself a grilled cheese sandwich, then walked around the apartment picking up the things I'd strewn about over the past forty-eight hours. I found myself staring blankly out my kitchen window at the snowdrift in the window well. I couldn't shake myself out of the story; I felt like an iron filing near a magnet. With a sigh, I threw myself back on the couch and picked up the book.

I was about a third of the way through it for the second time when the phone rang. It was my parents calling from Australia to wish me a Happy Christmas. They were giggling a bit giddily because they'd been up half the night trying to figure out the time-zone equivalents. Their Elderhostel course was going well, they'd reconnected with several of the people they'd met in Spain the year before, and they were shipping me a sheepskin vest.

"I hope you're not spending Christmas alone, Miranda," my mother was saying. She always uses my full name whenever I become an object of concern to her. It would be too costly—both in terms of long-distance charges and worry—to explain to her that being along didn't bother me. It was an old argument between us, anyhow. My mother still tried to unshackle herself from her '50s mindset, but she still couldn't fully accept that I might choose to remain single. I assured her that I was going out for brunch with a friend, and in a way I was; I could take *The Children of Magpie* with me for dim sum.

My folks promised to send postcards of Ayers Rock, which back then was what we were all calling Uluru, and rang off to throw a shrimp on the barbie.

I spent the rest of the week doing laundry and finishing a short paper on Marian Engel for my Canadian Writers seminar.

On December 29, Dr. Quinn phoned. We arranged to meet on January 3.

7.

I remember thinking Dr. Hilary Quinn was not a bit like I'd been picturing her for the previous six months. I'd had visions of a rather frail, older woman with her hair up in a bun. Don't ask me why; maybe my brain's casting director lumped all bookish characters—professors, librarians, authors, bookstore clerks—into one type. All I know is that Central Casting had to do a massive reshuffle when the office door swung open.

Dr. Quinn was just average height for a woman in her late forties or early fifties, but she held herself with such amazing posture that she seemed taller than me. She had shoulders I'd have killed for, the Joan Crawford kind but without the padding, and short dark hair that resembled anthracite with a few strategically placed veins of silver running through it. She wore a large red sweater over a black and red tartan skirt. I was going to have to fire my casting personnel; Dr. Quinn was altogether the quintessential professor.

"Miranda Craig?" There was something in her tone that kept

me from asserting my preference for Randy. I used Miranda, the name on my birth certificate, only when necessary, like on university applications. Randy was a better name to publish under, more androgynous. I'd rather be mistaken for a man, which often worked in my favour, than spend time fighting the preconceived notion of Shakespearean naïf.

Quinn smiled as we shook hands, but her face didn't light up. Fine by me, I figured. If cool and reserved was the way we were going to play it, I could try that. She motioned me into her office and closed the door before resuming her place at her large desk. I just had time to catch a quick scan of the room—floor-to-ceiling bookcases on each wall, two massive sideways filing cabinets, a few plants on the window ledge, a personal computer in the corner, and some very nice paintings—before Dr. Quinn focused in on me again. She caught me with my eyes on a painting of a lake that seemed to have about seventeen distinct horizons as part of the design.

"Interesting work, isn't it? It's a McNaught."

"I beg your pardon? I didn't catch the name."

"McNaught. Euphemia McNaught. A Peace River Country artist. Student of the Group of Seven."

"She's very … engaging," I stumbled. Art has never been my strong point. I feel as awkward discussing aesthetics as I would declaiming a wine as having "an unpretentious yet amicable bouquet." I was hoping that Dr. Quinn would let me off the hook, and she did.

"You're rather older than I expected from your note."

I tried not to bridle as I nodded. I'd forgotten that aspect of the career academic, the sort that teethes on Milton and has their PhD at fifteen. Of course I was older than Quinn had expected; how could she possibly imagine starting an MA at thirty? She'd probably been in the biz for at least six years by the time she was my age.

I plastered on a placating smile. "I spent some time freelancing before coming back to do an MA."

She nodded in a businesslike way and folded her hands together on top of her desk. "So, why don't you tell me what you'd like to work on? I gather it's something to do with Margaret Ahlers."

This was it. I took a deep breath and began to ramble immediately. After about five minutes of garbling terms like "regionalism," "space," "terrain," and "inner reality," my diatribe trickled to a halt. To my surprise, Quinn looked interested.

"I see. You want to tackle the metaphor of place and belonging in Ahlers' fiction within the context of Canadian regional dictates. Not a bad idea. There would seem to be enough scope for an MA thesis there. What graduate seminars are you attending at present?"

We went on to discuss my timetable and schedule, plotted a time to meet on a semi-regular basis, and ended up, forty minutes later, in the same place we'd started—in the doorway, shaking hands. I bounced down the hallway toward my own little hideyhole at the other end of the building. Things were rolling right along at last.

Or so I thought. Even thinking about it now makes me cringe, after all these years. For someone who prided herself on reading people and situations, I made a complete fool of myself. Too many 1940s college caper movies, I suppose. I should have just stuck to watching *Animal House.*

If I had expected to bask at the feet of the master, I changed my expectations in a hurry. While Dr. Quinn allowed for a meeting every second week, she didn't ever seem too het up over it. She'd sit and listen to my research so far; occasionally she would nod or say, "Hmmmm." I never did learn how to translate those "hmmmms"—they didn't appear consistently enough to denote triumphs or mistakes. After about an hour and a half, Quinn would unfold her legs, which she had wrapped around each other about three times during the course of the meeting, and clear her throat. This was my cue to stand up and say, "I'll see you next time."

She never marked anything except grammatical errors on any of the papers I handed in to her. I narrowed this sparse feedback down to two possibilities: either I was a genius or too stupid to waste intellectual time on. Having the self-confidence of a salamander, I proceeded to get spooked.

Guy was not the rock he thought he was. "Are you sure you've read all her articles? Maybe you've contradicted something she's written."

"Thank you, thank you. This is just what I need to hear. Shall I start humming 'The Volga Boat Song' now, or should I just go out and hang myself?"

"You're getting too worked up about this, Randy."

"Well, I just can't figure her out. One minute she's nice as pie; the next minute, she's staring off into space and ignoring me."

"Sounds like a godgame to me."

"A what?"

"A godgame. You know, one where you are the player, but you don't know the rules. You try to go one way, and the god who is the game-master lops off your arm because you've somehow transgressed an unwritten law."

"How could I have known about it if it's unwritten?"

"Exactly! The god toys with you. Like flies to wanton boys and all that malarkey."

"Do you really see Hilary Quinn as a god?"

"It's not about what I see; it's what Hilary Quinn sees when she looks in the mirror every morning."

"Hmmmm."

"What's that supposed to mean?"

"What? Oh, I don't know. Why don't you ask Dr. Quinn?"

"Why don't I just order more beer instead?"

So there I was. It was mid-March; my seminars were winding down in spirit as the workload increased proportionally. Meanwhile people around me were generally going a little crazy.

I had three major papers to submit, one presentation left to complete (in the course I understood the least), a thesis outline and chapter draft to hand in and two comprehensive exams to mark. I pitied my poor students; even I couldn't remember what we'd covered in September without consulting the syllabus.

Not only that, I was beginning to believe that my advisor was toying with me for her own bizarre amusement. Did I say "other" people were going crazy?

8.

When I am caught up in a project, such as grad school, I tend to turn off my need to stay current, and cease to watch the news or read newspapers. Knowing this, my mother, out of abject fear of my being caught without some vitally important piece of news, had been weaving tidbits into her letters. For some reason, it was the deaths of important people that she kept telling me about. It reminded me of a comedian I once saw who said his grandmother reads the obituaries every day and then crosses the names out of her telephone directory. I suppose that's what we want to hear about, though; it's somehow comforting to keep track of who's fallen out of the race while we're still running.

I didn't have to wait for Mom's letter to hear about this particular obituary. Maureen had thoughtfully left the page on my desk, and Guy came by about twenty minutes after I'd hung up my coat.

"Did you hear?"

All I could do was nod.

"You weren't planning on interviewing her, were you?"

I shook my head.

"Listen, let me buy you a cup of coffee." Guy led me out of the office and down the corridor. I felt numb, so numb that I hardly noticed my knuckles scraping against the stucco of the corridor wall. The architect obviously had his own ideas about the mating habits of English professors; the hallways were treacherous if not navigated single file.

Guy bought coffee, snaffled a table, and sat me down. "Here's to Margaret Ahlers. May she rest in peace."

"Oh, Guy. I can't believe it."

"I know what you mean. After all, her latest book just came out … what? A couple of months ago?"

I nodded. "Just before Christmas. It's not even that so much. I guess, really, it's because her name hasn't become a household word yet. I mean, who even knew what she looked like? There's no signature; no frizzy hair, or bowtie, or kilt, or wolf smile. Who was she?"

"That's not part of the bargain, Randy."

"What do you mean?"

"I mean that, unless you're Truman Capote, you don't write a book in order to become a celebrity. You write a book to communicate the ideas you have committed to the text."

"This is the part where you call me naïve again, isn't it? Because I don't care; I think people really do want to be able to recognize their bards on the street. Movie stars parroting someone else's words are celebrated, so why not those who wrote the words in the first place?"

"I suppose you want to know what Thomas Pynchon looks like, too."

"Damn right. And I want to meet J.D. Salinger."

Guy snorted. I think he was letting me ramble to work through the shock. He probably had seventeen different arguments to prove that the author is insignificant in the true course of events. I stared into my Styrofoam cup, trying to divine an answer to the universe.

Guy's voice startled me because it was so unexpectedly soft. "I was sitting in bed reading and listening to the radio when the news came out that Borges had died. The announcer stumbled over his name—it came out something like Georgie Louise Borgia—but I just started shaking my head because it couldn't possibly be true. Borges wasn't dead, he was right there with me! I'd been re-reading 'Death and the Compass.'"

I looked up at Guy. He was sitting across the table, looking vulnerable and hopeful and so damn nice. The greatest new Canadian literary voice had been silenced, and any hopes I'd had for eventually meeting her were shattered. I felt like someone had taken a cookie cutter and punched it through my chest.

"Guy, please get me out of here. I think I'm going to cry."

I don't remember much more of that day. I probably cried, and it probably wasn't pretty. Guy hovered a bit, then once he was sure I was just going to wallow in my sadness for a bit, left to get on with his writing. Back then, it was all about the work; we just fit our awkward little personal lives in between the chapter breaks.

And speaking of awkward, my next meeting with Dr. Quinn

could probably win, hands down, as *My Most Embarrassing Moment.* We were sitting stiffly, as usual, in her office, the large desk between us. I honestly didn't know what to say. I had mentally attributed to Quinn my grief tenfold for each article she had published on Ahlers. Since she'd really been churning them out, by all rights she should have been prostrate. It said a lot about her sense of dignity that she hadn't cancelled our meeting. I was, however, beginning to think she was made of ice; she didn't even mention Ahlers' death.

Finally, I figured I had to say something. "I caught your interview on CBC this morning."

Quinn tensed slightly.

"I thought it was very respectful of her work, very dignified."

"Thank you."

"It seems so awful to think there won't be any more."

"I beg your pardon?"

"Any more books. It's tragic to think there won't be any more writing by Ahlers."

"Well, I think the scope of your thesis will suffice on the three texts available."

It was like milking an icicle. I couldn't believe the chill in her voice. Maybe it was true what Dr. Ross, another prof in the department, had said: Never choose the writer you adore the most for your thesis work, because eventually you'll wind up hating them. Did Quinn feel antipathy toward Ahlers' writing after all the work she'd done on it? Or did she hate Ahlers herself?

I blurted out my next question. "Did you know her?"

Quinn looked at me for several long seconds without blinking, but I had the feeling I'd hit a nerve somewhere. "Margaret Ahlers? Yes, I was acquainted with her. The Canadian literary community is, after all, not that large."

Quinn was trying to bluff me, I could feel it. After all, I knew from experience how hard it was to get past Ahlers' publishers to gain access to the woman. Somehow I couldn't imagine her just happening to rub elbows with Hilary Quinn at a wine and cheese party.

"What was she like? Was she shy? Did she enjoy the writing process?"

I wasn't prepared for the sudden attack. If I'd been a cartoon character, my features would have melted under the blast. Now I have a standard by which to measure when people say that someone has "laced into them."

Quinn laced into me. "Really, Miranda, this is a literature department. Surely you don't expect to turn a thesis seminar into an excuse to indulge in coffee-room gossip. Perhaps we should curtail this meeting until you've had a chance to re-examine your priorities. Your confusion at this time is perhaps understandable, but that in no way condones your lack of intellectual rigour. Goodbye."

I collected my notes and blundered out of her office, into the hallway. Somehow, in some way I didn't quite comprehend, I suspected I had just diminished myself in my advisor's eyes. I wasn't sure what I had said to trigger it, but it felt as if Quinn had found me dreadfully wanting.

Quinn cancelled our next two meetings by leaving terse

notes in my pigeonhole. While this made life a little simpler, it also meant I was falling behind schedule on my thesis research. I thought about looking into a change of advisors, but the potential fallout had me worried. The further you go up the educational ladder, the harder it gets to say, "My teacher doesn't like me." Even couched by terms like "personality conflict," it still smacks of pettiness and failure. Besides, in April, absolutely everyone is complaining about something.

The halls were filled with people sobbing quietly on benches. Others were sobbing quietly in bathroom stalls; the lucky ones were sobbing quietly in the privacy of their offices. The unlucky ones did their sobbing on the High Level Bridge. Going crazy in April is common practice in academe; it's the way intellectuals measure the seasons from inside their climate-controlled buildings.

It seemed, though, that Dr. Quinn's sudden antipathy to me was not merely a product of my imagination. Dr. Peters, the graduate chairman, stopped me in the lounge one day. After looking over his shoulder, he asked in a muted tone, "Is there something wrong between you and your advisor?"

The only inheritance I ever collected from my pioneer ancestors was an inordinate desire to conceal my innermost feelings from strangers. I often suspected that a burning ambition to clean my house weekly would probably have been more useful, but my heritage nonetheless kicked in as I looked into Dr. Peters' sympathetic face. "No, not as far as I know. Is there something I should be aware of?"

"No, no—just checking." Dr. Peters' voice seemed to precede him nervously out of the lounge.

The very next day, the associate chairman of the department smiled at me for the first time ever, but I put my unease down to paranoia—until Guy cornered me.

"What has happened between you and Quinn?" he asked brusquely.

"I've been telling you for three months, she's weird. Haven't you been listening?"

"I'm talking about just lately. Did you two have a fight or something?"

"Not really," I said, recalling Quinn's tightly pursed mouth at the conclusion of our last meeting.

"Maybe the things you've been saying about her have got back to her somehow, then."

"Wait a second, what do you mean by 'the things I've been saying about her'? The only person I've talked to about Dr. Quinn is you, Guy."

"All right, all right, don't look at me like that. I haven't said anything, so we can cross that idea off the list of possibilities. I just don't know..."

Guy could be a sweetie. He could also be extremely annoying, especially when holding one of his conversational games for one player. I felt my temper beginning to fray. "You just don't know *what*, exactly?"

He looked slightly startled. "I just don't know why Quinn would turn down a full Summer Research Assistantship for her MA student to help organize a projected biography on Margaret Ahlers. Didn't you know?"

It's lucky I don't have an alabaster complexion, or my

face would have shattered as my jaw hit the floor. I couldn't believe it. No one could be that malicious. No one turns down a free slave, especially not when that slave would be absurdly grateful for the job. What did Quinn have against me anyway?

"You're kidding."

"Sorry, kiddo. That's the buzz among the office staff, and if anyone knows anything around here ... need I say more?"

"Who is she giving the job to?"

"No one, apparently. Says she can handle it, although the powers-that-be believe than an RA would help get the book published all the sooner. They offered, but the little red hen said she'd much rather do it herself."

"And so she did. Well, that puts the kybosh on my working with Quinn." One glimmer of hope began to shine in my brain. "Hey, with all this happening, maybe no one would question me about changing advisors. Peters seemed pretty worried about me the other day. Whaddaya think, Guy?"

"Can't hurt to try. Watch out you don't get stuck with Martin, though. I think there's a sale on him these days; Carrie just got saddled with him as a second reader on her thesis."

"Why would they do that? He's a medievalist, isn't he?"

"Yep."

"But Carrie's working on Norman Mailer."

"Go figure, eh? Maybe they thought there'd be enough of a scatological connection."

I winced. Spending time with Guy when he was in one of these moods could keep you buoyed up for hours if you were already in good spirits—but if you were in low gear, he could be as aggravating as a telephone solicitor—and about as persistent.

I mumbled something about the library, gave him a kiss on the nose, and beat a hasty retreat. I needed time to think about what Quinn had done to me and to my research. I would have given anything to work the biographical angle on Ahlers with her. It would fit right into my personal research, and I'd likely have got a credit on the biography when it did come out, which would bolster my slender curriculum vitae when I began looking for academic work later.

Not to mention, the money would have helped. I was running my prior savings pretty close to the bone. Just to not have to worry about each item in the grocery basket as I budgeted would have been a luxury.

I managed to get a measly two-month RA looking up citations for Dr. Bella Spanner, the chair of the department, who was writing her seminal book on Thomas Pynchon, but her short lists in my pigeonhole came only every other week. I had a feeling the money was a gift from a department looking on at the weird relationship between my advisor and me. I didn't care for the pity, but I had no pride when it came to paying my bills. The research didn't take up too much of my time, and I needed money, so I figured I'd better look farther afield to supplement my income.

I tossed a couple of resumés into bars and cafés between the campus and my basement suite, and landed three nights a week waiting tables at The Library, a basement bar under what had been a high end restaurant in a residential tower just south of the Law Building. The atmosphere was dark and leathery, with bookshelves lining the walls. The books themselves had been picked up in bulk from secondhand stores and auction houses, and were about seventy years out of date, but local businessmen, professors who couldn't be bothered to walk across campus to the Faculty Club and some of the more louche grad students patronized the place, because the conversation was good and the drinks reasonably priced.

Brad, the bartender, was a musician saving up to head back to grad school. I had bought his EP and personally thought he should become the next musical superstar, but he had a thing for James Joyce and perhaps he had looked the chance of long-term security in the eye, like I had. Now that I had chosen academe, though, it seemed far less likely to provide the security I had craved.

Guy would come in at least one of my nights each week, and sit at a table and read or scribble in one of his coil-bound notebooks. We considered this a date night. On my days off, I researched critical work on place in literature, applied for graduate monies, and pored over Ahlers' books, as if I would find an answer to everything between the lines somewhere. I dithered on whether or not to start the proceedings to change supervisors, torn between looking like a whiner and becoming orphaned. It wasn't as if supervisors were thick on the ground, and I couldn't see too many people on faculty wanting to get in Quinn's bad books.

By late June, I had enough in wages and tips saved up to make it through till the end of December, rent and foodwise.

I also received a magic envelope containing a $500 travel grant from Grad Studies to visit the area Ahlers had written about in her novels. Now, I just had to figure out which direction to take.

I felt like Trixie Belden, girl sleuth, as I revisited the notes I'd made. Anything that made a specific reference to place was copied onto an index card people normally used for recipes. If the reference seemed to be fictional, I jotted it down on a pink card. If it was descriptive of an area, it went on a green card. If it was bald fact, it went on a white card.

So far, the only bald fact I had identified was the section in *Two for Joy* where the two fat American tourists make the hitch-hiking girls sit on newspaper in the backseat of their El Dorado and yammer on about the fact that there's no sales tax. That was enough for me to get started. I bought a wall-sized map of Alberta, the only Canadian province without sales tax, and set my mind to narrowing my horizons. That can be hard to do in Big Sky Country, but I had determination on my side—determination, and three ambiguity-laden novels.

Throwing caution and care for my security deposit to the winds, I covered one wall of the kitchen with cork tiles from Canadian Tire. The map was tacked to one side, and various-coloured recipe cards kept it company. While the pink ones moved around a lot, the green ones began to seep upward, consistently moving above Red Deer, the bellybutton of the province. There was no mention of ranchland, badland, or scrub, and very few mountains, except for those sometimes mentioned as "looming on the horizon." The descriptions, as far as my well-thumbed copy of *A Nature Guide to Alberta* was concerned, seemed to be parkland all the way. My focus was heading north and west.

It was the river that clinched it. I'd initially been certain that the river mentioned was the North Saskatchewan, probably because it was the biggest river I'd ever seen. Any river that needs a bridge half a mile long to span it rates right up there in my personal "big" category.

That was before I read about the Peace River.

To give you some idea of how big the Peace is, let me quote a few facts. In graphs of annual water flow, most of the rivers of Alberta are measured in terms of cubic metres. While the graphs occasionally rise to the 200 mark, in July most of the rivers clock in around nil. The Peace River, alias the Mighty Peace, has a graph measured in *thousands* of cubic metres—all year long.

My reading turned up the fact that the Peace River Valley was one of the last areas opened up for homesteading in Canada. There were still people up there who remembered building the log cabin, let alone the sizable number who had been born in one and were still around to tell the tale.

I had no real proof, but something at the back of my brain niggled at me when I thought about the Peace River area. I couldn't quite dredge up the connection, but I knew I was on the right track. I needed actual connection to Margaret Ahlers' books, and I couldn't get that from flipping through the *Canadian Encyclopedia.*

Brad wasn't too happy to see me packing in my apron, but

he understood the reasons. After all, he was planning to head to Dublin for two weeks before classes started in the fall, himself.

The day after Canada Day, I rented a car and headed up Highway 43.

9.

Every time I get behind the wheel of a rented car I question my decision not to own one. I love the sense of power it gives me to know I could point this sturdy machine in any direction and just head off into the great unknown. Of course, most of the everyday elements of car ownership involve getting tied up in gridlock on the Whitemud Freeway, so I was better off renting. A couple of weeks of temporary car culture meant I could get where I needed to go or haul what I needed to haul but not have to worry about annual parking fees. Sometimes the places you needed to get to were a little off the beaten trail, and a bus pass just wasn't going to cut it.

Back then, I wasn't sure what the trail I was heading to find even looked like. All I knew was that I needed to head north. Just thinking back on my naïveté and haphazardness during that whole endeavour makes me want to cringe. Nowadays, I make a list before rearranging furniture. Then, I just grabbed a map of the province and turned the key in the ignition. Even with my general notion that Margaret Ahlers had been writing about the Peace River Country, I realized I was headed for an enormous haystack with only a vague idea of what the needle looked like. With my luck, when I did find it, it would be embedded in my foot.

I stopped in Valleyview for a coffee and reconnoitered with the map I'd found in the rental car's glove compartment. The highway split here, and I had to choose between going north to Peace River or west to Grande Prairie. There was another loop from Grande Prairie through Dunvegan and Fairview to Peace River, so it came down to a choice between travelling clockwise or counter-clockwise. I tossed a coin. Heads—Grande Prairie it was.

At that time, the only place I'd ever seen a live Canada goose was in Kew Gardens in London. The incongruity of it all had surprised me at the time, but not half as much as seeing swans all over this small, northern Alberta city.

Apparently, trumpeter swans migrate to nest in the lakes around the area, and the city council sure seemed dang proud of it. I passed three statues of trumpeter swans on my way to book into the Swan Motel, which I chose simply because it was in the centre of town and looked clean.

After a shower, I decided to stroll down to City Hall to see if I could access the archives and dig up a little local history. The weather was sunny and mild, a perfect summer afternoon. The sun was deceptive this far north, though. I'd mentally estimated the time at 3 p.m. or 3:30, tops, but I was greeted by locked doors and a sign announcing that City Hall closed at four. I checked my watch to find it was closer to five than three. I made a mental note to be back at nine the next morning and headed to the library.

I was figuring on finding a local history section to occupy my time until I could check through the registry, but my eye was caught by the bulletin board just inside the doors of the library. There was a large poster declaiming the merits of an Old Time Country Fair being held at the college on July 1, 2, 3. Crafts, artwork, baking, preserves, and readings from local poets were promised. I turned back to retrieve my car from the motel lot. If I was going to find anyone who knew whether Margaret Ahlers had been part of the local arts scene in Grande Prairie, I had a feeling the fair was my best bet.

Whoever sang "it's all happening at the fair" knew what they were talking about. Inside the rotunda, a woman with a full-scale loom was set up, demonstrating her warp and woof, while a macramé lady was explaining her use of "found art" to complement her hangings. I couldn't imagine just "finding" an entire fan of partridge tailfeathers, but who was I to question the artistic process?

I moved on. Tables were set up as booths down the hall that led to the auditorium. These were laden with cookies, pies, preserves, paper tole, and pottery. Grande Prairie, from all appearances, was a crafts mecca.

I headed for the auditorium. On a table at the doors was a wooden bowl for loose change, a pile of pamphlets indicating the order of performances within, and a few chapbooks that were presumably the published poetry of some of the readers. I was leafing through these with one hand and scrabbling in the pocket of my jeans for some loonies when the woman behind the table spoke.

She asked me if I was enjoying the fair, and whether I was from around the area. I answered yes and no as I sized her up. She was petite and, as far as I could tell, in her early seventies—but then again, she was sitting down and I'm bad with ages. I did notice well-behaved grey hair, a clear complexion, and an ashes-of-roses outfit that coordinated beautifully with the silk scarf draped around her shoulders. She had a lovely smile, too, which she was displaying as we talked.

"How did you happen to hear about the fair?" she asked.

I explained about seeing the poster in the library, and on impulse I told her I was searching for some history on a local author.

This news seemed to delight her. "Oh, I'd love to talk to you about your research. I'm a bit of a history buff myself. Perhaps," she glanced at her watch, "we could get together tomorrow sometime. I'm supposed to be judging the preserves right now, and then there will still be the ribbon ceremony and all the celebrations. Do you have a car?"

I said I did, and she whipped a pamphlet from the top of the pile, flipped it over, and sketched a quick but clear map to her farm with her name—Dorothy Lewis—neatly written in cursive underneath. We arranged that I should "pop by" at about 10:30 the next morning. She dashed off, leaving a hastily recruited teenager to man her table.

I checked the map and turned the pamphlet back over. After

scanning the list of poets and musicians, I decided to keep my loonies in my pocket and make an exit of my own. Back then I was of the mind that poetry was meant to be kept in a small book tucked into a picnic basket, not declaimed from the apron of a stage to a crowd of sisters and cousins and aunts. Of course, back then, I had never heard of poetry slams.

I paused to buy a jar of saskatoon jelly and a small plate of chocolate chip cookies on my way out of the fair, feeling satisfied that I hadn't been wasting my time. This might not have been how Ackroyd researched Dickens, but then again, they don't have saskatoon berries in England.

10.

I turned up at City Hall spot on 9 a.m., and by 9:30 I'd discovered that there was no record of Margaret Ahlers ever having paid taxes to the City of Grande Prairie. All in all, it wasn't surprising; it would have been somehow entirely too easy to have discovered that she'd run for mayor, but I was disappointed nonetheless. What had seemed like such a great project when I'd applied for the funding was starting to feel pretty thin. My great adventure needed a kick in the pants, so I found myself gearing up for my visit to Dorothy Lewis. My inner voice was warning me not to get my hopes up too high, but my inner voice had also been the one to get me into this situation in the first place.

I wasn't sure how the judge of preserves at the fair could help me, but Dorothy seemed to be my only lead. Following her sketched map, I easily found my way to her farm and was rolling down her drive at exactly 10:30.

"Farmyard" is not the word you'd use to describe Dorothy Lewis's landscaped showpiece. I'd seen things like it in

Better Homes and Gardens or *Architectural Digest*, but frankly I'd always assumed they were airbrushed or embellished somehow. A driveway of immaculate white gravel gave way to a front patio walk of flagstones that ran the full length of the house. On the borders of this welcoming stage was the most amazing border of foliage I'd ever seen. Many of the shrubs and flowers looked familiar, yet somehow out of place. I finally figured out that I was looking at a vegetable garden unlike any I'd seen before. Carrot ferns bordered purple kale like some sort of Japanese meditation garden; peas frolicked in a vanguard making way for troops of potatoes, rear lines of corn, and trellises of scarlet runner beans. Equally aesthetic arrangements of onions, marigolds, cabbages, zucchini, and pumpkins dotted the way to the house.

I suspect my mouth was hanging open as I walked toward the tidy woman standing in the doorway of the ranch-style house.

Dorothy smiled at me. "I've always felt vegetables get shortchanged by being lined up like criminals. They are honestly every bit as pretty as other plants. Why should they look dowdy just because they're useful, too?" She smiled again after this little speech, but I had a strong feeling I'd been checked out pretty thoroughly by those shrewd eyes. "Well, Miss Craig, I hope you found my map helpful."

"Call me Randy, please," I said, scuffing off my loafers in the doorway. "I had no problem getting here at all, Mrs. Lewis."

"If I'm to call you Randy, which must be a pet-name for Miranda—that is, unless you're Norwegian—then please call me Dot. Everyone around here does." She started off through the house, with me right behind her. "It's such a beautiful morning,

I thought we might have tea out on the deck. Come this way, dear."

What I caught of the house fit right in with my thoughts on the front garden. This was one seriously arty woman. Driftwood for a fireplace lintel, pretty-coloured sands layered in a jar for a doorstop, various oils and watercolours on the walls. When we got to the deck, I figured out what she had done with all the flowers absent from the front beds.

The deck had a half roof, and pots of flowers hung from each rafter—begonias, fuchsias, and lobelia. Staircase ledges had been set into the two walls, and on every step sat a potted flower. Sweet peas ran riot on the third wall, which was not a wall at all, but a stretched piece of netting that made it possible to peer through vines and flowers to the sky beyond. Geraniums guarded the stairs to the lawn, one to each side of the three shallow steps. African violets sat in hand-thrown pots on the table. It was like sitting down in the middle of a bottle of Chloé.

Dot poured the tea. Sure enough, the cups were pottery, and so was the matching tea set of pot, creamer, sugar bowl, and lemon plate. She caught me looking.

"This set was a little project of mine. I was so excited after Harold built me my own kiln that you couldn't pry me from my wheel for months."

I murmured something complimentary.

"You're not from these parts, are you, Randy?"

"No, I'm not. What tipped you off? My accent?" I've been told I've picked up a "Toronto slur" somewhere along the line.

Personally, I believe it's more of a western drawl, but then I don't have to listen to myself.

"No, it was your name. I've never heard of any Craigs from around here. Of course, you might have been associated through your mother. What was her name?"

The name Summers did nothing for Dot Lewis, either. It seems our Mrs. Lewis was something of an amateur historian for the area, having helped to organize one of those massive books that lists everyone, quarter section by quarter section. While I felt a little snubbed to be so summarily excluded without even being looked up, I was beginning to think I'd come to the right place. If anyone knew Margaret Ahlers and her stomping grounds, it was going to be Dot Lewis.

It turned out that the name "Ahlers" rang about the same numbers that Craig had for Dot Lewis. "It's not a local name, I know that much. Here, come with me." She led me out of the conservatory patio and back into the cool of the house. In the living room, on either side of a magnificent flagstone fireplace, were floor-to-ceiling bookcases. One entire shelf, it turned out, was filled with local history books. Dot handed me one and took out another for herself.

"Most of these books have indices at the back, dear," she informed me. "Let's check and see if we can find your friend."

"She's not actually my friend, Dot. She's an author I'm interested in."

"And she comes from around the Peace?" Dot beamed with pride of ownership. "Well, we do have a very active artistic community here."

"But you've never heard of Margaret Ahlers?"

Dot smiled. "You know how it is. I don't get much reading done, except in the winter, and you know how secretive writers can be."

"Tell me about it!" I was just about to expound on the secretiveness of Margaret Ahlers when I spotted something familiar on Dot's shelf. "What about this book?" I asked, pulling a twenty-pound tome off the shelf toward me.

Dot gave me a cursory glance. "*Beaverlodge to the Rockies*? No Ahlers there, and I should know. That's my old stomping grounds."

It was the cover that had attracted my attention. It was a wrap print from back to front, depicting a brownish-green landscape with about seventy-five horizons. Something about that picture was scratching at my memory like a potshard. Dot noticed my concentration.

"Lovely cover, isn't it? It was just super of Betty to allow it."

"Betty?"

"Betty McNaught. You've probably heard of her as Euphemia McNaught. She's a Beaverlodge girl. In fact, she was my Grade One teacher."

McNaught. Of course, it was the same artist whose work I'd seen hanging in Quinn's office. A Beaverlodge artist. Dot was amazing; I think she really did know everybody. At last, I had the feeling I was getting somewhere.

I flipped to the index. No Ahlers, but of course Dot had already told me to expect that. This time, instead of closing the book, I flipped to the Qs. Sure enough, there was a Quinn listed.

Dot looked at me quizzically. "Have you found something, dear?"

It turned out that Dot knew quite a bit about the Quinns of Huallan. There had only been one child, Hilary, who went off to the big city to "become somebody." Mr. Quinn suffered a stroke after his crops were hailed out two seasons running, and Mrs. Quinn had moved to Edmonton to be near her daughter. Apparently she held onto the family land for years, but finally sold the farm once she knew for certain that Hilary would never marry and come back home.

Dot had gone to school with Hilary's dad, but said she didn't know all that much about her. I figured if Dot didn't get to know everything about a person, there was something wrong. She already had enough material on me to produce a reasonable genealogical chart, and I'd only met her the day before. She could tell me quite a bit about the senior Quinns, but now the fountain of information was starting to dry up.

I offered to put the kettle on for another pot of tea. Dot would have none of it, and began bustling around the kitchen like a banty hen. Never one to be overly pushy about chores, I sat back.

"So Hilary went off to the big city and never looked back?"

Dot ran tap water into the kettle. "I wouldn't say that, exactly, dear. Her parents are buried here, and she still comes here every summer, after all. It's just that she never really socializes with any of us, and there's still a lot of us around who are rather active."

From what I'd seen at the fair, this was an understatement. That was the point that interested me though. "She comes up here every summer? But I thought her mother sold the farm."

"The farm, yes; the cottage, no. It was something else when they bought that property out on Trumpeter Lake. I mean, can you imagine wanting to spend your holidays cooking on a stove even more rustic than the one you use all year long on the farm? What is so relaxing about chopping wood by a lake when you can do that at home? It seems that Mrs. Quinn—she was from Ontario originally—had to have a 'summer place' as she called it. I remember a few of us howling when we heard about it."

"And you're saying that Dr. Quinn still comes out to this rustic summer cottage every year?"

"Hmmm. From what I hear, she's got it pretty winterized by now. The Giebelhaus boy had the job of insulating it, as I recall."

"So you see her up here quite often?"

"Not really. I mean, we know they're here, but they just don't seem to want to connect with anybody. There have been rumours, that, well..." For the first time since I'd known her, Dot looked rather uncomfortable wading through someone else's autobiography. "But then again, I suppose they always say that about brainy ladies who don't get married, what with Gertrude Stein and all."

"People here think that Dr. Quinn is a lesbian?"

I probably should have trundled out a euphemism; Dot looked uncomfortable with the "L-word" hanging in the air. There was something else bothering me about what she'd just said, though, something that hadn't come up before.

It hit me just as the kettle started to sing: "They?"

11.

I made it back to town, filled with tea and innuendo. I also now had a lead to something I wasn't sure I wanted to tackle alone. Maybe it was time to bring in the cavalry. The card beside the telephone in the motel room was too convoluted, and from what I could tell, it would cost fifty cents a minute to call Edmonton. I opted for a payphone I could see from the window, out on the corner by the parking lot. God, the trouble we went to before cellphones.

It seemed like ages before Guy picked up the phone. The operator cut in over my answering "Hello."

"I have a collect call from a Randy Craig. Will you accept the charges?"

"I suppose so," Guy drawled.

"Never try joking with paid officials, Guy, especially not when they have the power to cut me off."

"Hold on there, ma'am. Since when does someone instigating a collect call have the right to tell someone off without even saying hello?"

"I did say hello, and thanks for accepting the charges. I couldn't figure out the change system on this payphone."

Guy chuckled. "Whatever—it's great to hear from you. Where are you and what have you found out?"

It was so good to hear Guy's voice. I told him all about the rumours I'd harvested from Dot Lewis. Guy whistled over the phone, nearly deafening me.

"And you think the 'other woman' was Ahlers? What makes you so certain it's not her mother or sister or someone like that?"

"She doesn't have a sister, and her mother is dead. Anyhow, you should have heard the tone Dot's voice took on when she started tut-tutting about 'how people like to talk.' Besides, while 'far be it from Dot to spread a malicious rumours,' this other woman seems to be Quinn's partner—whenever they catch sight of her."

"What do you mean, catch sight of her?"

"Well, it seems that she never comes into town to go shopping, but the lake is pretty well overrun with pleasure boats during the summer, and people occasionally spot two women around the place." A wind blew at the phone booth door, and I suddenly remembered the cost of little conversation. "So anyway, I thought I'd just phone to let you know that I'd be in Grande Prairie instead of Peace River for the next few days."

Guy's voice took on a note of suspicion. "Randy? What are you planning on doing?"

"Oh, I thought I might take a little tour out to Trumpeter Lake."

"Alone? You must be out of your mind! You can't go snooping around Quinn's cottage."

"Why not?"

"What if she's out there? What kind of an excuse would you have? I can see the headlines now: GRAD STUDENT FOILED IN ATTEMPT TO MURDER PROF."

"Don't be so melodramatic, Guy." He wasn't even close to spooking me, but the wind whistled through the phone door again and I shivered.

"Listen, Randy, where are you staying?"

"The fabulous Swan Motel. Why?"

"Why? Because I'm coming up there is why."

"And why would you do that? Because you don't trust me?"

"In a word, no. But to be honest and lay all my cards on all the table, there's nothing much happening down here right now anyway."

"How will you get here?"

"I'll take the bus."

"It's a six-hour trip, Guy."

"Hey, what can I tell you? I care enough to send the very best. Just sit tight till I get there tomorrow, okay?"

I smiled in spite of myself.

"Randy?"

"Yes?"

"Scout around for a good pizza joint."

During the next fifteen hours, I did some heavy soul-searching and some light reading. I was examining why I'd called Guy with my discovery. On the whole, I hated to admit to myself how nervous Quinn or anything associated with her made me feel. It would be good to have a friend with me to navigate the unknown waters.

I wondered if my calling him had something to do with the lesbian connection to Dr. Quinn, too. Dot Lewis might have stirred things up when she spoke about academics and lesbianism in the same sentence. There used to be this smirking association between the two, as if women could only engage their brains if penises weren't preoccupying their minds. Maybe that was why I'd phoned Guy: to prove to myself that I could handle both at the same time. Or maybe I was scared it was something I couldn't tackle on my own.

On the other hand, there was a good chance I was overanalyzing the whole situation. Maybe all I needed was a friend to talk to. I decided to let Sherry Hite worry about that one, and proceeded to navigate the lumps in the mattress toward oblivion.

Waking up presented no problems. Birds were singing, Guy was on his way, and huge semis were roaring along the road outside my window. I showered, dressed, and went out to forage for breakfast. I spent the rest of the day rereading Atwood's *Survival* as a consideration to the environment in Canadian literature, making several notes that seemed applicable to Ahlers and the Peace Country. I also double-checked Guy's arrival time three or four times with the agenda the motel office had given me and finally went down to wait for him near the station.

Guy was Greyhound-grumpy for about an hour, but he cheered up after catching sight of his seventeenth swan. We tacitly refrained from discussing the next day's plans. Instead, we explored the town, ate an anchovy-free but otherwise laden pizza, caught a movie, and headed back to the motel.

I know that boxers and football players abstain the night before, but we weren't planning on battering anyone the next day, so what the hell. Maybe there were much simpler reasons than I had considered for why I had lured Guy up north to be part of my summer adventure.

12.

We'd driven down the road three times before I spotted two tire tracks meandering off the beaten path behind a large copse of Balm of Gilead. Guy started to protest as I nosed the car toward them. "What are you doing?"

"This has got to be it. The grocer said it was between the Bide-a-while and the Dew Drop By, and we've been back and forth between them."

"But this isn't even a road. Self-respecting goats would turn up their noses at this thing!"

"I'm sure this is the road in."

"You did take out complete coverage on the car, didn't you?"

"Guy!"

It seemed that "summer places" had caught on since old Mrs. Quinn's day. Trumpeter Lake was surrounded by cabins. Some of the larger places on the far side of the lake had that all-year look, but those on this side were charmingly unkempt and identified by silly names, like proper cabins should be.

We made several sharp turns through the long grasses and bushes before suddenly popping out into a clearing. The cabin looked much like the others we had passed, just a bit older. There was a wooden porch leading to a screened door, a wooden door behind the screen. Small windows looked over the parking green. I presumed the picture window faced the lake beyond. An outhouse, painted the same rusty red as the cabin, sat off in the woods to the left. A lean-to shed next to the cabin housed storm windows, a push mower, and cobwebs.

There was no other car in sight, but I was nervous anyway. When you're persona non grata with someone, it doesn't do to just drop in for an unannounced visit. Breaking and entering takes that to a whole new level.

I hadn't discussed a game plan with Guy, but he was beginning to sense where my mind was headed. He cleared his throat. "Cat burglary isn't one of my fortes, you know."

"Who said anything about stealing cats?" I countered, with more breeziness than I actually felt. "I just want to look around."

"Oh sure, isn't that what Hitler said about Poland?"

"Since when did you turn in your Amoral Anonymous membership card?"

Guy rose up in his seat, wounded. "Just what is that supposed to mean?"

"Anyone who is so into games should have no problems with playing on the fringes of danger."

"I'll have you know that anyone with a true love of games is a most moral person. To whom else are rules of such vital importance, I ask you?"

There was no way to win this one, so I let it drop and put the car into Park. I turned the key off, and the birds immediately sounded as if they had turned up their volume knobs.

I felt as if I was trespassing as soon as I stepped out of the car. And, I guess, technically I was. I've never quite figured it out; if they don't put up a "No Trespassing" sign and then shoot you anyway, are they legally in the right? Since then, I guess I've done more than my fair share of bending and entering, but I've never felt quite so intensely vulnerable as I did up in that sunny glade.

Despite his compunctions, Guy followed me around to the lakeview side of the cabin. I could see why old Mrs. Quinn put up with being teased about her summer place. The view from the front porch was gorgeous.

There is something about the colour green in the Peace River County that is unlike a green in any other place on earth. Maybe it's the combinations of all the different verdant shades put together; whatever it is, it's enough to knock your eye teeth out every time you turn a corner and come up against it.

The grass was lighter than the leaves of the poplars, which was lighter in turn than the Balm of Gilead, which gave way to darker pines. The lake reflected all these hues and added a bluey-green of its own to the spectrum.

The dock was unpainted and accessible straight from the cabin's back door. There was a small, sandy beach, a lawn with an old picnic table, and a canoe that had been drawn up and turned over next to the trees. A picture window took in the whole scene. It was to this window that Guy was gluing himself, shading his eyes to peer into the cabin.

I came up from behind. "What do you see?"

"Not much. A fireplace, an overstuffed couch, some wicker chairs, a desk, and I think this thing, over to the right here, is the edge of the kitchen table."

He was close to being a complete cataloguer. Two doors led off from the room he'd described, and the kitchen seemed to take up the corner to the right of the window. I rattled the door beside the window, although I knew it would be useless; there was a newish-looking Yale deadbolt gleaming at me from shoulder height.

Guy, in the meantime, had headed around the far side of the cabin. "Randy, come here! I think I found what you're looking for."

I picked my way through the long grass and found him removing a screen from a high window. The butterfly bolts appeared disinclined to budge, but Guy soon had the screen leaning beside him. He then pulled out a Swiss Army knife and inserted it into the lock mechanism of the window. With one twist, the window was unlocked and Guy was shoving it open.

"What are you doing?"

"Finding you a point of entrance, which I presume is why we are here."

"But that is illegal."

Guy looked at me as if he was disappointed in me, the way high school teachers would look when they'd called on you for an answer you couldn't muster to their satisfaction.

"You are digging into the background of the author whose body of work you are studying. If anything, this amounts to social anthropology. And don't tell me you weren't planning something like this in the back of your mind."

"What do you mean?"

"Why would we drive all the way out here only to peer through windows? We might as well go in. Just driving onto the property is trespassing, and we've already done that. It's not as if we're planning to steal, damage or even disarrange anything. No one will even suspect we've been here, so what are you waiting for?"

I was impressed, both with his argument and his lock-twisting skill. "Where did you learn to do that?"

"Oh, I've developed a plethora of skills over the years."

"What happened to all that hoo-hah about morality?"

"Really, Randy. Morality is a choice one makes, not a blind compulsion. If one were not cognizant of the options, how could one make an informed choice?"

I shook my head at Guy's semantics.

"Oh forget it," he replied. "It's a long story involving junior high curfews and monster movie marathons. Now are you going to climb in, or do I stand here holding up this heavy sash all day?"

Put that way, I could hardly refuse. I hooked one foot onto Guy's bent knee and hoisted myself up over the sill.

I've never been the most graceful of people, but I don't think there is a delicate way of entering a house by means of a window. I was stranded with my arms and torso dangling in forbidden territory and, for a second, I felt like giving up. It was the realization of what Guy's perspective must be on this scene from below that inspired a burst of scrambling and an awkward somersault onto a bed about two and a half feet below the window.

I was in a small, dark room, presumably behind one of the two doors we'd spotted. The only light was coming from the window. Guy's voice was coming from the same direction. "Do you think you can find your way to the deck door, or do I have to follow your example of delicate little cat feet?"

I groaned and slid off the chenille bedspread, making a mental note to myself to straighten it before we left.

Lazy motes of dust hung in the air of the main room. They were probably everywhere, but there was more light by which to see them in here. I headed for the deck. The deadbolt slid back and clicked open. Guy entered the room like Inspector Clouseau pursuing Cato, but he ruined the effect by sneezing several times in a row.

I shrugged. "There went the atmosphere."

"It's the so-called atmosphere that's making me sneeze," Guy protested, after blowing his nose into an oversized hankie. "Doesn't that woman ever clean the place?"

"It's a summer cabin, Guy. Who knows when she was here last? All the grocer said was that she closed up the house late last fall. That could mean anything from the day after Labour Day till Hallowe'en."

"All right. So what exactly do you expect to find here?"

"Evidence."

"Evidence of what? Slatternly housekeeping?"

It was hard to answer Guy's question, so I sniffed and turned my back on him. I honestly wasn't sure what I was looking for.

I just had a feeling that I would know it when I found it. Guy began to open kitchen cupboards. Like a magnet, I made for the desk. In contrast to the rest of the dusty cabin, this area was pin-in-place perfect. Pens and pencils were arranged in the top drawer. Letter and legal-sized pads of bond paper were in the second. I found a couple of packages of carbon paper in the third drawer.

I wonder what space aliens, or students today—and yes in some ways those two categories are interchangeable—would make of carbon paper. I remember being amused by finding it, since I had left off having to wrestle a piece of the messy blue paper between two sheets of typing paper in order to create a second copy the minute my trusty Kaypro personal computer came into my life. Now, of course, I back everything up on flash-drives and email myself copies of works in progress to a variety of mailboxes, in case my laptop crashes.

Carbon paper was the flashdrive of its time. One always made a copy of everything, because you never knew when some well-meaning assistant was going to tidy the editor's desk and lose your masterpiece. I wondered why Dr. Quinn didn't just bring her Compaq computer from her university office up to the cabin with her. Then it occurred to me that I couldn't see any grounded sockets in the cabin, so maybe she just left high-tech to her urban run.

Guy had continued from the kitchen through to the second bedroom, the one I hadn't used as an access point. "Randy, come here!"

I entered a larger space than the first bedroom. There was

an iron-frame double bed covered with the requisite chenille spread; a large closet was set into the wall. Side tables stood on either side of the bed.

Guy was grinning in the open doorway of the closet.

"What is it?" I asked, trying to sneak a look around the bulk of my fellow investigator.

"Evidence," said Guy drily, stepping aside to allow me to peer inside.

The closet was divided as dramatically as I've always imagined the Red Sea parted; hangers were shoved to either side. On the left were assorted cotton tops and pedal pushers—standard cottage garb. On the right was a collection of very frilly, feminine dresses.

I could understand what led Guy to identify this as evidence. In a million years, neither of us could imagine Hilary Quinn in one of those frothy concoctions—it'd be like sticking a carrot into a Singapore Sling. They actually reminded me of what Carol Burnett used to wear as her television character Eunice.

"They aren't hers, are they?" Guy asked.

"No. In fact," I said, checking some labels, "they are at least a size bigger than the clothes on this side."

"Maybe her mother's?"

"They couldn't be. I mean, I'm not sure when she died, but these dresses are current style—if you can use the word 'style' to describe them."

"So they're someone else's."

"Yes."

"And they could be Ahlers', is that what you're thinking?"

"Well, why not, Guy?"

"Because it fits too neatly."

"What do you mean?"

"I mean that, if this were a mystery novel, then these would be Ahlers' clothes. We'd discover that Quinn was her lover and Ahlers had been murdered in a fit of pique. But there's one problem: this is real life. Things like that just don't happen."

"Joe Orton was killed in real life."

"That's close to being a perfect oxymoron, Randy. And you're overlooking one other reason why they can't be Ahlers' clothes."

"And what's that."

"How could such a tasteful writer dress so tackily?"

I smiled inwardly at Guy's superficiality, but he did have a point. There was something a little too loud, a little too strident, a little too gaudy about these dresses. They practically screamed from the confines of the closet. Dresses like those could make a statement from three counties away. No wonder the grocer was so sure there had been folks around the cottage. From his vantage point across the lake, he wouldn't have been able to miss these walking flower gardens.

While my eyes recovered from staring at the brightly printed frills, Guy continued to poke around. I shook myself and went after him. A storage closet contained an ironing board, brooms, an old dressmaker's dummy, and the water heater. I confirmed my suspicions of Quinn's—or perhaps Ahlers'—low-tech needs by noting a pale green Hermes portable typewriter standing next to a mop pail.

The small bedroom had no closet, just a chest of drawers and the small iron bed I'd encountered previously. I was grateful

Quinn hadn't put the dresser under the window. I straightened the bedspread, opened and closed the dresser drawers, and pulled down the window sash and relocked it.

By this time Guy was outside, refastening the storm window. I closed the bedroom door behind me. Everything looked the way we'd found it. I checked the big bedroom and was glad I had. I must have dropped the open packet of carbon paper on the bed in my surprise over Guy's discovery. I picked it up and double-checked the closet door, even though it appeared to be well and truly closed.

"Randy, let's get out of here."

Guy sounded strained. I glanced around once more, shut the bedroom door and made my way to the deck. Guy had tripped the lock and was waiting for me in the doorway. I stepped out into the freshest air I'd ever breathed. It felt as if I'd been holding my breath the entire time we'd been inside. Guy pulled the door closed and shook it to be sure it was locked up tight before he turned back to me. His smile did a reverse-Cheshire and disappeared from his face.

"What's that?" he asked.

"What's what?" I looked down to see what he was pointing at, and my heart plummeted down around my appendix. "Oh my god." I stared at the packet of carbon paper, still in my hand. I looked around frantically. "We have to go back in and replace it."

"You've got to be kidding. We have just spent half an hour making sure we haven't left signs of our awkward break in, which may I remind you took us long enough to hoist you through that window, and you want to try that all over again?"

"Well, then I have to find somewhere to throw it away."

"And have someone wonder what's up if they find it? The object was to make it seem as if we've never been here, not to broadcast the fact."

"Well, what should I do?" I wailed.

Guy looked pained. "Oh, bring it with us and we'll ditch it somewhere. No one ever remembers how much carbon paper they have. She'll probably never miss it."

"There's another whole unopened packet in there," I volunteered.

"In that case, we're home free." Guy opened the passenger door and stepped back to let me in. I handed him the car keys and sank over into the bucket seat, clutching the only item I'd ever stolen in my life. I was a burglar! I wondered if some cosmic Victor Hugo would sic a Javert on me for a half-empty packet of carbon paper. I had a feeling Dr. Quinn wouldn't like it one bit.

13.

I didn't notice much of the ride back. I was too immersed in the problems I seemed to have created on this trip. I had travelled here to discover a setting for Ahlers' life, and instead I had stumbled upon a reason for her death.

"Let's review things, okay?"

"Fine by me," said Guy with his eyes straight ahead.

"Ahlers seems to have been writing about the Peace River Country."

"Check."

"Quinn comes from, and still maintains a cottage in, the Peace River Country."

"Check."

"No one knows Ahlers, but they all know about Professor Quinn and her ladyfriend."

"Check."

"And Quinn, the stolid professor, seems to have some sort of 'in' with Ahlers."

"What do you mean?"

"Well, she has scooped everyone with an article just as each book comes out. It's as if she's the first person to read them."

"So?"

"Well, maybe she actually is the first person to read them."

Guy snorted. "Why would a world-class writer hand over her manuscripts to a by-and-large unknown English professor? That's a pretty pricey proofreader, isn't it?"

I refused to rise to Guy's ribbing. "All I'm saying is that Hilary Quinn and Margaret Ahlers are close."

"Ah, the Dot Lewis lesbian theory."

"What does it matter? They're close enough to be intimate about their work. Maybe Ahlers just let her best friend read her novels first, to give her a break in the academic game. Why are you slowing down?"

"I thought I'd pull in here so we could stretch our legs a bit."

The campground sign identified this as "Waskahigan River Campsite." I checked the map to determine where we were. The only campground on this side of the road was marked "House River." I asked Guy what he thought that meant.

"I don't know—it's a very old map?" he offered.

"Or that's a very new sign," I countered.

After he'd pulled up by a picnic table, Guy took a closer look at the map. "Hmmm, same place, as far as I can tell."

"What do you think 'Waskahigan' means?"

"Probably means 'house.'"

I snorted and went off to the little waskahigan marked

"Ladies." When I got back, Guy was alternating touching his toes and stretching his arms over his head.

Stretching looked like a good idea, but I've never been much for joining in on good ideas. I prefer to come up with them. Instead of exercise, I set myself to cleaning out the junk from the floor of the car. It's amazing how quickly juice boxes and gum wrappers can multiply. I took one handful to the garbage bin and headed back to shake out the floor mats.

As I was pulling out the first mat, the fateful packet of carbon paper came with it. I'd shoved it under my seat and forgotten my shame. Now it surfaced again like my own peculiar albatross. The only thing to do was get rid of it. I pulled the lot out forcefully and sheets of flimsy blue paper escaped, flying everywhere.

"Shit!" This exclamation got through to my campground Charles Atlas. Laughing, he began to chase carbon paper like an actress chasing butterflies in a tampon commercial. I was scrabbling at the sheets nearest me when something brought me up short.

Most of the packet had never been used, but someone had shoved a little-used piece of carbon back into the plastic. On it were centred the words:

Feathers of Treasure

by

Margaret Ahlers

I screamed.

Guy paused in his Catherine Deneuve dervish routine. "What's the matter? Did you see a snake?"

I was so excited I barely registered the semi-chauvinistic tone. Guy's consciousness could get raised later.

"What do you think of this?" I shouted, waving the incriminating carbon in Guy's face.

"I think it's carbon paper," he said.

"No, no—look what's cut into it!"

He squinted at the paper and then whistled slowly. "It looks like you may be right after all."

"Of course I am. As if there was ever any doubt," I chirped. But deep down, I was not sure whether or not I was pleased or terrified that I'd been vindicated. After all, it's one thing to suspect that a person has been murdered, but quite another thing to have it proven.

It was if Guy was reading my mind. "It's not exactly irrefutable proof, you know."

"What do you mean?"

"Just because you found that in Quinn's cabin doesn't mean she killed Ahlers. God, it doesn't even mean she knew Ahlers—she could have just been goofing around on the typewriter."

"With carbon paper? That's like doodling in oil paint."

"You know what I mean," he said.

"No, I don't. First of all, this means that it's very likely there's a fourth novel, for all Quinn's hot air. For another thing, it makes a direct link between Quinn and Ahlers. And, it corroborates the reports of the two women and explains the two different wardrobes in the cabin. I think it's incredibly significant."

"Okay, so it's incredibly significant. What are you going to do about it?"

I stopped and stared at him. There was a moment or two of pugnacious silence before we began to laugh. It really was a silly scene; Guy was glowering and I was trying to stare him down, clutching a dirty piece of carbon paper. It's lucky we were the only ones at the campsite. People would have been burning their marshmallows left, right, and centre watching us.

"I haven't the faintest idea," I finally admitted. "What do you think I should do with it?"

"The logical reply would be that you should go home, write your thesis, and forget all about this."

"We may be talking about murder, though."

"We may be talking fantasy. You really have no justification in assuming that Ahlers was murdered. You barely have proof that they knew each other. If you start spreading these accusations, we're almost certainly talking slander."

"You really are hung up on the rules, aren't you?"

"Well, if you don't want to follow my advice, what do you propose? Go to the police and say you've discovered a murder on the grounds that you broke into a summer cabin and stole some carbon paper?"

My elation crumbled. Of course I had no proof. All I had was my theory that Ahlers had been describing the Peace Country in her novels and a crumpled piece of carbon paper with an odd new title on it.

I was beginning to feel very foolish. I sat down on the picnic bench and scuffed my shoe in the gravel, feeling all of seven years old.

Guy sat down next to me and draped a long, warm arm over my shoulders. "Don't take it so hard, Randy. I'll bet Sam Spade had his off days, too."

"But Guy, it was making so much sense."

"Which is exactly why you should stop and question it. Nothing should make that much sense in this day and age. We are living in the world of open texts, after all."

"Oh, give me a break." The last thing I needed was a lecture on post-modernist theory. What I did need was a bath. The blue from the carbon paper was all over my hands. I looked around, but the only source of water other than the river seemed to be the hand pump. I opted for the river.

When I came back up the bank, wiping my hands on the back of my jeans, Guy was already sitting in the car—in the passenger side.

The next four hours were taken up with white-knuckle driving. My fellow drivers, most of them in eighteen-wheelers, took the speed limit signs merely as suggested minimums. I wondered how many of them were wired on caffeine and uppers. I kept flashing onto images from Spielberg's *Duel*, alternating the scenes of the truck driver hauling a semi full of toilets in Edward Abbey's *The Brave Cowboy*. When I finally hit the Yellowhead's divided stretch, I felt like I'd been given a reprieve from death row. We'd all but ceased conversation by this time, so Guy's voice startled me a little.

"Supposing there was a fourth novel. Where do you think it is now?"

14.

It seemed like the next few days after our trip to the Peace River Country blurred into still photos with weeping sepia edges. Nothing seemed to connect and nothing seemed to get done, either. I was in a fog, wandering from my apartment to the English department and back again. Every now and then, I'd punctuate my time with a coffee break at Java Jive with Maureen or whoever else was headed that way.

Summers on campus are a strange thing. There's a distant bustle of spring and summer session students, but the upper office floors could be used as bowling alleys most of the time—they're that empty. A lot of professors traipse off to conferences or to visit special collections or, heaven forbid, to actually go on holiday. Most grad students start taking things a little bit easier than they have done in winter session. In fact, by the middle of July, the Rasputin-on-a-bad-day look had faded from most everyone's eyes. For all I knew, it might have even faded from mine.

I hadn't been seeing too much of Guy since the trip. I wasn't sure, but I felt a coolness that hadn't been present before the long car ride back to Edmonton. Since the weather had turned nice, I wasn't staying inside all that much when I was home, and the library had better air circulation than my office, so who knows—maybe he had been phoning me without getting through. I didn't really care. I was feeling too preoccupied to be worrying about our relationship, if you could call it that, and the sight of him reminded me of breaking into Quinn's cabin—an incident I wasn't feeling overly proud of. At the same time I was trying to put Guy out of mind, I was still pondering what he'd said to me about the fourth manuscript.

Suppose there was a fourth novel somewhere. Where would it be? Had Ahlers left a will? Was there any way of finding out? It occurred to me that Garth, my publisher, might know about the laws of wills —and especially about the willing of copyrights and manuscripts. I was just about to pick up the phone and call him when another publisher's name leapt to mind. If anyone would know about Margaret Ahlers' literary effects, it would be her publishers, McKendricks. A call to directory assistance got me the number in no time. I contemplated what sort of reason I could make up to get them to give me the information I wanted.

A male voice answered the phone. I tried the truth on them; I was a graduate student working on Margaret Ahlers and could they please tell me where her papers were being sent?

I made a mental note to try the truth more often; I was connected straight through to Duncan McKendrick. From what little I recalled of the Toronto literary scene, Duncan was the son and heir apparent to Daddy's empire. I didn't know how old he was, but since Angus McKendrick was still whooping it up in the celebrity pages, Duncan was probably only in his mid-forties. I tend to group people into three camps: under fifteen, over seventy, and in-between. Duncan was part of that "older than me, younger than Mom" in-between category. I'd had him pointed out to me at a couple of wingdings over the years, but I'm sure he had no idea who I was. And why should he? I had been a writer for hire, not a name author when I was freelancing. That was okay with me. I figured I might get farther on the innocent student ploy.

"How may I help you, Ms. Craig?"

I launched into my grad-student dilemma. I could almost hear him nodding sagely over the phone.

"I see. Well, of course you would want to examine Ahlers' papers for your study. The only problem is that we're not free to divulge any information concerning the placement of the papers until it's been officially announced, and that won't be for—let me see—several months yet."

I had been puffing up expectantly throughout his little speech, but now I sagged. Months? My silence must have been loaded, because Duncan McKendrick leapt into the breach with an inspired suggestion. "Why don't you write your request, care of us here at McKendricks, and we'll see that it's passed on to the executor? After all, I can't see why anyone would want to stymie an academic interest in Ms. Ahlers' work."

It was grasping at straws, but I thanked him and hung up the phone. What did I have to lose? I drafted a quick letter asking for an opportunity to examine the papers, then went down to the department office to get an envelope. After opening several empty drawers that had once held envelopes by the gross, I finally asked one of the secretaries where they were being kept.

"Under lock and key—part of the new budget cuts. Sorry!"

I trudged down to the mall to buy a package of envelopes, feeling hard done by. My run of luck continued—the business envelopes were out of stock. I bought a package of ten designer colours and mailed off my letter to McKendricks in a neon fuchsia special. I hoped that Duncan and old Angus kept sunglasses handy.

15.

The character business came to me at about eleven on a hot July night. I was sitting at the kitchen table, drinking iced tea while watching a spindly-legged bug dart around the standing lamp in the corner. Even in my basement suite, it was too humid to move, let alone kill anything. I was idly thinking about redecorating, which in my case meant moving the tacky furniture from one dim corner to another. I wondered if the landlord would contribute toward the cost of wallpaper, and pondered the walls to see which one I should attack first.

The bulletin board with the big map of the province was still staring down at me from the opposite wall. I'd have to do something about that. If I took down the map, the cork would be too dark for the room. Maybe I could spray-paint the cork a lighter colour; I was getting sick of staring at Big Sky Country.

A slight breeze riffled the curtains and gave me the impetus to heave myself out of the chair for more iced tea. On the way to the fridge, I yanked the pins out of the map. A bunch of file cards tumbled down with it. As I bent down to pick them up, it occurred to me that the system I'd created on this wall had been what sent me to the Peace River County in the first place. I started to remove all the cards from the board. It was ridiculous to even contemplate throwing them away—at the time I was such a packrat, I had trouble pitching out egg cartons—but I wasn't quite sure of what order to put them in.

Should I order them by location, or by which novel they came from, or alphabetically by the first word in the quotation? Idly, I began to cut and shuffle the cards like a poker dealer. I finally decided to order them by novel. I'd written the title at the bottom of most of the quotations, but on some I'd just jotted page numbers.

It became a game. Would I be able to recognize the novel from a cryptic, area-specific quotation? I was doing pretty well until I came to the part where Andrea is picking saskatoons and becomes disoriented in the bush. For the life of me, I couldn't remember whether that was from an early childhood sequence in *One for Sorrow* or one of the flashbacks in *The Children of Magpie*. It was driving me crazy. So, even in that stultifying heat, I plodded into the living room to pull out my copies of the novels. Pouring myself some more iced tea, I began leafing through the third novel. Even before I hit page eighty-three, I realized my mistake. The passage had to have been taken from *One for Sorrow* because the heroine in *The Children of Magpie* was Isabel, not Andrea.

I checked through the first novel, now dog-eared and heavily penciled throughout the margins, just to make sure. I was right.

The quote came from the passage where Andrea has gone to the farm for the summer and her grandmother sends her out for saskatoons with two honey pails strapped to her waist. She dodges a hornet and trips, spilling berries everywhere. After a good cry, she looks up and realizes that she's lost all sense of direction there on the ground among the bushes. For the first time in the farm context, she is pacified rather than frightened by the experience. She limps home eventually, with next to nothing in the pails and purple stains all over her matching shorts and pop-top.

It was a great sequence, and it finally occurred to me why I had mixed it up with the third novel. In *The Children of Magpie*, Isabel travels back home for her grandmother's funeral, and keeps travelling back in time to flashbacks similar to the saskatoon scene. There's the day her grandmother pushes the lawn chairs together and throws a quilt over them to make a playhouse for Isabel, and the time Isabel tries to be a home help for her grandmother when the old lady is laid up with arthritis. No wonder I'd mixed up the quotation. Grandmothers and saskatoons were laced through both. I closed the book and returned to staring at the now-empty cork wall.

Andrea and Isabel. They were the same woman. And, of the two central characters in *Two for Joy*, Eleanor was far closer to the mould than her friend Marie. Andrea, Eleanor, Isabel—A, E, I. Why hadn't I seen it before?

The answer was simple. I'd been looking for locations before, material for my thesis. Now I was looking for Ahlers herself, any clue that could bring this author "to life" for me now that it was too late to ever encounter her in person. I don't know if I was already thinking of myself as some sort of literary Mrs. Peel at this point, but my urge to find out whether Quinn had anything to do with Ahlers' death had been simmering ever since I'd first connected them in Dot Lewis's living room.

I know that authors are never completely autobiographical, and that most of the characters they create are amalgams of various people they have met, observed and imagined. I wasn't going to let that stop me, though. There was a definite through-line in these novels, and I was going to navigate it. In the same way I'd let the novels lead me to the Peace River Country, I was now going to let them lead me to their author. Maybe knowing how she'd lived would tell me how she'd died.

I decided to use the pink cards for physical descriptions, green cards for thoughts and dreams, and yellow cards for activities or events that might leave a mental or physical mark on the character. Starting tomorrow, the corkboard would have a purpose once more. I set my glass and empty pitcher in the sink, and then carefully straightened the pile of novels and cue cards.

For good measure, just before I turned out the light, I swatted the bug. I was back on track.

16.

Will Rogers once said that being on the right track was fine and dandy, but you could still get run over by the train if all you did was sit around. I was not intending to sit around.

I began preparing first thing the next morning. I washed the floor, cleaned the apartment till everything was either gleaming or a reasonable facsimile thereof, dragged my folding grocery cart out of the storage closet, and lugged home provisions from the Safeway. I also picked up fresh packages of cue cards and pushpins, three new pens, and a jumbo bag of strawberry licorice from the Shoppers Drug Mart next door.

It took most of the day to do all the chores I'd set for myself. Some people might find it ridiculous, but I'd discovered through experience that I had to clear everything else out of the way before beginning a new writing project. If things got rough, defrosting the fridge might look inviting, and a trip to the store could be extended with ease to fill an entire afternoon. I therefore had to get rid of externals before I could put my head down to concentrate.

I switched my telephone ringer to mute and left my machine on to field calls. These days all I really expected were calls offering to clean my non-existent carpets, but even telephone surveys had been known to distract me in the past. This was vital research and I wasn't going to take any chances on being sidetracked answering questions about instant coffee.

I had decided to start at the beginning and reread all three novels with pen in hand. I figured that since this would be at least my fourth time through each one, I should be able to spot character delineation without missing anything crucial to the plot.

It was harder going than I'd expected. The narrative kept winding around me, making me forget what it was I was looking for. I found that I'd have to back up constantly to find references that my eyes had swept past. If nothing else, I could testify that Ahlers had been a spellbinding storyteller.

One for Sorrow reminded me of a quirky Alice Munro with a dash of Iris Murdoch thrown in to keep things jumping. Andrea, the main character—whom I was betting had been patterned on Ahlers herself—starts out as a child of eleven and ages about fifteen years over the course of the novel. Each section focuses on an annual event: summer vacation, birthday, Thanksgiving, Christmas, Easter, first day of school, university exam week, convocation, Valentine's Day. The context reveals how old she was in each situation, and they were roughly chronological.

Explaining it makes it sound pretty complicated, I know, but it flows pretty naturally when you're reading it.

I was getting a feel for Andrea the physical person, but the original essence that I'd felt on first reading the book was still overpowering. No matter what happened to her directly—like falling in the saskatoons or meeting the trick motorcycle carnie at the fair—it was as if Andrea was always watching more than participating. Her glasses, which were constantly described because the frames seemed to change in each section, seemed to act as portholes or proscenium arches on the world. Andrea just wandered around behind them, not particularly selective with the channel switch.

I knew I was reading far more into the character than I could justify with page references, but at this stage that was fine with me. If I could get the groundwork done on Andrea, actualities and gut feelings together would give me a sense of how Eleanor and Isabel fit into the picture.

I finished *One for Sorrow* just before midnight. It had taken longer than usual with all the stops and starts for jotting things down. When I looked up, the kitchen table was littered with cue cards of various colours. I grinned with self-satisfaction; I'd start pinning them up in the morning.

Sitting in one position for such a long time had taken its toll on my back. It was as if I had to go through a refresher course on human evolution just to stand up. I took a shower and went to bed. I figured I could expect dreams of Andrea and her antics all night, but the gods smiled on me and I woke up feeling refreshed and with no recollection of rapid eye movement whatsoever.

I spent the first hour after breakfast futzing around with organizing my cue cards on the wall. I'm not by nature a morning person; I have to edge into a day sideways. I start really cooking at about 11 a.m. and usually run out of mental steam around 3 p.m. I figured that if I got all the chores out of the way quickly, I could get through *Two for Joy* by about 2:30.

It was obvious this time around that Eleanor was an extension of Andrea. Even the glasses figured again from time to time. It took me till chapter fifteen before I understood why I hadn't picked up on the connection before. Eleanor wasn't officially the heroine; Marie was front and centre as soon as she came into the picture.

Two for Joy focuses on the friendship-cum-rivalry between two women who have known each other for many years. It's written in limited omniscient, from the point of view of society watching the two of them. Every now and then you come across a bit in italics written from the point of view of one of the women. For the longest time, you think the voice is that of Eleanor, the retiring one who seems to adhere to everything Marie does. After a while, and I'm still not sure how she manages it, Ahlers shifts the focus subtly and you find yourself hitting your forehead in the classic "I-could-have-had-a-V8" action and shouting out loud, "It's Marie!" All the time the reader is certain that Marie is the leader and Eleanor the follower, Marie is actually milking Eleanor for ideas and making a splash with them herself. She has fooled Eleanor, she has fooled the world, and she has almost fooled herself into believing that she's the innovator.

Once the reader cottons onto the fact that Marie is actually using Eleanor and sapping her of all her strength, you'd expect the book to go for the jugular. There Ahlers goes and fools you again. The book becomes almost lyrical in its treatment of Marie after this point. Eleanor's willingness to let Marie use her only serves to condemn Eleanor in the eyes of the reader, and even Marie herself is convinced by the end of the narrative that her hand has been forced by Eleanor's passivity.

It's a complicated little plot, and what with having to remember to juggle the italics back to Marie instead of identifying them with Eleanor, it took me some time to get through it again. I'd almost gauged it correctly, though. At 3:30, I looked up from the novel to find I'd managed to cover about fifty cue cards with notes and page references.

About half of these corresponded exactly with references from the first novel. The rest were what you'd expect to find of Andrea grown up a bit. I estimated the ages of Eleanor and Marie to fall into the twenty to thirty-five range as the story progressed.

I'd also had to create an entirely new category along the way. I turned the pink cards over to the unlined side and wrote down things that other characters (in this case, mainly Marie) said about Eleanor. The authorial voice wove in and out of the narrative so much, it was difficult to distinguish it at times from that of Marie.

For various reasons, I had figured that *The Children of Magpie* would be the easiest of the three to get through. For one thing, Isabel is front and centre as the main character. Not only do we get her in the story's present, at about age thirty-five, we also get her flashbacked as a child and younger woman. I jumped right in after scoffing down some Kraft Dinner, estimating that I'd have at least half the book covered by the time my eyes gave out for the night.

As usual, I'd figured wrong. By 8:30, I had only managed to fill eleven cue cards, and I felt myself bogging down. I set the book aside and tried to figure out where I was going wrong.

I knew it wasn't the character; Isabel was obviously the extension of Andrea and Eleanor. She was quiet and very internalized. Unfortunately, for my purposes, there was not enough time spent on Isabel—she acted more as a lens for the action. Any information I did glean was mainly old Andrea-covered territory. *The Children of Magpie*, which had practically led me like a Baedeker up to the Peace River Country, was not taking me anywhere close to Isabel. In fact, if there was anyone I got to know well in these pages, it was Isabel's grandmother.

Sure, there had been a lot of focus on her in the first novel, but that was from the viewpoint of a child. The grandmother in *Magpie* was seen in hindsight, which they say is 20/20. I've never been completely convinced of that old fallacy, but how else to judge what a character written by a specific author does or doesn't remember about another character on two different occasions?

To make a long story shorter, I didn't find any glaring character discrepancies in the cue-card reportage I'd culled from the third novel. The books obviously formed a loose-knit trilogy—*One for Sorrow, Two for Joy*. If only there were a "three" in the third title. I looked at the titles again, where I had been doodling them on a yellow cue card. Together, they looked like some sort of nursery rhyme, but not one that I was familiar with. And why "Magpie" anyway? There was no reference to it in the novel, and I'd not come across any magpie references up in the Peace Country. Now, if it had only been a trumpeter swan in the title, we'd have been cooking. Was it some Aboriginal legend, perhaps? I was going to have to hit the reference library tomorrow, and the realization deflated me. What if I wasn't on the right track after all?

17.

Google and Wikipedia may have changed the game, but back when research required physical movement instead of Boolean searches, the place to go was the library. I loved libraries, especially the open-stack variety. I'm a lot better off combing the shelves, once I've zoned in on the general area, than whipping through card catalogues. Closed stacks are sort of like those fishing games at the county fair; you cast your hook, but you never know what you're going to get, or what's sitting right next to what you hooked that you should have been asking for. I headed for the subject card drawers, figuring I would focus on which floor to aim for after narrowing down the search. I ended up with three main places to look: children's literature, ornithology, and Aboriginal legends.

I riffled through nursery rhymes with no luck. Four-and-twenty blackbirds was as close as I could get to magpies there. I headed next for the birding books, from Audubon to local editions. Still no luck, although I learned that the magpie is a scrappy, thieving bird that has taken to city life like helzapoppin'. It was also apparently a nickname for an Anglican bishop. I had a sneaky feeling this wasn't the kind of information that would help me. Reading through First Nations studies on legends got me no further. The Micmac have a legend about some geese and a turtle, and the coastal nations favour the Sunbird and the Thunderbird, but as far as I could figure, neither of these feathered deities even slightly resembled a magpie.

After a discouraging hour or two, I wended my way back down to the reference table, knowing that I should have headed there first. I was also armed with the self-righteous knowledge that I had done my level best not to bother the reference librarians.

Seriously, my advice to anyone who wants to know something, and doesn't have all the time in the world to soak up lots of other information along the way, is to make a beeline straight for the reference librarian or archivist's desk. Not only do these people know their information storage systems backward and forward, they are also goldmines of information in their own rights. I'd once met an archivist in Kingston who was an expert on the history and craft of taxidermy, and there's a woman at the Glenbow who knows the words to all the old Wobbly strike tunes.

I wasn't expecting miracles this time, but I sure wasn't going to leave an unturned stone in my wake, either. The woman smiled as I approached. A university library can be a lonely place to work in the summertime. She looked to be about fifty, and when she said hello she gave away her origin as somewhere in England. I can't often pinpoint regional dialects, but I felt safe enough in guessing she was from the southern part of the island nation. I flashed what I hoped was my winningest smile and began what I knew was going to sound like a very strange request.

"Magpies? You mean the black-and-white birds that you see all over campus?"

"Yes, those are the ones. I was wondering if you knew of any legends or local stories attached to them, or where I might find such stories."

"My goodness, I'm not sure I know of any. Wait a moment … they're the birds my Auntie Jean used to count on, aren't they?"

"I beg your pardon?"

"She'd spot them in groups and count them off with a rhyme." Her smile faded as she furrowed her brow. "Now, how did that go…"

While it was a long shot, I figured I'd give it a try. "It wouldn't go something like, 'One for sorrow, two for—'"

"That's it!" she exclaimed. The desk librarians shot a judgmental glance our way. Her voice modulated down quickly in embarrassment, but her words hung in the air for me anyway. "Yes, that's her rhyme:

One for sorrow, two for joy,
Three for a girl, four for a boy,
Five for silver, six for gold,
Seven for a story never told.

I suppose it must be odd to see seven of them together. It's a little fortune-telling game, you see? Silly, I suppose. Now where else might there be something?"

She turned to her computer to see if she could locate anything else about the squawky birds, but I thanked her and wandered out of the library in a semi-daze. I needed a cup of coffee. I'd happily have substituted a beer, but it was only 10 in the morning.

One for sorrow, two for joy. Three and four became the children of the magpie. I knew then that there had to be a fourth novel. The carbon paper was not lying. This wasn't planned as a trilogy, it was a quartet. Somewhere, somehow, I was going to find a copy of *Feathers of Treasure*—silver and gold.

18.

I probably over-caffeinated myself the rest of the day, but I was too preoccupied to notice or count cups. By 10:30 that evening I was pacing around my apartment, feeling like a computer cursor buffeting through its program on sensory overload. I was almost literally bouncing off the walls trying to figure out what to do next. It was really no wonder I almost had a heart attack when I spotted the face peering in my window.

Though not as far north as Grande Prairie, Edmonton still boasts long summer nights. Around the solstice, the sun doesn't set completely till after 11 p.m. By 10:30 on the 28th of July, though, there is enough shadow cast to make even your mother look like the Garneau Grabber, in the right context.

I screamed. The face didn't disappear.

I screamed again and began pawing for the phone, which was supposed to be somewhere on the wall beside me. I had the receiver in my hand before I realized that the face belonged to

Guy. With my heart still doing aerobics, I made my way up the stairs to let him in.

"You scared me half to death," I sputtered at him.

He was too busy chewing me out to notice. I was crazy, I was impossible to reach; I put people in the awkward position of worrying about me. Why hadn't I answered my phone messages? Now I was overreacting and making him feel like some kind of peeping Tom.

I had a feeling that blame for the greenhouse effect was going to be laid at my feet at any minute—no doubt it had something to do with the deodorant I used. I am always amazed at people's capacity to designate blame. There was really nothing to do but let Guy's tirade run its course, so I turned my back on him and plugged in the kettle.

I had mugs and milk out on the table and the water was nearly boiling when he finally stopped for breath. Because I knew it would really bug him, I apologized. It had been careless of me to disregard my phone machine, but the truth was I'd forgotten about it. I'd only bought it in the first place because people were always harping on at me about my not being available when they wanted me. Now I was getting chewed out anyway. Life was not fair.

My meek reply deflated Guy's pomp like nobody's business. I grinned as he sat down and accepted a steaming mug of tea. Even after the tongue-lashing, I was glad to see him. I was longing to tell him about the magpie verse, and the character connections, but something warned me to keep my trap shut. After all, he had been pretty distant recently. Besides, I was curious to know what had brought him here out of the blue. I couldn't even attach a date to the last time I'd seen him. Maybe my mother did have cause to worry about my marital future.

"So, do I have to go rewind my phone machine, or are you going to tell me what you want?"

Guy looked smug. "Do not ask what you can do for your fellow grad student. Ask what your fellow grad student can do for you."

"You came over in the middle of the night, scaring me out of my socks, to do me a favour? I think it's time you brushed up on your Emily Post, my boy."

"You neglect to realize that had you, like a reasonable human being, deigned to look at your answering machine, I wouldn't have been forced to stoop to the ignominy of tapping at your basement window."

"That's as may be, but you still haven't told me what you want."

"Let me savour the moment, Randy. It's not that often I find myself in the position to be magnanimous."

"Hmmm. Maybe I will go listen to the phone machine after all."

"Nice try. It's full of cryptic but urgent messages from yours truly. Believe me, this is not the sort of thing you just spill over the phone."

"Guy! Will you tell me already?"

"Okay. As you may have noticed, I've been spending a wee bit of time with my third reader lately."

"Your third reader?"

"Hilary Quinn." He read the puzzlement on my face. "Oh, I assumed you knew. She has no position even remotely close to my dissertation, but for some reason it seemed politic at the time to ask her."

"Hilary Quinn is your third reader."

"There's an echo in here, kiddo. You should have that seen to." Guy crossed his long, hairy legs, making himself more comfortable. He really did have very nice legs, especially in shorts—a soccer player's legs. He caught me staring and grinned. "Are you even listening?"

"Of course I'm listening. You were just telling me how you've been consorting with the enemy."

"I had a feeling you might take it that way. Let me explain. Think of me not as a traitor so much as an infiltrator. Kind of a Trojan Horse, if you gather my meaning."

Guy went on to explain that he had talked the Ice Lady into lending him her office for the rest of the summer while she was off doing some research. The upshot was that he had access to Quinn's office—and he was offering me a wallow in forbidden mud. Would I like to see the interior of some fascinating filing cabinets?

Would I? Would I ever.

19.

To say I was too excited to get much sleep that night could be a winning entry in the *Guinness Book of Records* as "understatement of the year." I could almost taste victory. In less than twenty-four hours, I would be inside Hilary Quinn's office where I was certain I would lay eyes on Margaret Ahlers' fourth novel. She had killed Ahlers and stolen her work, and would somehow gain superstar status by "discovering" her posthumous work. And I was going to stop her.

I wasn't sure what kept me from telling Guy about my discoveries. Maybe it was my suspicions about his motivations. I tried my best to shake the feeling; after all, he was doing me an incredible favour. All the same, I was uneasy. How loyal should one be to one's third reader? I honestly didn't know the answer to that question, and the whole set-up felt odd. MA candidates don't usually know their third readers at all; typically, they come from another department on campus. And of course PhDs were a whole other ball of string.

Could Guy have been tagging along this whole time on Quinn's orders? Was there really something sinister going on, or was this all in my imagination? How could Guy wangle permission to use Quinn's office without being close to her? That last was no mystery, I suppose; I'd seen Guy working his charms on all and sundry, provided they were female. He often had a trail of them simpering behind him. On the other hand, wasn't Quinn supposed to be gay? Would Guy's effervescent charms work on her at all?

I decided—or rather my body decided—to give the puzzle a rest at about 4 in the morning. I set my alarm for 7 a.m., and woke bleary-eyed to a rainy day. Half of me was rejoicing; the much-needed rain would cool down my stuffy basement suite. The other half was wondering how on earth I was going to sneak into Quinn's office wearing my bright yellow sou'wester.

I needn't have worried. Guy met me at Java Jive and bought me a seventy-five cent cup of heaven. He told me Quinn's nearest office neighbour was away on naval exercises and that he hadn't spotted anyone else in the hallway all morning. Quinn's office was in the far northeast corner of the fourth floor. All I had to do was take the far eastern stairwell up from the mall level two flights of stairs and duck into the office. None of the English department staff who knew I shouldn't be there would be around to see me, Guy claimed, and the Religious Studies folks across the hall wouldn't know me from Adam. I countered that this last was an unfortunate choice of words, because Religious Studies types were more likely than most to recognize Adam if they spotted him. Guy gave only a nod for what I felt was a rather witty remark under the circumstances. I couldn't believe how nervous I was feeling.

Guy had been right about the ease of access to Quinn's lair. No one saw us go in, I was sure of it. He looked me straight in the eye. "You've got one day in here, and be neat about it. If you have to go out for any reason, unlock the door and close it behind you, but make sure it's locked tight when you leave for good."

"Aren't you staying?"

"No. One felony per term is enough for me. Besides, I have a dissertation to write."

"Where will you be?"

"I'll be in the library most of the day. I'll phone you later, shall I?"

"Yes, call me tonight, after ten. If I don't answer, please come find me."

Guy must have seen the sudden panic flashing across my face. "Hey, don't worry about it. What can possibly happen to you in the Humanities Building?"

"Right," I laughed, a little shakily. "I'll talk to you later."

"Yes, you will," he said, and gave me a swift kiss. "Good luck, Randy. I hope this is what you really want." He strode down the hallway, leaving me to curse his cryptic soul. Just what had he meant by that remark?

I closed the door behind him and leaned against it, surveying the uncharted landscape I was about to dive into. My mouth felt dry and my hands were sweaty as I reached out for the drawer of the filing cabinet nearest to me.

Three hours later, I was no longer nervous—just tired and dusty. I had finger-crept surreptitiously through every drawer and file in Quinn's territory, and there was nothing on Ahlers apart from a few file folders with rough drafts of Quinn's previously published articles on the novels. I plonked myself down in Quinn's swivel chair and began to spin myself around aimlessly. There had to be a clue to the fourth novel here somewhere.

I had been through the filing cabinets, desk, and computer table. The only other pieces of furniture in the office were the bookcases, which lined the walls with even a shelf above the door. Maybe the manuscript was in a hollowed-out book. I chuckled and tried to recall where this rather silly piece of detective trivia had come from, but by this point anything seemed worth a try. I decided to flip through all books more than an inch thick. I was going to concentrate on books that were larger than eight and a half by eleven inches, or big enough to hide print pages, but then I remembered the photocopy reducer in the main office and decided that any size book was fair game if it was thick enough.

Before long, I spotted a book that protruded a bit from the others on the shelf. The dust on the shelf in front of it had been recently disturbed as well. In my eagerness, I tried riffling from front to back, but it was a no-go. The pages seemed to be stuck together. My heart began to beat faster. I sat the book on the desk and opened it to the first page. As I leafed past the frontispiece and the table of contents, I got more and more excited. As my elation built, I slowed down my actions to accentuate the anticipation. I just knew that in a page or two, I would be looking at Ahlers' final novel, *Feathers of Treasure.*

I was wrong.

What I found in the book safe, for that indeed is what it was, were four floppy disks. All they had for identification was a number in the upper-left corner: one, two, three, and four. Was this what I had been looking for? Why would Quinn input an entire manuscript onto floppy disks? And where were the two paper copies of Ahlers' last novel? I knew there had to be two copies—otherwise, why bother with carbon paper? But inputting a whole novel that had been typed out as hard copy originals? That was one humungous load of typing. It was, however, the only lead I had. I had just hoped Quinn hadn't taken her command disk with her.

I quickly located the command diskette, the floppy containing the operating system for her word processing program, in the left drawer of her desk. Thank God, I thought, she used Wordstar. The last thing I needed was the challenge of figuring out another computer language.

My happiness was short-lived. Quinn may have guilelessly relinquished her office keys to Guy's big green eyes, but she had most definitely locked down her computer work with passwords.

Second-guessing an enemy can sometimes be easier than second-guessing a friend. That said, having to second-guess anyone is a pain in the ass.

After about two hours of steady plodding, I had worked my way through all the characters' names in Ahlers' opus and most of the place names as well. On the theory that the vowels would fall in order, I tried every girl's name that I could think of that begins with an O. I tried all forms of the magpie rhyme that I could think of, including the word "magpie." My vision was beginning to blur from staring at the blinking green of the screen. I leaned back in the chair and tried to relieve my tired eyes by focusing on alternating far and middle distances. I looked out the window at the High Level Bridge, and then moved my head slightly to the right and stared at the Euphemia McNaught painting of the lake with the mega-horizons, then repeated the sequence again and again. Suddenly, something made me stop and focus more intently on the McNaught.

I hadn't looked at the painting closely since I entered the office, but now I couldn't seem to take my eyes off it. When I'd first seen it, I'd been captivated by the stylishness of the work. Armed as I now was with first-hand knowledge of the Peace Country, I recognized the realism behind the abstract lines. That was Trumpeter Lake; I'd stake my life on it. It was, in fact, almost exactly the same view I'd seen from Quinn's cabin.

A devilishly simple idea stole through my brain. The floppies had been found in a book subtitled *Art and Artifice.* Obviously, things were not what they seemed in this office. Well, two could play at that game. I wasn't looking for an Ahlers name; I was looking for a Quinn name. I turned back to the computer keyboard and typed EUPHEMIA.

For a moment, nothing happened. Then the screen went temporarily blank. I was beginning to think I'd destroyed Quinn's computer when the cursor at last began to move across the screen. Trailing in its wake, like a banner behind a biplane, were the words *Feathers of Treasure: A Novel by Margaret Ahlers.*

I checked the length of the files on the disk. The novel ran about 350K. As much as I wanted to read it right away, I knew that the best idea was to get a copy. It would be an easy matter to copy it all onto another diskette, but that wouldn't do me much good once I was out of Quinn's office and away from her command disk. I'd have to get a hard copy. I glanced at Quinn's old-style dot-matrix printer. Why didn't they equip profs with laser printers, or even bubble jets? This was going to take forever.

I checked the printer ribbon and paper supply, and then set the ON switch alight. The PRINT program was a single-command affair, and pretty soon the office was echoing with one of the most irritating sounds known to modern man. Pages were churning out at the rate of about two per minute. I calculated that I was in for about three hours of this cacophony. If I could get hooked into a story, I could distract myself from the sound. I settled into Quinn's easy chair with her copy of Rita Donovan's *Daisy Circus.* As much as I wanted to be reading Ahlers' novel instead, I wasn't about to scan it line by line as it fed out of the printer. That kind of behaviour was enough to drive you mad in hurry.

I must have dozed off, lulled to sleep by the mechanical drone of the printer. I woke to a loud pounding. My first thought was that the printer had run amok, but it seemed to be fine. In fact, it seemed to have completed the task. I just had time to quickly check my watch and glance out the window into the dusk to ascertain how long I'd been out before the pounding started up again. My brain finally woke up enough to realize that someone was at the door. I crept up to the door as quietly as possible and peered through the keyhole.

A few years ago, it seems there was a lot of trouble in the Humanities Building with nutjobs harassing the female staff who worked late at night. In a fit of brilliance, the maintenance department had installed peepholes in the doors of all the female members of the staff—and only those of the females. I figured it was probably cheaper than flashing neon lights—but equally effective at identifying the proper doors to any wandering weirdoes. Even so, tonight I was grateful the peephole existed.

Maybe it was Guy, piped a hopeful little voice in my head. No such luck. What I saw through the fisheye lens was a stern-looking man in a brown uniform—campus security.

"Who is it?" I called through the door.

"Just checking, ma'am. Someone reported seeing a stranger in the building. I saw your light on and thought I'd check to see if you needed an escort out of the building."

A stranger in the building? All my worst nightmares were coming true—the ones about being locked up in a dark hallway with a serial killer. Unless I was the "stranger," in which case I was miffed. I glanced at the printer—it was definitely finished. "Please give me just a minute!" I yelled. I yanked out the floppies, popped them back in their booksafe, turned off the machinery, and was in the hallway out in the corridor, clutching the manuscript under my arm, in less than a minute. "Let me just make sure I've got everything," I smiled at the guard, praying he didn't know Dr. Quinn on sight.

I turned and gave the office a thorough visual scan to double-check that everything was as I'd found it that morning. I caught sight of a pile of mail on Quinn's desk that I'd shuffled aside but not paid much attention to earlier in the day. "Wait just one more moment, could you?"

"Sure, but I'm going off shift now," he said with that added tone of belligerence that high school graduates reserve for those of us who've thrown away honest monetary pursuits for a more esoteric quest.

"I won't be a sec," I promised over my shoulder, dashing back into the room to pull something from Quinn's mail pile. Guy must have been emptying her pigeonhole in the main office. Nothing had been opened, and it was just as well. Among plastic bags containing the *Times Literary Supplement* and departmental fliers was a bright pink envelope I recognized in an instant. It was my letter to Ahlers' estate, re-labelled and sent via McKendrick Publishers. What was it doing in Quinn's office? Was she the executor I had guilelessly written to?

The security guard coughed behind me. I stuffed the envelope into my pocket and turned back to him, pulling the office door shut and locked behind me.

Within five minutes I was on a bus home, feeling like Jack sliding down the beanstalk. I didn't miss the irony that I was equating myself with a hero who was also a thief, and who by doing so had placed himself in grave personal danger. Fee fie foe fad, I smell the blood of an English grad.

20.

If McKendricks had forwarded my request to Hilary Quinn, it meant that Ahlers had made her executor of her papers. I wondered what Ahlers would have thought of a professor who denied access of such materials to her own grad student. Was that the sort of person who should be made executor of an important literary figure's work?

My irritating little inner voice piped up: "You broke into her summer cottage, ransacked her office, and have practically accused her of being a murderer, and you're annoyed that she hasn't shared Ahlers' papers with you?"

All right, all right, so I'm easily wounded. All I knew was that Quinn's disregard for the virtue of sharing had wiped out any residual guilt I'd felt about my puny crimes toward her. Reading Ahlers' last novel was going to be especially sweet because I knew Quinn would writhe if she knew about it.

I had just settled into the one comfy chair in my apartment, the accordion of computer paper stacked on my knees, when the phone rang. It was late, and I wasn't expecting to hear from anyone. I was just about to let the machine answer when I remembered that Guy was supposed to check on me. I raced to the phone, barking my leg against the doorknob as I rounded the corner.

"Hello?"

"Did you leave any signs that you'd been in there?"

"Hello, Guy. Always nice to hear from you."

"Quick, Randy, I'm serious. Should I race over there and tidy up, or what?"

"Not to worry. Of course I left it tidy—no tell-tale signs that anyone has been in there at all, with the exception of you taking the mail in." Guy's voice didn't usually carry such a tone of panic, which made me highly curious. "Why do you ask?"

"I got home about an hour ago and there was a letter from Quinn in my mail. She's coming home earlier than expected. In fact, she'll be back on Wednesday. I just wanted to make absolutely sure that everything is as it should be, because I have to spend the next two days down in Interlibrary Loans, filling out forms."

"So there's no pressing need to get the wagons in a circle?"

"No, I guess not. Why do I feel like everything gets a little cloak-and-dagger whenever you're involved in things, Randy? Did you at least find what you were looking for?"

"I found plenty of evidence that she's not gifted in the filing department. Apart from that, not much."

"Ah well, I thought it was worth a try."

"Yeah, well, thanks anyway."

"I guess I'll see you soon."

"Yeah. Take care, Guy."

"You too, Randy. G'night."

"G'night."

I hung up with a sigh and stared at the phone in front of me. Why had I lied to Guy? It must have been a reflexive action, because consciously I'd had every intention of telling him about the manuscript. But there had been something in his voice, something odd. It made me wonder again if he wasn't a little closer to his third reader than he liked to let on.

That was ridiculous! If he was Quinn's henchman, why would he have let me into her office? Quinn certainly wouldn't have wanted me there. Again I thanked the heavens that I'd been able to rescue the fuchsia envelope. I certainly didn't need to telegraph my moves to Quinn any more than I already had.

I wandered back into the ersatz living room. Waiting by the chair was a cup of decaf and three hundred pages' worth of Pandora's box. Was I worried?

I smiled and went for it. A person can't spend her life ruled by fairy tales and superstitions.

The first thing that struck me was that *Feathers of Treasure* was a mystery novel. I couldn't believe what I was seeing at first, but as I turned the pages it became clear that the character Ophelia wasn't kidding when she introduced herself as a private eye. It was the first of Ahlers' novels to be written completely in the first person, and I wasn't initially sure that I cared for the change.

About midway through the book, I realized that not only was I enjoying myself, but that this was no ordinary mystery novel.

If you can imagine Paul Quarrington getting together with Italo Calvino and reworking an idea by Dashiell Hammett, you'd have some concept of what I found myself reading. There were mysteries within mysteries, and Ophelia wasn't much good as an investigator. In fact, she was turning out to be a much better victim in a "Perils of Pauline" sort of way. The evil characters kept splitting into twins; as the story became increasingly confusing, it also began to take on more and more characteristics of the old hard-boiled detective novels.

Ophelia wore white all the time. She had a theory that being very showy was in itself the best camouflage. No one would suspect her of being a private eye if she was so obvious. The trouble was, absolutely everyone knew she was a private eye—they just didn't take her seriously.

Ahlers had turned the entire genre on its ear without malice. In fact, even though it was a wicked parody of the form—even the title was a parody, based on plucking and trussing *The Maltese Falcon*—I wouldn't be surprised if *Feathers of Treasure* wasn't good enough to be at least nominated for an Arthur Ellis Award by the Crime Writers of Canada.

I wondered what the academic circles would make of this shift of genre. And I was willing to bet that Quinn didn't like it one bit. In fact, it made me chuckle out loud to imagine Quinn's reaction to this final book from Ahlers. My laughter died in the air as my thoughts shifted clear; Quinn's reaction to Ahlers' last novel might indeed be what motivated the tragic events that had ensured it would be her last.

I grabbed my legal pad. Scribbling always helps me think.

Quinn knew Ahlers. Quinn was making her academic reputation on Ahlers' back, in a manner of speaking. Quinn was finally getting some recognition in her field. Ahlers, her so-called friend, turns around and writes a mystery novel—a form considered "sub-literary" by most academics and literary snobs the world over. Quinn would be apoplectic! And suppose Ahlers had intended to write more mysteries, perhaps even make Ophelia a series detective. It could be done, I supposed. She was a pretty rich character; maybe not quite Hercule Poirot, but certainly comparable to Peter Shandy.

That kind of thing could hamper Quinn's career more than a bit. She'd have to branch into the study of genre work, and then who knows—she could attract hordes of pimply honours students, whose only virtue was having seen every episode of *Star Trek*, wanting to do their tutorials with her on the grounds that she was sympathetic to popular culture. I was beginning to see grounds for murder, all right.

So, if I was to assume Quinn read *Feathers of Treasure* and came to the same dire conclusions I had just reached, she would then murder Ahlers, become executor of her late friend's papers, and sit on the mystery novel to maintain her ideal of a standard.

I bought it as a motive, but I wasn't persuaded the police would. I couldn't see them taking the mentality of "publish or perish"—or in this case, "publish and perish"—in its literal sense. Would anyone believe me? What I really needed was proof of the crime itself. Or perhaps a signed confession. Hey, I'm not fussy.

I woke up on Monday morning in a cold sweat.

I have always prided myself on bringing assignments in on time, no matter what. While it may mean a sleepless night or two, it also guarantees future business. Nobody wants to go searching for their hired-gun freelancer while technicians and typesetters twiddle their thumbs with nothing to do. There may be flashier writers in the business, but there are none more dependable.

Yet here it was Monday, and I had to have a chapter in to Quinn for Thursday.

I had to admit it was anti-climactic to be thinking about essay deadlines when there was a possible murder to uncover, but on the other hand I figured that even Miss Marple had to do her ironing on Tuesdays. I might as well dig in and get to work instead of wasting more time griping about it.

Guy phoned just as the coffee was perking. He was a lot easier to put off than enticing thoughts of the mysterious mystery novel, but even so it took twenty minutes to convince him that I wasn't interested in driving out to see buffalo in a paddock at Elk Island National Park. I was laughing at his usual inanities as I got off the phone, but as I poured my coffee I began to wonder why he suddenly seemed so fancy-free. I thought he'd claimed to be slating in a long stint in periodicals or something. I dragged myself over to my Kaypro and leaned forward to find the ON switch at the back. Pretty soon I'd forgotten all about Guy, Quinn, and everything else—including my cup of coffee, which tasted horrible cold—in an attempt to pull together my thoughts on regionalism.

The more I worked, the more I realized that this was going

to be a down-to-the-wire job. Not only was my pride a factor in all of this, I had to make the chapter good enough to convince Quinn that I'd been working on it for the past two months. The last thing I needed was my advisor suspecting I'd been exploring her past instead, burglarizing her cabin and ransacking her office.

It was past 9 in the evening on Wednesday when I hit the twenty-page mark. I was exhausted, and I'd been over the same passages so many times that any attempt to objectively proof the chapter would have been absurd by this point. There was no one to call at this time of night, although Maureen probably would have proofed it out of the goodness of her heart. I figured a whisk through the spell-checker would have to do the trick.

Finally, at 11:10, I was holding a printed copy of Chapter One. It wasn't the best thing I'd ever written, but it was by no means a disaster. Quinn might be able to find fault with my argument, but there was no way she could sink me on not knowing the material. I knew those books inside out. Upside down. Backwards. In fact, if hypnotized, I might even be able to quote most of Ahlers' opus verbatim. That's how immersed I was.

That's one thing they don't put in the "welcome to graduate school" materials: close textual analysis can sometimes get you killed.

21.

The university was mired in that stalemated, becalmed time of the year; the stretch that hits just around the tenth of August, when it's too hot to party, too late to make summer travel plans, and far too close to all the fall deadlines you set yourself back in May. I had about five hours left to complete as a research assistant for Dr. Spanner. RA work is never fun and rarely interesting, but at least Dr. Spanner's requests seemed to have a purpose behind them. She would deposit detailed requests in my pigeonhole and leave me to ferret out the information from the MLA.

It now appeared that she'd received some rather ambiguous feedback from a reviewer when submitting her most recent article on the sonnets. The reviewer made some comparison to a fellow who'd made some comparison to Petrarch—it was all rather convoluted, and they'd neglected to provide a reference for the citation. It thus fell to me to find everything this fellow had ever written and locate the article the reviewer had drawn from.

I had a list of about nine titles dating back to 1968, which was the date of the fellow's dissertation. I know, I know, some people publish while still in grad school, but I always assume those folks are either aberrations who are true geniuses or folks who just couldn't get dates in grad school. Besides, the MLA makes me sneeze. Armed with my meagre list, I left Rutherford North and headed for the Periodical Library in Rutherford South.

I love the Periodical Library. For one thing, it's housed in the older part of the library, which makes me feel like I'm in an old Jimmy Stewart movie just by walking through the doors. The marble stairs have grooves worn in them from seventy-odd years of academic trundling. The librarians' counter is made of old oak, and the microfiche machines are tastefully tucked out of sight around the corner. As for the periodicals themselves, they are housed in rabbit warrens that can only be reached by climbing up and down narrow stairwells and sidling along ceiling-high metal stacks. Every time I came here, I promised myself that I would drop by weekly to read the *Times Literary Supplement* or browse through old copies of *The New Yorker.* I never seem to get around to it, though. Somehow, once I left the Periodical Library, it always vanished back into the mist like a bibliophile's Brigadoon adjacent to HUB mall—reappearing only when I had another article to find.

I'd found three of the rather ponderous-looking journals on my list and decided to head upstairs to locate the fourth before lining up to photocopy them for Dr. Spanner's files. I was so busy juggling tomes that it wasn't until I was halfway into the tiny aisle that I realized I was no longer alone. I looked up, expecting to see a librarian or another grad student. Unless you had to be here, or suffered from sun allergies, no one would pick a beautiful day like this to visit the stacks. But it wasn't a staff member, and I guess melanoma fears are underrated in Alberta. I was alone in the stacks with Hilary Quinn.

My startled gasp sounded louder than it should have been. Perhaps it was an echo effect, or maybe I feared this woman—whom I at least half-suspected as a murderer—more than I'd even let on to myself. I found myself wishing it back, partially because it sounded so rude, and partially because it seemed to affirm something for Quinn. Something about me. I wished to hell I could read what it was in her icy eyes.

"Dr. Quinn! I didn't expect to see you here. Well, I guess I didn't honestly expect to see anyone here." Oh great, my mental editor sighed—when cornered, babble. Quinn seemed to take stock of my discomfiture and moved closer to take advantage of it.

"This is a fortuitous meeting, Miranda. I was thinking of setting up a session to discuss the implications of your chapter."

"Oh, really? I didn't think you'd be able to get on to it so quickly. I've hardly begun the next one."

"Well, that's rather fortuitous, too, actually. I certainly wanted to talk with you before you went too far down the wrong track."

The wrong track? What the hell was she talking about? I knew my chapter wasn't a masterpiece, but it did lay out the basis of a thesis we'd discussed and agreed upon in our prior meetings. It was a little dry, sure, but that quality was *de rigueur* for this type of construct. After all, academic writing doesn't tend to be edge-of-the-chair stuff.

"I notice," she continued, "that you seem to have readjusted your thinking on the concept of Ahlers' trilogy of place."

There was something in her tone of voice that was making me sweat. But I still couldn't figure out what she was getting at. Trilogy of place? A warning light was starting to glow in my head; when she hissed at me, the sirens came on.

"How did you get hold of the fourth book?"

"Fourth book?" I stuttered. For the briefest of moments, I felt thrilled and justified in my reasoning—until I realized that I hardly needed this kind of confirmation from Quinn. After all, it was her computer I'd lifted the manuscript from. Still, how did she know I'd seen it? My confused thoughts must have flashed across my face, because she laughed—grimly.

"You mixed up the character names in your chapter. It happens all the time when working closely with more than one novel, especially when the characters are all fabrications of the same author. I even find myself mixing up Isabel and Andrea at times. But you really left yourself wide open when you mistakenly referred to Eleanor as Ophelia. Really, Miranda—that's rather clumsy. How did you find out about Ophelia?"

I'm accustomed to thinking on my feet. Years of freelance interviewing—to say nothing of a session spent teaching freshmen—had inured me to off-the-wall and trick questions. Still, how do you lie convincingly when your hand is caught in the cookie jar? She was on to me. She knew, thanks to my weary brain doing a sloppy job of editing, that I had seen *Feathers of Treasure*. Where could I have seen it without risk of being charged with a felony?

I tried my best to paste on a smile bright enough to couch the bluff I was about to attempt. "I have a friend at McKendricks who let me peek."

"You're lying. McKendricks has never seen the fourth manuscript. I suppose the ins and outs of your knowledge are not really the point; what is important to me is how much you know. Your curiosity might be a very dangerous thing, for both of us."

Any doubts I'd had about her murdering Ahlers faded to black. She appeared before me as the most thoroughly cold-blooded mammal I'd ever seen. With that realization, a funny sort of calm settled over me. Otherwise, I'd never have asked her my next question.

"When did you decide to kill her?"

Quinn looked at me and laughed. It was an eerie laugh—part mockery and part crazy. "Margaret? Oh, I always knew she'd have to die."

I've heard about people who can talk terrorists out of planes, jumpers off bridges, and crazies away from their weapons. People like that must have some innate grace that overtakes them in moments of crisis. Having confronted such a critical moment, I now know one thing: I'm not that sort of person.

Dropping three volumes of *The International Symposium of Petrarchan Studies*, I turned and ran with Dr. Hilary Quinn at my heels.

22.

I dashed out of South Rutherford Library with the knowledge that at least one hound of hell was right behind me. I could hear her heels clattering on the marble steps and she was hissing my name. It just goes to show how deeply the training not to shout in libraries is embedded in our psyches. Murder was one thing, but raising a ruckus in the library was still off limits. Once outside, I turned automatically south toward the bus stop. I wasn't sure how close Quinn was to catching up with me, and I had no intention of taking the time to check.

My running must have struck a prehistoric sympathy chord in the lone bus driver there, because he paused to let me on before pulling away in one graceful motion. Fumbling with my wallet, I spotted Quinn standing at the receding curb, squinting into the sunlight to read the number on the back of the bus.

The thought that she knew where I was headed made me shudder, and was closely followed by the realization that she was one up on me; I had no idea which bus I was on.

"Where does this bus go?" I asked, over the clatter of the nickels and quarters cascading into the change box. The bus driver seemed to think my question absurd. After all, how many people rush for buses in the generic?

"West Edmonton Mall," he growled, as if I should have been able to assume as much from the tilt of his cap. I thanked him, and stumbled back into the moving vehicle to find a perch.

Oh God, not the Mall. This bus would actually go right past my home on its way to the mega-mall, but I was sure Quinn would have either looked up my address or have easy access to it. I didn't want to be cornered in a cramped basement suite with just one entrance past the furnace and laundry room. Even worse, my copy of Margaret Ahlers' unpublished novel was sitting right out on my kitchen table, and all my cue cards would clue Quinn in to the full extent of my activities. But let's be honest: she'd already figured out that I knew enough to need silencing.

I shook my head to clear the gothic thoughts that seemed so incongruous on a lazy August day in suburban Edmonton. Hilary Quinn, a respected scholar at the University of Alberta, was out to murder one of her graduate students? It didn't sound credible. But I remembered the chill feeling of dread when I'd been alone with her in the periodical stacks, and I knew I didn't want to be alone with her again. I'd take my chances at the Mall.

I've never understood the urge to hide away from other people in unpopulated areas. Humans tend to stick out, rather than blend into nature. My best shot at anonymity was to disappear into the biggest crowd I could find. If that kind of crowd was anywhere in Edmonton in the middle of a summer day, it would be at West Edmonton Mall.

I got off the bus at the terminus and scurried through the parkade to the door of the Zellers discount store. Gosh, I miss Zellers, the last of the discount stores you didn't mind getting caught shopping in. Getting caught was exactly what I didn't want, though. I figured I'd need a different shirt; my striped aqua top was too distinctive, and it's what Quinn would be looking for. I riffled through the first rack of tee-shirts I came to, picking out a black short-sleeved shirt with no advertising on it. I hate paying to be a sandwich board for a brand, band, or cartoon figure on principle, and now I needed to fade into the scenery without any catchy message or visual focus that would blare out and render me memorable to sales clerks—or easy pickings for murderers. I paid cash and hurried to the public washroom near the skating rink so I could discreetly bite off the sales ticket and whip on the shirt. It was a little loose, but I figured frumpy was better than skin-tight when I was trying not to draw attention. I pulled the elastic out of my French braid and finger-combed my hair around my shoulders. I stuffed my old shirt into the Zellers bag and froze—someone was coming into the washroom. Only when the stall door next to mine banged shut did I gather the courage to creep out of my cell.

My heart stopped again as I tried to leave the washroom. My strongest urge was to hole up, to take no chances on being seen, but I knew that I'd be crazy to sit and wait here where I could be cornered. Besides, it's one thing to see two teenage girls hanging around in a mall washroom, quite another for a lone thirty-year old. If Quinn didn't find me, I'd likely be reported. I had to keep moving.

It's all well and good to hide in a crowd, but I couldn't stand the thought that Quinn could also be somewhere among this overwhelming mass of people; I could just as easily tread on her toes as avoid her. I had to find a place where I could see without being seen first. I also really needed to sit down, gather my wits, and think. I couldn't run forever. If only the panic could subside, I might be able to formulate a plan. At this point, all I wanted was a strategy that would save my own skin. Margaret Ahlers was already dead, and there was nothing to be done for her.

I bought a coffee at the food court next to Fantasyland and sat as near as I could to the back wall. I could keep an eye on both entrances from my vantage point, and quickly make a beeline in either direction. Sitting among the tourists, tired shoppers, and overstimulated teenagers calmed me down for a bit. Everything was so ... ordinary. In a way, that was the most macabre thing about my whole flight from the library—it was so clean and bright and non-threatening. Sort of like the Bates Motel the morning after.

I noticed a kid with curly blond hair and thought about Guy. Could I trust him enough to let him know where I was? What was his connection to all of this mess, anyway? Why had he tried to get me off campus today? Did Quinn know about our collusion—or was it really collusion at all?

Call me a hopeless romantic, but intuitively I couldn't accept Guy as some sort of double agent attached to me. For one thing, Quinn had no reason to suspect my motives, or at least hadn't until the lousy Freudian slip in my thesis chapter. Freud now had even more to answer for in my books. It occurred to me that if Guy weren't in cahoots with Quinn, she would soon enough twig to how I'd got my hands on Ahlers' manuscript; only Guy had the keys to her office. But even he didn't know what I'd found there, because I'd held back on the information. If Guy really was innocent, I'd made him a sitting duck. I had to get hold of him, fast.

I carefully checked the scene before I got up to stow my coffee cup and find a phone. This would be the dangerous part. All the phone kiosks were located in highly visible central areas near the centre of the concourse. I made sure I had quarters in my hand and was jiggling them like worry beads as I nervously made my way into the middle of the mall.

I tried calling Guy at home. No answer. I tried the general office. The secretaries hadn't seen him today, and no, I didn't wish to leave a message. I didn't want to create any sort of trail for Quinn to follow, no dots connecting Guy to me. I hit the payphone in frustration. Where the hell was he? Had he really gone out to Elk Island Park on a whim? And if so, did that mean he was out of harm's way?

I don't know what made me dial the number to Quinn's office. Maybe I was still fearful of a conspiracy with Guy. Maybe I just wanted to get a bead on her logistically. If she was there, answering her phone, she couldn't also be stalking me through the mall with a butcher knife.

A mixture of relief and horror flooded through me when her voice came on the line. I was too paralyzed to say anything.

"Hello?" she repeated. She waited a beat or three and then said, "Miranda?"

I must have breathed idiosyncratically, because she continued with certitude.

"Miranda, we really must talk. I'm sure you'll want some sort of explanation, and I suppose, under the circumstances, you're entitled to one. I'm still not certain how you obtained access to the manuscript, but I have to assume you've read it."

There was silence from me, which she took as confirmation.

"Well, then I'm sure you'll understand that after this novel, there was no more need for Ahlers. Can't you see that it was best for me to silence her before her work took on second-rate signs or reduced in strength? Look what happened to Tennessee Williams in later life. He really should have been stopped after *The Rose Tattoo*."

I couldn't believe the cold-blooded way she was talking. Silencing a writer before she lost it artistically? I've heard of censorship, but this was really taking it to the limit.

"Perhaps if we could talk," Quinn continued, "I might be able to explain. It would do me good, probably, to talk about it to someone. Would you come to the office tonight, around seven? I'm sure I could make you understand my position."

"Dr. Quinn," I finally said, "I've been to Trumpeter Lake. I don't think there's anything you need to tell me."

Her voice changed somehow. I realized with hindsight that she'd been pleading with me, and she was now through. The supplication, what little she'd been able to muster, was gone from her next words.

"You've been up north. I see. Well, perhaps you're right. Perhaps there really is nothing more to say."

The dial tone began to buzz in my ear.

I made my way back to my neighbourhood with my mind on Nancy Drew. She always got clobbered in the line of busybody-ness, but she managed to spring back time after time to get the baddie. Maybe it wasn't possible to ferret out truth without getting bludgeoned. Of course, I was alone in this venture, I thought, as I rounded the house to reach the back door to my suite. Nancy always had her Ivy League boyfriend to help her out of jams. What was his name…? "Ned Nickerson!" Thrilled at being able to retrieve this bit of trivia despite my fear and exhaustion, I must have said it out loud.

"I beg your pardon?" a voice spoke from the shadows.

My heart jumped in my chest, but then I saw Guy unfolding himself from his perch on the back steps. "I know it's been a couple of days, but surely you could make a pretense of remembering my name."

I was so relieved to see him that I gave him a big, tight hug that neither of us had been expecting; we almost toppled backward onto the steps.

Guy regained his composure and balance first. "Really, Randy, what would the landlords say? Why don't we go inside so you can further demonstrate how happy you are to see me at our leisure?"

Relief at seeing him turned quickly into anger, the sort mothers demonstrate to kids who have managed to lose themselves in grocery stores. "Where the hell have you been? Do you realize what I've been through? I've been trying to call you, and..." My hand was shaking so much I couldn't direct my key into the deadbolt on the back door. Guy took the keys out of my hand like the take-charge men did in movies from the fifties, and soon we were sitting at my kitchen table. I stared at my knees as he busied himself with kettle and mugs. The next thing I knew I was drinking very sugary hot tea.

"Ewww. What's this?"

"The only part I remember from my first-aid course at St. John's Ambulance—sugar in the tea for shock. I'm assuming this is shock and not the DTs you're exhibiting, right? Where have you been anyway?"

"West Edmonton Mall."

"Ah! Then it's shock, all right."

I laughed, in spite of everything. Guy looked so concerned, so helpful, so downright nice that I decided at that moment he couldn't be some kind of evil cohort of Quinn's. Maybe it was just that I was too weary to expend energy on being suspicious of people. Ahlers had been murdered. I'd been chased. I'd been forced to change clothes in a mall toilet stall. It was all getting to be too much for me to process.

"I suppose you want to hear the story thus far," I sighed.

"If you're up to it."

"I honestly think I'll go mad if I don't talk about it."

Guy sat on the edge of one of my teetery chrome chairs while I told him of finding the hidden diskettes, my forwarded letter from the publisher revealing Quinn as the executor of Ahlers' papers, and the discovery of the fourth novel. I continued by recounting my slip in nomenclature, Quinn's admission of murder, the chase to the bus, and my terrifying flight through the mall. Piece by piece, it didn't sound like much, but connected in the torrent spilling over my tonsils it all seemed to add up. Most importantly, Guy seemed to agree with me. At least he looked captivated by my wild tale. Or maybe it was my tee-shirt.

"And then she hung up on you?" he asked finally.

"Click. Final."

"But what did she mean by 'there's nothing more to say'? What do you think she wanted to explain to you in her office?"

I shrugged. "Her relationship with Ahlers, I guess."

"But what about her relationship, specifically?"

"Guy, it's obvious—she and Ahlers were lovers. Ahlers was the creative writer, Quinn the academic. Sounds like a love/hate relationship from the outset. Real Eleanor-and-Marie stuff, if you think about it. Anyway, Ahlers allows Quinn first crack at her work, probably even before the proofs stage, so that Quinn can get a jump on everyone else in the field. Then, when the books are published, Quinn moves into the fore with her incisive critical work on the novels."

"Then why kill the goose that's laying the golden egg?"

"Because the fourth novel, the one yet unpublished, is a detective novel. It's a brilliantly subversive detective novel, but a detective novel nonetheless. Don't you see? All that territory staked on the next Margaret Laurence, or Margaret Atwood, and she turns out to be the next Margaret Millar!"

"I don't know, Randy. It feels like something's missing from the argument."

"Like what?"

"I'm not sure. But why would Ahlers write a detective novel under her own name if she was so concerned about her lover's critical reputation?"

"Maybe they fought. Maybe Ahlers ditched Quinn and got herself killed because of it."

"Or maybe Quinn ditched Ahlers and she intended to get back at her by writing a 'sub-literary' text."

"Then why show it to Quinn at all? Why not just publish and have the last laugh?"

"Maybe she just died naturally, and Ahlers' papers went to Quinn automatically from an unchanged will."

"No!" I banged my tea mug down on the table for emphasis. "I may know nothing else about this whole mess, but I do have one fact straight from the horse's mouth: Hilary Quinn killed Margaret Ahlers. Maybe it was a lovers' quarrel. Maybe it was jealousy on the part of a writer manqué. Maybe she did it to 'edit' Ahlers' work permanently. But I know she did it; she told me as much. If I want to find out why, there's only one thing left to do."

"And what's that?"

"Meet with Quinn at seven tonight."

"You can't be serious! You're actually thinking of bearding a confessed murderer in her den?"

"I have to do it, Guy. The story's not over till it's over."

"Some stories are perfectly fine without closure, you know."

There was more than theoretical argument showing on Guy's face; he was worried about my safety. But I had somehow moved beyond fear and into the realm of pure, unquenchable curiosity.

23.

The Humanities Building was locked up tight as a drum by six on summer evenings, but I was armed with my pass-key and the knowledge that Campus Security was out there, somewhere. Guy had refused to let me tackle Quinn solo, but had agreed to remain in the Grad Lounge while I kept my rendezvous. It made things easier knowing there was help within convenient screaming distance, but not enough to calm my nerves. For all my earlier bravado, I was getting seriously spooked. Guy had told me he'd wait half an hour, and then come in with metaphorical guns blazing. I took what comfort I could in that knowledge.

There was no air moving in the building, and the banners that normally looked so cheerful hanging among the skylights at ten in the morning appeared mildly malevolent in the dusky light. It was the same sort of feeling I got when visiting the Glenbow Museum's military gallery. I was clearly in an ideal state of mind to meet up with Dr. Quinn.

"Come in," was the command elicited from my hesitant knock at her office door. Quinn was expecting me. She sat behind her desk like a besieged zealot. The visitor's chair was centred in the remaining floor space. I half-expected arc lights to blaze into my face as I sat down. What the hell was I doing here?

"Thank you for keeping this appointment, Miranda. I wasn't sure you would come."

"I wasn't sure I would, either, but I thought I should get all my facts straight before I … before I do anything." I found myself stumbling over my words and thoughts. And what was I going to do with this information? Should I go to the police or the Dean of Arts?

"I suppose you'll be eager to publish, and I would prefer you got all your facts straight, as you say. I suppose it's the scholar's dilemma; does one bluster through and deny culpability in this sort of situation, or does one determine the accuracy of the presentation against one?"

I was stunned. Here was a woman on the brink of jail time, and her only concern was being quoted correctly? What the hell was she talking about? And what did she assume I was preparing for publication, anyway? This was quickly turning into more of a seminar than the dramatic showdown I had anticipated. Admittedly, I don't have much experience with murderers, but this behaviour wasn't at all what I'd imagined. I decided to blunder on through the fog.

"We are talking about the murder of Margaret Ahlers?"

To my surprise, Quinn laughed. It wasn't an attractive laugh, and there seemed to be no joy in it, but then I didn't have much of a basis of comparison, considering I'd hardly ever seen her crack a smile before.

"You sound like Conan Doyle's mother. No, of course not. I'm speaking about the creation of Margaret Ahlers."

My face must have betrayed my astonishment, because this time Quinn did more than chuckle.

"Oh ho! Now I understand! You have been cast as a modern Don Quixote, Miranda. You are out to avenge the death of a fiction. I'm sorry to have to tell you that your giant is nothing more than a windmill."

"What are you talking about?" I stammered, even as a glimmer of truth was beginning to take forth in my mind.

"I assumed you knew the truth when you spoke of Trumpeter Lake. I thought you'd found the dresses and the dummy."

"The dummy?"

"I kept a dressmaker's dummy there. I'd put flashy clothes on it, and situate it around the cottage and the grounds so people would assume there were two women up there, instead of just me."

I flashed on poor Dot, stumbling over the "L-word."

"It worked," I admitted. "I heard all about the two ladies who came to stay every summer—you and your shadowy lover."

"My lover? How wonderful. I wasn't sure my clever neighbours would make that connection. Well, I suppose it's hardly any wonder that I never had any nosy visitors traipsing over to introduce themselves."

"But why? Why go to all the bother of creating a second woman?"

"I needed the solitude to get as much work done as I could. And in case it became necessary, I needed to create the illusion that Margaret Ahlers actually existed. Now I see that it was, in fact, necessary. You must have been quite industrious to follow such a meagre trail."

Finally, I was getting some praise from my advisor! This wasn't quite what I'd had in mind, but it kept me in a state of shocked silence nonetheless. Quinn noticed it, and continued in a more professorial tone. It occurred to me, somewhat irrelevantly, that she must be a pretty good lecturer.

"There never was an Ahlers, Miranda. I created her, and then disposed of her when she had fulfilled her purpose."

"You wrote the novels?"

"You still don't understand, do you? It was the only way I had to make a name for myself in this business. Oh, we hate to call it a business, but behind the ivy-covered walls lies a cutthroat industry like any other. To get tenure and advance, one must publish. To publish, one needs a topic—preferably a topic that no one else has exhausted with their own minutiae. There simply aren't that many suitable topics to go around, in case you hadn't noticed."

The trouble was, I had noticed. Why else would I have been so eager to tackle Ahlers? Because she was so fantastic, or because she represented virgin territory? Quinn was convincing, but one thing still didn't make sense.

"But if you can write like Ahlers—or, I mean, like you did—why didn't you just publish the novels under your own name? Why hide from that kind of talent?"

"You mean, why hide from the glory and the honour of being a lauded author?"

I nodded.

"All I have ever wanted, my entire life, was to be an academic. Always. Even before I first came to university. I knew that someday I'd be here, where I belong. Not all critics are failed writers, although that's what most people assume. Some of us truly revel in exploring the words of others—what those words say about the authors, the readers, and our civilization. I had to get into the enclave. Perhaps it was cheating, but I knew that this was the only place I belonged, the only place where I could function properly." She looked slowly around her office, this precious niche she had carved for herself in the fortress of great minds. "I was finally granted tenure six months ago. I no longer need to be novel, just insightful. In short, I don't need Ahlers anymore."

"Then why the mystery novel?"

"Oh, is that worrying you? I was already playing around with a bit of magic realism and postmodern tweaks, trying to expand Ahlers' realm. After all, Atwood is making inroads into speculative fiction and Kinsella has a whole ghostly baseball team popping up in a cornfield. It seemed like the right move, while I was working on it. Then I got wind of the tenure committee's decision. Since I was almost done, I finished it. Perhaps it was the hint of skullduggery behind my own actions that inspired it. I don't suppose I'll have it published by Ahlers posthumously, after all, though. It really doesn't fit the oeuvre, does it?"

I was no longer afraid of Quinn. She inspired disbelief, and a bit of pity, but no fear. If what she said was true, I held her future in my hands like Alice's pack of cards.

"If I expose this fraud, what will happen to you?"

Quinn returned to reality and stared at me. "If you publish what you know, my career ceases to be. This would not be entirely your fault. I knew the risks involved when I conceived of the shortcut. I won't beg you not to tell; I've never begged for anything in my life. I'll have to wait and see what you decide. But do remember: whatever you decide will affect your windmills, too."

I was being dismissed.

I left Quinn sitting behind her hard-won desk, staring at a Euphemia McNaught painting that must have reminded her, every day, just how far she'd come.

The meeting had taken twenty minutes. I turned down the hall toward the Grad Lounge to retrieve my Sancho Panza.

24.

Guy and I were up most of the night, going over everything we knew and some of what I'd learned from Quinn that evening. Even thought I'd sworn him to secrecy, I wasn't letting him in on everything—at least until I decided what to do about it all. What I had told him was that Quinn had access to an unpublished manuscript that Ahlers hadn't lived to publish, that she had been hyperbolizing and I had misunderstood her when I thought she'd confessed to murder, and that she was considering suppressing the new book to preserve Ahlers' reputation as a mainstream writer.

"I still don't see where the conundrum lies," Guy said, continuing the argument he'd been presenting for the last hour or so. "This could set you up for life. You expose the suppression of a literary work and it nets you a thesis, a mass-market book, and maybe even an interview with Vicki Gabereau. So what's the problem?"

"If I expose Quinn—and really, how much of a crime is it

to not publish a friend's manuscript if you think it is substandard?—then quite apart from what happens to Dr. Quinn's career, what becomes of Margaret Ahlers' work? People would be forever after measuring one work against the other." I was spitballing, offering Guy half-truths and hoping I didn't stumble over myself in doing so. I did feel a commitment to Ahlers more than Quinn; the two were still separate in my mind, no matter what I had just had confessed to me.

"So what are you saying?" Guy broke through my silence.

"I guess I'm saying that I'm not going to do anything about it."

"Okay, but what about the next eager bloodhound who comes along? Secrets never stay buried. Ahlers probably said something to someone about a fourth book. Someone's going to come up with the goods eventually, so why shouldn't it be you?"

"Because I have to live with myself." I shook my head and shrugged myself into motion. "I'm beat. I need about twenty hours of sleep and then some. Go home, Guy. I'll call you when I get myself back in gear."

"You do that. I'll come and take you out for a sinfully large breakfast at Uncle Albert's."

"Yum." I gave him a quick kiss. "And Guy—I know you don't understand, or approve, but thanks for the solidarity."

"No problem, comrade. You know me, always one to play by the rules."

I went to sleep thinking about Guy, who didn't really understand me, and Quinn, who did. And I also dreamt of a shadowy woman in a flowery dress, standing on the far side of a lake.

No matter what Quinn thought, she did exist. And no matter what Guy thought, it was she to whom I owed my loyalty.

The phone woke me. It was Guy.

"Randy?"

"I said I'd call you, Mr. Eager. What time is it, anyway?"

"Randy, I'm over at the English Department. I thought you ought to know right away … Dr. Quinn killed herself last night. Here, in her office." Silence. "Randy?"

I hung up the phone. There was nothing to say.

As a detective, I'd been worse than E.C. Bentley's Trent. The most you could say for me was that I'd been persistent. And finally, after all the digging, I'd succeeded where a lot of literary critics fail.

I spent the morning with Guy at the English Department. The police were there, but Dr. Quinn had left a note giving her motives as grief over the death of a friend amid stress-related job pressures, so they didn't seem too interested in questioning hordes of people. She'd had a shotgun, something I hadn't found while searching her office. She had likely brought it with her from home. Apparently no one seemed to think it unusual that she would have a shotgun, being an Alberta girl. According to the officer keeping gawkers from traipsing down the hallway, shotguns were the weapon of choice in western Canadian suicides. He also was the one who let us know that the blast had been enough to pull a goodly chunk out of the concrete wall behind her chair, and she had been found amid a flurry of gore-covered books. She was identified by her clothing and a signet ring on her baby finger. The general scuttlebutt and gossip machine was running overtime. People at the other end of HUB were likely talking about the incident already.

Though we identified ourselves as her students, the police weren't interested in talking to us about Quinn's state of mind. Detectives were seen heading into Dr. Spanner's office, and that was that.

I needed to walk. I found myself on Saskatchewan Drive, looking past the emergency response vehicles parked along the road, back at the Humanities Building. I counted off the windows to find hers. It felt appropriate for Quinn to have died in her office; she'd spent her whole life getting there.

The responsibility I felt weighed like an anvil on my heart. If I hadn't been digging, if I had only said something to assure her I wouldn't be revealing her secret to the world, maybe she'd be up there, clinically dissecting my next chapter. How could I face anyone again? People would be able to look at me and sense my guilt. I had driven someone to take her own life. I was a monster.

What could I have said to assure her of my silence? Maybe nothing. Maybe Guy was right and Quinn had realized it; one day, someone else would discover the hoax and blow her tidy life right out of the water. At least now, Ahlers' work would have a chance to survive and Quinn would maintain some dignity.

I thought about my thesis, which seemed inordinately anticlimactic. Should I finish it? I could foresee second-guessing myself, having to obscure my own research to muddy the trail from Ahlers to Quinn. Was it worth it? Or should I let the world know what I had discovered? People would revel in the ingenious planning and work that went into creating a successful academic career and somehow the brilliance of the books would be lost.

I would follow Quinn's drastic lead, I decided. She had always insisted on calling me Miranda. Well, I'd take my cue from Prospero's daughter and "drown the book."

I put together my thesis quietly and efficiently in another couple of months of concentrated work, and the department rewarded me with my degree and about seven years of steady work as a sessional before it grew too crowded with other post-secondary students needing a TA stipend.

And day after day, it grew a bit easier to not think about my part in another person's death. Guy moved away, I met Steve, life went on. And I had managed to put all of it behind me, mostly.

But now, there was a new Margaret Ahlers novel? From all I had gone through, I knew it couldn't be written by Hilary Quinn. So, who was behind it? And what did they hope to do? Would they be cashing in on Ahlers' cult status as one of the greats cut down in her prime? They certainly wouldn't be receiving royalties from the earlier works, but the reputation of those earlier books would do a great deal for the new book, I was certain.

I wondered if Guy Larmour was out there somewhere today, reading the same news item, and asking the same questions? As far as he knew, of course, Ahlers was a dead writer. I had never confided Quinn's last conversation with me to anyone.

Most people knew of her as the dead professor who had written about Ahlers. Guy knew of her as the dead professor who had had a lesbian relationship with a dead writer.

Only I knew they had been one and the same person. Or so I had believed.

Now I was really curious to know if Guy was coming to Homecoming.

25.

Denise was overjoyed with my more enthusiastic help with the class reunion, and tasked me with sending out invitations to her English mixer. Because we had decided to broaden the invitation to a couple of years on either side of our twenty-year date, we had to be a lot more manual in our combing of lists of people to invite. The Alumni Association had great algorithms for address lists of particular class cohorts, but we were asking a bit much of them to be so bohemian and bizarrely inclusive in our approach.

The Faculty of Graduate Studies had very nicely complied with a list of all English specialty postgraduates, and it became my duty to cross those lists with the Alumni Association's list of members, to see if I could get current addresses and phone numbers.

The Alumni Association was nicely supported on campus, and properly so. The VP of Finance knew which side the butter was coming from, after all. My happy chore for the day was to walk across campus to Assiniboia Hall to get a current printout of the alumni.

It was no hardship to get out into the late summer air. On the whole, my favourite time of year is incipient fall—August through to the end of October. You could taste the air, and with it the anticipation of new and great things to come. Birds were still singing, the more vibrant flowers were shining in all the boarders and beds, and best of all, there were very few students wandering around getting in one's way or tossing Frisbees at one's head.

Assiniboia Hall is one of the first buildings on campus, and stands in redbrick glory with its sister buildings, Pembina and Athabasca, along the western side of the main quad on campus. The smell of Murphy's Oil and old books wafted in the air, which was golden with the hints of sunshine through stained glass. Once you got past the foyer, the building was modernized to look like any other cubicled business territory, but if you looked beyond the fabric half-walls, you'd get to a real sash window, often with pots of African violets sitting on the sill.

Sherry Brownlee, the head of the Alumni Association, came out to the front desk personally to meet me. She was just the sort of person I would have chosen for the job if anyone had asked me in the first place. She had a streak of silver hair braided and tucked behind her right ear, but the rest of her shiny brown hair hung straight, halfway down her back. She was wearing a coral shift dress with little turquoise turtles printed along the hem, and a short-sleeved turquoise cardigan to match. Her high-heeled flip-flop sandals were a tangle of straps over her big toe and instep, showing off coral toenails. She had matching turquoise earrings and silver and turquoise bracelets and yet somehow it wasn't too much Santa Fe on her. She smiled and shook hands with me, and invited me into her inner sanctum, laughing at the term.

I liked her immediately.

"I've been in conversation with Denise Wolff about your plans, and I think it's wonderful to expand things to all English majors. You never know who is waiting to be asked back to Homecoming. Not that anyone has to wait to be invited, of course," she trilled. "We try to make sure people realize they are welcome back any and every year. But class reunion years are very special, aren't they?"

"I think we're trying to focus on people who did grad studies, mainly," I inserted cautiously, worried about hurting Sherry's expansive plans.

She smiled. "Yes, but on the whole, how many people would that be? What about adding in the Honours English grads? They are easily discernable on the list, so it wouldn't take too much more effort. More stamps, of course—unless you're planning to go entirely digital on the invitation?"

"We were thinking so, yes." I couldn't imagine licking the number of stamps Denise had begun with, let along the myriads Sherry Brownlee now wanted me consorting with.

"I can understand that. Of course, you have to balance that with the findings that people respond more positively to personal mail in the post. Our suggestion is that if you can, do both, with handwritten addresses on the envelopes. Add in a self-addressed card to mail back along with an email address for connection to you, and you cover all bases," she nodded. "That way, they can respond in whatever way is most comfortable for them and you can feed it right into your computer database on receipt." She was now getting too technical for me, event non-planner that I was. I decided to smile and nod, which seemed to be all she needed. She smiled back and settled herself in front of her computer, and began humming to herself as she input a variety of "open sesames" from her keyboard. She was probably the sort of person who hummed as birds and forest creatures braided her hair and dressed her each morning. There was something beautifully protected about Sherry Brownlee, and I realized it might be that she had never been made to leave school. She had continued to exist within the hallowed halls, a place that was merely a respite or way station for most of us.

I envied that serenity of spirit that I was sensing. Maybe that is what I had been looking for through getting my MA, a re-entry into the safety and serenity of the university. Maybe that is what I've always been looking for. Who knew it was all happening in the Alumni Association Office?

Pretty soon Sherry was sliding a printed list into a manila envelope for me, and seeing me to the door of her sanctuary.

"You'll want to ask for an automated response to your initial email, even though some people really hate those, because we cannot guarantee the validity of all the email addresses on the list." She shook her head, demonstrating for a moment what a sad Sherry would look like. "There is nothing worse than waiting for someone to answer, only to find later that they never got your initial message." I nodded in companionable sadness, though I could think of plenty worse things than not getting an answer to an invitation to a class reunion.

"Call me if I can be of any more assistance to you, Randy!" Sherry Brownlee waved brightly as I descended the steps into the hot August afternoon. I trudged back across campus toward Denise's office in the Humanities Building, intending to drop the list off with her, but as I passed the Old Power Plant Bar, I veered right instead of left and headed up past South Rutherford Library, where I had run from Dr. Quinn all those years ago, and homeward to my cozy apartment.

I had moved to my present address directly from my initial basement suite, exactly a month after I'd crossed the stage as a newly minted MA. At that point, it had been owned by the City, but they had sold it to a nice small consortium who continued to offer good landlording services. The place had been broken into once, and I discovered the folly of having collected objects when everything I owned had been trashed.

Now, I lived a more modest life, not monk-like, but definitely less acquisitive. It had been important to me at the time to rebuild my existence there on my own, even while Steve had been pressing me to move in with him. I didn't want that step to feel like a contingency plan, and he finally understood my reasoning. Another couple of years into our relationship, and that ship seemed to have sailed. They were writing articles in the mainstream press these days about two-household and two-bedroom relationships. While we were more than happy to share space when we were together, a secret to our long-standing relationship might well be the space of twelve long city blocks between our respective homes.

I unlocked the several locks that had made me feel safer since the break-in, and did my routine of checking my mail at the door, depositing the dross in the recycle bin I kept by the shoe stand, kicking off my sandals, and heading to my dining room to dump my bag on the spare chair.

Once the teakettle had been filled and clicked on, I made a quick trip to the bathroom before settling in with the two letters that weren't please-or-buy entreaties.

The first was from Leo, whose penmanship was probably still so great because he eschewed email in favour of little handwritten notes. Or perhaps he figured the best part of his missives was his cursive writing. Chicken, egg. The real issue was he was definitely coming back for the festivities and was trolling for a cheap place to stay.

I no longer had my long sofa, but I could possibly shift things around to accommodate one of those high air mattresses. I took a hard look at my apartment. Why was I even thinking about it? There was hardly enough room for me in a calm state of mind. It would be mayhem during Homecoming, helping Denise to keep things running. Why complicate matters by adding in the most flamboyant person I'd ever known? Leo was a big boy with a full-time gig in Newfoundland. He could pay for his own hotel.

I made a quick note on the envelope to send him the number of the Campus Towers Suite Hotels right across from campus, and picked up the other envelope. It was from my mother, who delighted in embedding photos into her letters but refused to make the leap to emailing them. So, every few weeks I would receive a thick envelope of colour commentary on my parents' lives.

I noted that their hydrangeas were completely blue this year. My father must have been digging in the coffee grounds and eggshells diligently. His ideas on gardening felt a lot more like science experiments than restful meditation, but whatever. It got him out of the living room for hours at a time, and my mother loved the blooming garden results.

After two cups of tea I felt ready to tackle the list Sherry Brownlee had sent me off with. I grabbed a yellow highlighter and plunked myself down onto my loveseat. I figured a first pass to find all English grads would take me an hour.

It was getting dark when I turned the last page of the list over. Who knew there were that many English majors in the world? You'd think there would be far fewer apostrophe problems on signage.

I flipped back through the pages, seeing splotches of yellow on pretty well every page. There was no way we could manage if we sent invites to everyone. For one thing, there wouldn't be room enough in the English grad lounge, where Denise wanted the mixer to be held. For another, I couldn't imagine most of these people knowing each other.

Sherry and the Alumni Association had provided Denise with a checklist of things to think about when she had stepped forward to be a class organizer, and they were very particular about how actual printed invitations were more successful than email invitations. Denise was determined to foot the bill for the mixer herself, instead of asking people to send in a contribution, so I couldn't see her wanting to invite more than a hundred strangers. It's not like anyone in grad seminars had actually known any of the Honours students. They were a tribe unto themselves.

I pulled the papers together and thumped them straight into a tidy pile. Denise would have to be the one to decide if we would only target MAs and PhDs, or if we would open it up to Honours English grads. But then, what about double Honours folks? A lot of people had done English/French or English/Comparative Literature or English/Classics. In fact, going through this list was making me feel entirely inadequate.

I pulled my venetian blinds shut, and debated turning on a light or two and watching some television. My immediate reaction was to yawn, and I took it as a sign to get to bed.

Perhaps I was leaving too many decisions for another day. My sleep was restless and my dreams vivid and disturbing. I woke up feeling as if I'd run a marathon. Away from a killer with a shotgun. My sheets and nightshirt were drenched in sweat.

My subconscious was trying to tell me something.

I had to figure out what was happening with the new Margaret Ahlers book before strangers from my past started showing up on campus.

Someone out there knew things I figured only I was privy to. I had to figure out who, and just how much they knew. And whether or not they knew that I knew anything.

Hilary Quinn had killed herself because she thought my knowing meant I would tell the world her secret. If someone else out there thought I had a secret about Margaret Ahlers that might make problems for this new book, then maybe my dreams were trying to tell me something.

Maybe someone out there was dangerous.

26.

It took riffling the list in her face to show her the vast number of highlighted names, but Denise finally settled on our sending out mixer invites only to Grad Studies in English who had already indicated they'd be coming back for Homecoming, and BA Honours in English who had graduated within a three-year span on either side of our graduating year.

"That way, we'll have possibly seen each other in the hallways," she reasoned.

I was fine with that. It was still more people than I could imagine forgetting, let alone remembering, but I had promised to help. Besides, embedded in that list was one specific name—Guy Larmour. It pained me to think about bringing an old flame near the relationship Steve and I had forged. After all, both of us had shown signs over the years that we could be jealous of each other's attentions. Still, if I were to find out anything about this new book of Ahlers, it would help to talk with Guy.

So many questions were swirling about in my head. Had

Quinn written a fifth Ahlers manuscript before she had died? Had Quinn been lying to me about having created a false front in order to write the books she could then dissect critically? Did someone else who knew Quinn was no longer around capitalize on the situation and slide in a new manuscript? Was Quinn really dead, or had she faked her suicide and run off only to eventually succumb to the need to write a fifth manuscript? Had Guy been complicit with Quinn all along?

Was I overthinking things?

Dutifully keeping my receipts, I purchased several booklets of self-stick stamps, and a gross of envelopes. Within two days I had managed to knock out the invitation to our event, which looked very official with the approved logo of the Alumni Association and the Homecoming Golden Bear in the upper corner. Sherry Brownlee had explained to me that the joy of getting a personally written letter in this world of forms and emails was worth five per cent more uptake in the chance of attending. Who was I to argue? She had been inviting the whole campus back on an annual basis.

I folded my personally written notes around the return postcards the Alumni Association had given us. A number on the card apparently sorted our replies into one batch. It was great. No one had to know my address and the fact that in twenty years I had managed to move only five blocks from the Humanities Building; the university could keep track of the actual numbers attending the overarching Homecoming, and the postcards were pre-stamped, ensuring a greater likelihood of response.

I had been hoping to do the email invites as well, to make

it even easier for the wired, but was astonished by the number of entries on the list without an email connected. These were university graduates who had stayed in contact with the Alumni Association, who presumably had been in contact with computers. Hell, I had written the final draft of my thesis on one some twenty years ago. Why were they leery about offering up their emails?

Perhaps they really were Luddites. I had heard enough screeds about the death of the book and the rise of electronic illiteracy to fill an ebook. I wasn't having any of it. To me, the link was the word, not the medium.

I felt like crossing myself and whispering an apology to St. Marshall McLuhan whenever I thought this way. Of course I agreed with his theories that how a message is delivered can change the way people perceive it. That wasn't what I meant. I just felt that too much time was expended worrying about whether or not people read fiction or non-fiction in large units. My theory was that no one was going to stop imagining and crafting any time soon. There would be plenty of novels for me to read, lots of movies to watch, and the musical theatre genre was on the rise once more.

No, using a computer was not going to be the end of us as a species. If anything, it would bring us closer. I still kept in touch with people from all around the world I had met while monitoring in a chat room years ago, and now various video chat programs made the Jetsons' television phone a reality. If we could see and talk with each other, surely we could learn to cooperate with each other, right?

Leo would probably disagree with me. He was immersed in media studies and had recently written an article on scams and cheating in university studies, citing computer facility as the primary reason for plagiarizing and falsifying of information to occur. Denise had been at the session where he'd presented a year or two ago, and came home raving about the way he had handled the Q-and-A after. Leo knew his stuff.

In fact, maybe Leo could help me with the manuscript issue. If his plagiarism studies had brought him information about good programs to run passages through to authenticate the authorial voice, maybe I could send some of Ahlers' earlier works through and then the new text. Of course, if there was such a program, all it would take would for some industrious person to run some of Quinn's own writing about Ahlers through to discover the secret I'd been holding on to for the last twenty years.

Maybe that wasn't such a good idea.

It would be great to see Leo, anyhow. He and I had enjoyed each other's company back in the days of our thesis writing and early sessional work. I could always count on Leo to be game to trek out to Audreys Books for Christmas shopping, or to Uncle Albert's for pancakes.

Leo hadn't been back to Edmonton in years. He might be devastated to find that our favourite breakfast haunt had burned down several years ago. Whyte Avenue had undergone quite a significant change over the last decade or so. The eccentric little businesses like the Basket Shop, that never seemed to have shoppers in it, and the hundred-year-old, wooden-floored version of Hub Cigar, the city's quintessential magazine store, were both gone as well. Now, a couple of boutique hotels, some fancy optical shops and some grunge fashion stores, a lot of bars, and coffee shops had taken over the strip.

I liked Whyte Avenue during the Fringe Festival when the theatre crowd took over, and during the Artwalk, when local artists would set up all along the Avenue and adjacent streets. Otherwise, now, I mainly headed downtown, or to one of the malls, if I wanted to do any shopping. Mostly, I shopped online, to be truthful.

Leo would probably have something to say about that, too.

My use of online banking and shopping would have him in security conniptions. I didn't care. If Steve didn't see anything wrong with me ordering through encrypted sites, I figured I was safe. Besides, no one in their right mind would steal my identity when they could go after someone who actually had two RRSPs to rub together.

Leo better be coming to this shindig, was all I could think. Even though I had been fabricating his side of the argument, I figured he had some explaining to do. I laughed at myself, thinking about how startled he would be if I started in on him right there at the airport.

That would be another thing, the need to pick up various of these people. Denise could do some of that, but I didn't have a car. Maybe they were all so successful they could cab it in from the airport. Or maybe they could all take the airport bus to the south end of the LRT, and ride the train to the university. Denise was suggesting most of them stay in Campus Towers or the Garneau Hotel, but I was willing to bet that other Homecoming groups were targeting those hotels, as well.

Let the neurosurgeons stay downtown at the Macdonald Hotel. Unless any of our cohort had invented an app or a game that had netted them millions, they might be looking for one of the more reasonable motor hotels along Gateway Boulevard. It would be fine. Edmonton is a relatively easy city to navigate, and aside from a new bridge here or there, nothing much had changed in the manner of road works in the last few years.

I wondered how many people usually returned for Homecoming. Would the city feel fuller? Would it be hard to find a cab that week? While campus tended to fill up with a lot more white hair than usual, I wasn't totally clear on how many people came back from far-flung places and how many grads had just settled nearby. Denise would know. Speaking of Denise, I had promised to call her when I was done the mail-out. I sat back to look at what I had accomplished.

Three piles of envelopes sat before me. Two of them were substantial, folded, stamped, addressed to seven years' worth of English graduates, many of whose names were unfamiliar to me. I had also placed the invites to the professors emeriti that Denise was anxious to invite, such as Drs. Spanner, Wilkie, Samson, and Demers.

The third pile contained fewer envelopes, but every name was known to me. This was the bunch who had already received full Homecoming packages from Denise earlier in the summer. These were the people who had been in seminars with me like Axel Hamner and Shannon Mason, who had shared office space like Maureen Kelly, who had worked in the older houses that had been turned into sessional office space like Leo and Alan

Knight. This was my cohort, and on top of that pile was the invitation to Guy Larmour.

This could be wonderful, as I knew Denise believed it would be. Or it could pull apart everything I had built for myself over the last twenty years. There was only one way to find out.

27.

Denise was tickled to hear I'd got the mail-out ready, and offered to come pick me up to haul it all to the post office. We could head out for a meal after and catch up, she said. I wasn't all that sure what we needed to catch up on, but the company was always good, and the promise of food had never failed to get me on board.

We dumped the letters inside a post office outlet on the possibly misguided notion that another set of hands on the process would make it faster and more secure. Then we headed over to City Hall, to eat at The Kids in the Hall restaurant, a lovely place overlooking the fountain that served fantastic food for breakfast and lunch. The other great thing about the restaurant was that it served as a training ground for teens at risk, helping them adapt to workplace conventions like showing up on time, looking customers in the eye, speaking politely, and working in a group environment. Not all of them went on to service careers, but most of the kids who had been through the program were employed and stable now.

The fellow who managed the restaurant, Calvin Avery, was at the desk when we arrived, and gave me a quick hug. We went way back. His family had lived next door to us the first time I had lived here, when my dad decided not to live on base but to buy a house in north Edmonton. In fact, I had babysat Calvin and his sisters from time to time. This really was getting to be a time of reunions.

I introduced him to Denise and then he let a young woman lead us to our table. Throughout our meal, I saw him supervising all over, a calm and dependable presence in the lives of the youth surrounding him. He'd done well for himself in my books. I wondered briefly what he would think of my career path, if he indeed thought of me at all after greeting us.

It wasn't the clear trajectory his seemed, and perhaps I hadn't done as much good for the community, but I certainly couldn't call it boring. On the whole, I didn't dwell overmuch on the past. At least not my past.

Denise was deliberating between their daily soup, which today was carrot ginger, or the special, which was a seafood jambalaya. I was thinking of sticking to a salad for my main course, in order to justify a helping of their amazing bread pudding. At the last minute, I added a serving of chicken to the salad, which would likely tip the balance into the red zone calorie-wise. Oh well, if I didn't think about the past, I was obviously equally uncommitted to the future.

Once our orders were in to the lovely girl with two metal

studs on her cheek and a tattoo of a treble clef on her wrist, Denise and I settled back to enjoy ourselves. It was nice to take a break before all hell broke loose in the weeks leading up to the new term. If students only knew how much prep time goes into the courses they take. She asked about my timelines.

"I think we start classes the same Wednesday as you do, it's just that we have a faculty meeting, then a department meeting to attend on the Thursday before the Labour Day weekend, and then we are required to be around for an orientation day on the Tuesday. The new vision is that we are the 'accessible choice,' though I am not sure what being in our offices a day before classes start proves. I would think it would be more effective to have us all downstairs helping pack and bag purchases in the bookstore if they wanted to make us the truly accessible spot."

Denise laughed. "Oh God, bookstore lineups. I certainly don't miss those. I lost all feeling in my arms one year, and my books crashed to the ground seven people back in line, after standing there for an hour. They rushed me to the front of the line to get me out of there, but I remember the cashier glaring at me, because I am sure she thought I had just dropped them all on purpose. If only she'd known how irritating the bent jacket on my Chaucer has been, all through that course and even today. I would never drop a book intentionally."

"A Muslim friend once told me that his tradition was if you dropped a book, you had to kiss it when you picked it up, to apologize, for learning was sacrosanct, and books represented learning."

Denise nodded. "Good tradition. We need to foster that

reverence in the kids we teach, I think. And to get them inured to buying books. That is perhaps our greatest role as educators, turning them into happy consumers in bookstores."

"I can dig it," I said. "I doubt I have ever looked at the price on a book I wanted, but I can't even count the number of times I have put back cuts of meat once I checked the price. It has to be my being required to buy long lists of books back in university."

"Maybe we should make that one of the questions at our homecoming: how many books do you buy per year to this day?"

"There's going to be a quiz?"

"More like a survey. Don't worry, I've got Alvin Morrison handling all that. He says he can collate the answers online and have it all printed out in time for the registration at the Telus Building on the Thursday. People just fill it out as they sign up."

I was thankful I wasn't the only one being roped into things by Denise. Alvin was on campus daily, and obviously way more invested in computers than I.

My contributions so far were far more old-school in terms of manipulating data bases, in that I'd used a highlighter instead of an algorithm to sort my invite set.

"Old-school," mused Denise. "Makes me think, all this reunion stuff, of how young we really were. I look out at my classes sometimes, and I just want to stop the lecture and say to them, 'You are so beautiful and lithe and the possibilities are endless, so stop worrying about your skin and your hips and your empty dance card and just enjoy yourselves—you will never be this glorious again.' Not that they'd listen, of course."

"I know. I was looking at some old pictures of us the other night, trying to put a face to someone on the list named Rudy Semple, and I was thinking the same thing. Even at thirty, we had such vigour, and shiny hair. And I must have been at least two sizes smaller."

"It's all relative," Denise mused. "In a year or so, we'll remember this lunch and both of us will wonder why we worried about eating these desserts."

"Well, I'm not wondering now. This is divine."

"I know, what do you think they put in this sauce?"

"I think it's the cinnamon from the bread that makes the difference."

"Mmm, you might be right."

Once we were finished our rich and wonderful bowl of bread pudding, we settled up and made our way back into the foyer of City Hall. The fountain was arcing, casting rainbows into the air, and children were wading and squealing in it. Their mothers lined the sides of the pool, some of them holding squirming babies on their laps. I loved this part of our city, where the decorous element was pushed to the side in favour of the community sensibility. Water was for splashing in, not just to walk past and admire. In the winter, this pool was turned into a community skating rink, and a set of benches outside the restaurant we'd just been in were placed there specifically for skate donning and removal.

Denise asked whether I wanted a ride home, but I declined and gave her a quick hug. I needed to walk off the dessert, and pick up a book from the library on the way. I promised to check in with her for more homecoming preparations in a week or so. She headed for the elevator to the car park level, and I pushed open the glass door, exited the glass pyramid and headed past the water play toward Sir Winston Churchill Square and the Stanley Milner Library across the cemented park.

Our library had recently won the title of North American Library of the Year, a first for a Canadian library, and we were all justifiably proud of it. They deserved it, too. They had launched a colourful campaign to make library use cool, installed a multi-use room that included a print-on-demand press, a 3-D printer and all sorts of other neat gadgets, and their children's library was a warm and welcome corner. I loved the banners declaring "We make Geek Chic" and "Smart is the New Black." The logos showed up on tee shirts, drink bottles, travel mugs, book bags and library cards, which probably helped funds. My own card reads, "I'm happy and I know it."

I went off in search of the holds shelf, where I picked up the copy of James Cawelti's *Adventure, Mystery, and Romance* that I wanted to source for my notes on popular culture. I was going to be teaching a section on graphic novels and formula fiction later in the course, but I figured that by the time I got to it, some first-year would have already taken out every copy of what I considered the seminal text on genre studies.

Once I had found the book, I wandered over to a computer terminal to search some other titles. On a whim, I typed in Margaret Ahlers, to see what came up. The computer listed all the books I had: *One for Sorrow*, *Two for Joy*, *Children of Magpie*, and *Feathers of Treasure*, which the University had seen to having published after the floppy disks had been found next to Quinn's headless body. There had been some clause in the tenure contract that dealt with intestate research materials, and Dr. Spanner had determined that this included novels. I recalled reading something about McKendricks and the U of A having "discussions," which we had all figured was a diplomatic way of saying "fighting it out for the royalties." After all, as the literary executor, the English Department benefited from an annual stipend, so it was in their best interest to be sure the manuscript was published.

The library computer screen also listed Dr. Quinn's posthumously published critical work gathered under the title *The Next Margaret: The Works of Margaret Ahlers*. At the bottom of the second screen I found several other titles, two of which gave me pause. One was the unreleased book, *Seven Bird Saga*, which I knew about, but still gave me a shock to see included. According to the library listing, it would be published and in circulation before Christmas.

The other listing that created a rock in the pit of my stomach was another critical work, one of about seven on file. Ahlers studies were steady if not robust. The one in question, though, had me pole-axed.

The title was *The Voice in the Enigma: A Study of Novels by Margaret Ahlers*. The author cited was G.D. Larmour.

28.

I left the library with the book I'd come for and one I hadn't even known about. It wasn't all that surprising. As an MA, it wasn't likely that I'd ever be able to teach my specialty, so why keep up to date on your thesis topic? I had spent more of my time reading contemporary Canadian novels, and boning up on computer skills, in order to fit into the sessional work of distance teaching and freshman survey courses.

So Guy had stolen my thunder, had he? I refused to look into the book on the bus, because I had a sense this was something that needed to be done in private. I got off by the Garneau Theatre, which I noted was playing *Down By Law* and *The Station Agent,* two films I enjoyed for their odd characters. I walked through the alleyway toward the backdoor of my apartment.

Once I was settled in my own sanctuary, with a glass of iced tea from the fridge, I sat in front of the short pile of books on my kitchen table, almost afraid to open the cover.

I checked the publisher page. Rosetown Press, Indiana. I'd

vaguely heard of Rosemount College because one of my sessional buddies from an online adjunct site taught there, but nothing on a Rosetown Press. Maybe it was a private press, or maybe it was a press associated with a college close to Rosemount. Maybe Guy was teaching there now. His dedication page was to his father, a sappy message about looking for where we come from. Men rarely managed to get dedications right in tone.

The table of contents was next. I swallowed and turned the page.

The first chapter was just titled "The Great Canadian Novel." The second and third were what really caught my eye. "Facets of Faces: Similarity of Character in Ahlers' Novels" and "The Last Frontier: The Peace Country in Ahlers' Novels." Those two chapters were my entire thesis. If he had lifted from it, to further his career, without any recognition or citation to my work, I would be beside myself. I was already finding it hard to catch my breath, and I hadn't even turned the page yet.

Guy must have been working with Quinn the whole time. He had lied to me about the scope of his own dissertation on godgames. Or this was the ultimate godgame. Befriend and seduce a fellow student and then steal her work. I flipped back to the publication date on the textbook in my hands. This had come out nine years after I'd graduated and he had left U of A. Ten years after Hilary Quinn had been found dead in her office, and I had sworn him to secrecy about her connection to Ahlers.

Was he laughing at me the whole time? Had he set me up to do his dogsbody research from the beginning? Was he in cahoots with Quinn? Had he murdered Quinn, to pass it off as suicide? Was that even Quinn's body?

I read through the chapters with a sadness that would likely turn into rage later on. It was familiar territory. While he hadn't plagiarized word for word, he had lifted my argument completely. It sounded a little more condescending in his archer tone, of course. There was an underpinning of judgment on Ahlers' work: that somehow she was less than she was thought to be.

His other chapters dealt with comparing Ahlers' shyness from the limelight with Salinger and Pynchon, which was accurate but sort of slim in heft, since their writing didn't offer any commonalities to use as clues as to why they would shun the prestige of public appearances.

I pushed the book aside finally. I was feeling flayed. Twenty years ago I had worked my tail off to put together many of the threads of the argument I had just read. I had confided in Guy, and I had been vulnerable in his presence.

All this time, I had believed we had just faded apart with the distance. He had taken a post-doctoral position with McMaster for a year, and then moved to the States when a position came up in a well-considered teaching college. We had lost touch after that.

Now, it occurred to me that my Christmas cards had gone unanswered just about the time this text was getting published. Of course, that would have also been around the time that Steve and I had got together, so I might have not noticed the lack of communication quite so quickly.

Who could I talk to about this? What could I do about it?

Nothing could likely be done about the stealing of my ideas at this point that wouldn't just be ugly, but what about if he were to show up at Homecoming? My name wasn't anywhere on the invitation, so for all he knew, I would be well out of the picture, off getting conned by some other smooth-talking charlatan.

Or maybe he knew exactly where I was, and had been keeping tabs on me all along. After all, he had a vested interest in me not getting all efficient and trying to publish any part of my old thesis.

Thinking about this made me turn quickly to look behind me, checking to see whether anyone was looking in at me through my kitchen window. It was ridiculous, of course. Not only was Guy Larmour miles away in Indiana or somewhere equally remote, there was a film on my window that detracted from people being able to see in. Still, the thought of being monitored and used was strong.

I couldn't talk about this in any great detail to Denise. She might see it as annoying of Guy to have stolen my thunder, but she would have no idea of the barrel he thought he'd have me over, since I'd never confided in her. So, telling her now might hurt her feelings. I had kept the Ahlers secret from her, and she might see that as a betrayal of our friendship.

The one person I would be able to tell was Steve. Of course, the fact I'd not ever told him before this, in the dozen or so years we'd been together, might make him rethink the openness of our relationship, too. But I'd have to risk it, because right now I felt unsafe.

All the things I had thought were true might not be. All my certainties were shaky and the uncertainties I had learned to live with were looming too large once more.

Guy had used me and may have been in cahoots with Quinn all along. And as Margaret Ahlers, the enigmatic and mythical writer who had started it all, Quinn might have had another book in her. After all, the children's counting song hadn't been completed.

One for sorrow, two for joy; three for a girl, four for a boy; five for silver, six for gold: seven for a story never told.

One for Sorrow; *Two for Gold*; *The Children of Magpie*; *Feathers of Treasure*; *Seven Bird Saga*. The story never told. Until now, presumably.

I needed to know who was doing the telling.

29.

Steve was almost through his shift when I called him, and promised to get to my place by six. I in turn promised him dinner.

It was good to get my mind off of the shock of Guy's treachery, and focus on trying to cobble together a decent meal out of what was in the fridge and freezer. It had cooled off a bit outdoors, so I wasn't too bothered about heating the oven. I sliced up some oranges and set frozen tilapia fillets on top of them in my glass dish. I poured in enough water to lap at the orange slices but not cover the fish, tented a roof of foil over the dish, and popped it into the oven to poach.

I'd shopped at the downtown farmers' market and Earth's General Store the past weekend, and still had some parsnips and Swiss chard in the crisper. I peeled the former, sliced them into coins, and set them to steam. I stuffed washed chard into a pot with a cover, to boil up at the last minute. As soon as the chard went limp, I'd drain it and toss it with butter and vinegar.

I checked my watch. If I started the oven in ten minutes and the appropriate stove burners in twenty, everything would be ready as Steve walked in the door.

That was the trouble with me and cooking for guests. I could never figure out how to make a meal work so that company could arrive, have an aperitif, chat for a while and then walk into the dining room to eat. It always ended up with me taking someone's coat and guiding them straight to table.

Maybe you needed a cook and serving staff to manage the former scenario. Once more, Hollywood had lied to me.

I was just putting the cut glass bowl with tossed salad greens onto the table as Steve knocked on the door. I pulled the door open, and smiled. He was just so damned good-looking and the extra beauty of that was that he was all mine.

Standing six-foot-three in his regulation boots, which he wore whenever on duty, he almost grazed the doorframe coming in, and had by habit learned to enter a room with a bowed head. Aside from the boots, which he was presently unlacing to set by the door, he was in civilian dress: casual navy trousers, and a striped navy, red, and yellow polo shirt. His socks were red and yellow stripes. I laughed at his socks, and he gave me a mock wounded look.

"I took a lot of time coordinating this look, I'll have you know!"

"And I appreciate it. Come on, dinner is ready."

I bustled through to the kitchen to get the fish out of the oven. I served up from the stovetop, and brought the dishes to the table. We added salad where we could on the plates. My table wasn't big enough to afford extra salad bowls, though I did have a nice wooden set on the top shelf somewhere—another gift from my mom.

"This is great, Randy. I've been grabbing too many burritos on the go this week. It's nice to sit down to a proper meal." Steve wiped his mouth with the cloth napkin I'd folded by his setting. Cloth napkins were my addition, not my mother's, who still used printed paper towels. I figured a stack of napkins bought at various times from yard sales and thrift shops and dumped in the laundry regularly were better for the environment. Every time I used them, I knew David Suzuki was smiling.

"It's good to see you. I feel like, with the prep for the school year and Denise's Alumni Weekend demands, I've not seen you face-to-face in ages."

"It's been over a week, for sure."

"And I miss seeing you. Texting and emails are all very well, and thank goodness for them, but geez I miss you when I don't see you from day to day."

My toes reached under the table to rest in the arch of his feet.

Steve smiled broadly at me. "Why don't I help you with the dishes and then we can figure out how to make up for lost time?"

I laughed at his attempt at a wolfish swagger.

"I hope you can stay, but I need to talk to you first. And the dishes can wait." There must have been something in the tone of my voice, or perhaps Steve could read something in what he always called my transparent face. His joking Lothario look disappeared, replaced immediately by intelligent concern.

"What's the matter?"

In response I removed the plates from the table, and brought Guy Larmour's book from my desk to place before him. He read the title quickly, and then looked up at me quizzically.

"Isn't this who you did your thesis on?"

"Yes, and Steve, oh gosh, do I have a lot to tell you. It goes back a long, long way."

"Best place to start is at the beginning."

And so I did.

By the time I got to finding Guy's book earlier in the library, we were sitting in the living room drinking beers I had retrieved from the fridge. We'd pulled the blinds an hour earlier, and Steve had even started taking notes to keep things clear in his mind.

I finished talking and leaned back to look at him.

He took his time looking up. The longer he stared at his notebook, the more worried I got. Perhaps he wouldn't want to be with me anymore; after all, I had kept quiet about Margaret Ahlers for so long. Maybe he wouldn't see any difference between my actions and those of Guy Larmour's.

Finally he spoke.

"So this book has been out there eleven years, and you just now found out about it?"

I nodded.

"And you stopped hearing from Guy around the same time?"

"I guess so. I just wasn't thinking much about it at the time. You and I had just met. Crazy things were happening in the department."

"How normal is it that a critical work on your writer could come out and no one would think to tell you about it?"

"I've been trying to consider that, and I think it might be quite normal. I don't hang out with a load of Ahlers scholars, after all. Denise is a Shakespeare prof, and most of the reading I do critically has to do with work I teach in my freshman courses. There you get to teach one classic work, and one modern work. I've never taught Ahlers in any of my classes. It would be too problematic for me, I think. I was too close to it when I was teaching at the U of A, and now over at MacEwan, they encourage you to teach their Book of the Year as your modern Canadian text, since they pay to bring the writer in for a set of lectures, and so on. And it's not like they could ever bring Margaret Ahlers in to speak, eh?"

"So, Larmour may have figured he could get away with this forever? Or perhaps, he was ready for your attack a decade ago, but has determined you're not a threat to him now?"

"Or maybe he just figured that as a lowly MA, no one was ever going to take my word over his, especially as he had helped me with my work enough to go into my acknowledgments. Maybe he'd tell them I had used his notes, for all I know."

"One thing we need to do is check the police records for aything about Quinn's death. If Larmour was responsible, or if they both conspired to cover up her disappearance, we may find some anomaly in there that will help us."

My fears and hollowness were dissipating now that Steve was speaking as if we were still a team. "I'm so glad I told you all this."

He shook his head and smiled sadly at me. "Randy, I can understand why you kept this secret all this time, but I am glad you let it out, too." He set down his notebook and opened his arms. I moved into the bear hug that made me feel both secure and strong. "Don't worry. We are going to get to the bottom of this."

I decided not to tell him then that I was still worried.

After all, if I was the only other person who knew the truth behind Ahlers' non-existence, I was a threat to Guy's scholarship.

I really needed to know if Guy Larimour was intending to come to Homecoming.

30.

Leo Desrochers really was a cheapskate. As well as the card he had sent begging a bed from me, he sent a long letter to Denise, which she brought over to show me the day after I had unburdened myself to Steve. I read it while she pored over Guy's text, which I'd handed her silently.

By the time I finished reading Leo's chatty missive, where he pointedly also asked if he could crash on her couch rather than shell out for a hotel room, Denise was finished flipping through the book. From the look on her face, I figured she had come to the same conclusion I had, that our former friend had ripped off my research.

"How could he think he could get away with this?" Denise sputtered. "He'll be drummed out of academe."

I shrugged. "The truth is, he's gotten away with it for more than a decade. He didn't publish it here, and what university publishing arm in the States was going to comb through old masters' theses to see if there were any correlations? It's not as if he has lifted it line for line, either, so how would they have caught it?"

"If that is a university press at all," Denise mused. "I've never heard of them. It could be a small publisher operating without the rigour or staff of an academic press."

"The thing is, now that I have come across it, what do I do? And what happens if he comes back for Homecoming? How do I face him?"

"Maybe you should talk to Steve about it," Denise suggested.

"I told him last night, and he thinks I need to be careful in the way I approach things. A lot depends on how much I want to pursue it, after all, he could lawyer up, and so could the university press. Reputations are at stake." I didn't want to get into the whole secret of Ahlers with Denise if I didn't have to. Keeping that sort of information from her for twenty years might be more than our friendship could handle.

I had made a decision that night, after speaking with Dr. Quinn for the last time, that I would tell no one about her authorship of the Margaret Ahlers novels. I hadn't even told Guy. Until I spoke of it to Steve, I hadn't even shaped the words in my mind. If Guy knew that Quinn had written the books, he knew it from Quinn herself, not me.

I wanted to tell Denise now, but something held me back. It was bad enough to share the possibility that someone we were inviting back to her reunion preparations was a plagiarizer. She'd already discovered another of our crew was still a moocher after twenty years. If I was going to add on my complicities in hiding a literary fraud all this time, she might just throw in the towel.

"Leo can stay with me if he pays for an air mattress," I offered, trying to make things easier on my friend. "After all, it will feel like old times." All throughout grad school, Leo was constantly showing up just around mealtimes, ostensibly on his way home. To his credit, he had also been there when I had moved to this apartment, and had brought champagne over the day Denise had defended her dissertation. Leo himself had bundled himself out of town and off to Newfoundland and into what sounded like a very solid job teaching North American Literature. That's what a comparative dissertation featuring Sinclair Lewis and Sinclair Ross will get you: how the west was won in two parallel studies. I think he also branched out into popular culture studies once he received tenure, and could safely dabble in the "sub-literary."

It would be good to see Leo. Hell, it would be good to see anyone who made it back for Homecoming. Of the entire list of invitations we had sent out, only about fifteen were still in Alberta. The rest were scattered all the way across the globe. Quite a few were along the eastern seaboard in the United States, and others clumped in Upper Canada. That made sense, considering just how many universities and colleges were found there.

I wondered if anyone would be coming from Europe. Katherine was in London. She might show up, if it coincided with a visit back to see her mother, whom I think still lived here. Richard was retired early to Amsterdam, having taught in New York for twenty years. I had a feeling he wouldn't show up, even out of prurient curiosity. He had not enjoyed Edmonton much, finding it too provincial.

Edmonton had done a lot of maturing in the last several years. The downtown had revitalized itself, and more and more people were living in the core of the city. Our film festival, comedy festival, improv festival, and rodeo brought in just as many people as did our mainstays of jazz, folk, and fringe festivals. Edmonton had nothing to be ashamed of, and people returning for Homecoming were going to be more than pleasantly surprised, I was thinking.

Denise was still fuming about Guy's stealing of my research. "You could take this book to the Graduate Studies office and see what they had to say about things."

I shook my head. "I am really not sure I want to get into any of that. After all, it's not as if I'm up there with the Ahlers scholars. Most of the work I did was already touched on by the work Quinn did before she died."

Denise made a moue of a face, the sort of look that said either "I disagree with you heartily but don't have the energy to pursue this now" or "I've just eaten a bad apricot." I could tell the conversation was over, and I was just as glad it was. I didn't want to get into the reasons why I didn't feel up to waving the Ahlers flag too strenuously. I still had too much to hide on that score.

Denise insisted on helping with the dishes, which was kind of her. I swirled rinse water through the teapot and set it back on its trivet. Our tea mugs and toast plates were done in a jiffy and pretty soon I was seeing her to the door.

"Thanks for offering to put Leo up, Randy," Denise said, as she pulled on her slouchy boots. "With all the stuff to organize, I will be running that entire weekend, and I know that if I left

Leo to his own devices, he'd end up reorganizing my kitchen shelves on me."

We laughed, but it was true. Leo was the sort of person who just took over under the guise of knowing best. No wonder he was still single—he was probably way too picky to settle for just anyone, and I just couldn't imagine a man out there who would meet his standards. Poor Leo, he should have been born a hundred years earlier and hetero, and he could have happily married my grandmother, who used to extend her dusting into the root cellar weekly.

Once Denise was gone, I pulled out my laptop, with a view to seeing just how much I could discover about what Guy Larmour had been doing in the last dozen years or so.

I might not be on top of every nuance of academic pursuits these days, and I certainly wasn't in the know as far as what the graduate students of today were tackling, but I did keep up with work on theoretical approaches and articles to do with writers I was presenting in my freshman classes. Guy and his work on Ahlers had never cropped up in any of that general sweeping I did on a regular basis.

Of course, I'd been making my rent money for the past few years doing research on all sorts of topics that weren't my own. Surely I could take some of those skills and apply it to snooping out what Guy might have been up to.

I checked his profile on a couple of the academic and business networking sites. His CV of publications was up on one of them, and he appeared to have been working on research to do with magic realism for the first few years after he graduated. He had two papers on a couple of South American writers, and then a book comparing W.P. Kinsella to William Cobb called *Beyond the Margins: Magic Realism as a Response to Centralism.* From the write-up, I gathered his argument was that writers outside the hubs of New York or Toronto were far more able to experiment with form, and that the Canadian West shared similarities with the American South in terms of recognition from the publishing centres.

All this work seemed in keeping with the work he'd been doing on Borges and godgames and metafiction in his dissertation. It wasn't until about a dozen years ago that he'd moved into examining the works of Ahlers.

Sure, she was a western Canadian writer, so I suppose no one batted an eye as his interests seemed to shift. But really, she was to Borges as cashmere is to steel wool. Aside from her posthumous detective novel, there was merely the similarity of putting words together between the covers of a book. Had I been the dean of Rosetown State, which seems to have been where Guy had been located for at least fifteen years now, I think I might have questioned the shift. Of course, the dean might be so immersed in his own studies of James Fennimore Cooper that he didn't really care what his faculty was working on.

So, after an article about Ahlers' duplicity in point of view in *Two for Sorrow,* which went out in a periodical from Hamburg dealing with Western Canadian literature, he had presented a talk about Ahlers' sense of place in a colloquium in New Zealand geared to Commonwealth literature. I'll bet he was pretty sure I wasn't going to show up in the back of the hall there, like some avenging Richard Mason out to stop Rochester's marriage to Jane Eyre. And he was right. I hadn't even been aware of a Commonwealth conference in the University of Waikato.

I had been in the trenches of sessionaldom at the time, just prepping and teaching and marking essays, too busy to keep up with my own interests in research, too broke to even think of going to a conference in New Brunswick, let alone New Zealand. And I had been unable to even sustain that sort of academic continuum. The last few years had been a patchwork of different jobs, mostly research and writing in tone, with ties to academe, of course, but nothing that would make a CV zing. No, I was pretty much the gypsy tinker, in comparison to Guy's steadfast knitting of himself into the fabric of the university mainstream. Who would even care to believe me if I raised a voice of dissonance against his scholarship? I hadn't even kept up with the literature; who was going to care about my measly thesis in the face of more than a dozen years of work by others?

That night I dreamt of Dr. Quinn, chasing me through the stacks of the Periodical Library and down the groove-worn stairs of Rutherford South. As I looked over my shoulders to see if she was gaining on me, I saw that where her face was supposed to be, there was nothing but a smooth surface, as if she was wearing some sort of flesh-toned fencing mask. The absence of features was even scarier than the pursuit. I woke up sitting bolt upright in bed, pretty certain I had screamed loud enough to wake the neighbours.

I sat there in the dark, willing my heart to calm down, listening for movement beyond the walls. When I was certain no one was stirring, I looked at my clock-radio. It was 4:30 a.m. In another three hours it would be light out. Already the nights were getting longer. If this had been July, the birds would already be singing in the sunny branches.

There was no way I was going to risk going to sleep again, so I padded out into the kitchen to turn on the kettle. I sorted out the Melita filters and funnel to make strong coffee. Thank goodness I had already ground enough for two or three days the last time, because my neighbours really wouldn't have forgiven that noise. The walls were thick, but somehow noises flowed all over along the pipes that heated the building and brought water to each suite.

Coffee and a small bowl of cereal later, I was back at my laptop, combing through responses that were already trickling in for Homecoming. As suspected, the local people were deciding first. There was far less at stake to cross the river for an evening, after all. Unless you'd gained four hundred pounds or lost all your hair, that is. Of course, given the last century's penchant for big hair, that latter aspect might not be a bad thing. You never knew what would keep people from reuniting with folks who "knew them when." There was bound to be some nerd who had parlayed his English degree into a role-playing game that had made him millions or a fascinating government job. There would be a couple who had gone on to be high-powered lawyers, or who had married into well-set families. There might even be a writer or two.

There weren't all that many local who had become academics, or Denise and I would know them. Most of those had gone further afield, and I wasn't sure whether those who had become illustrious professors at Yale or Stanford would bother with a reunion weekend. Still, one never knew.

I was starting to see Denise's point. There came a time when you did get curious about those with whom you'd shared strong developmental times. I was beginning to wonder about all the people I'd been in seminars and coffee-lines with. I hoped enough of them decided to come back to make it worthwhile.

At 8 a.m., I closed my laptop. Intending to head through to the bathroom and have a shower, the lure of my unmade bed was too powerful. Nightmares be damned. Hilary Quinn couldn't bother me with the sun streaming through the rice paper blind. I fell asleep almost immediately and slept without dreaming till noon.

31.

I awoke feeling as if I'd got away with something, and after a quick shower and a grilled cheese sandwich for lunch, I felt pretty perky. After all, I'd already got half a day's work in, so I was still on schedule.

I opened my laptop to discover the world had conspired to fill my email inbox while I'd been sleeping in. Sherry Brownlee had sent along a list of people who had responded directly to the Alumni Association. Her cover email had been friendly, too, bordering on the point of bubbliness. I made a note to give her a call and see if there was anything I could do to make the process easier on her end of things.

Leo had responded to my invite with enthusiasm and sent along a list of things we could do in addition to Denise's very full schedule. Just reading it made me want to go back to bed. I added "vitamins" to my ongoing mental shopping list in order to keep up with my reunion houseguest.

Steve had emailed to see if I'd like to catch a movie and dinner downtown. I sent back a quick "sure thing" and continued down my list. I consigned newsletters to a file to be read later, zapped shopping ad emails into the trash the same way I dumped fliers out of my mailbox into the receptacle the landlords left there for all junk mail, and responded quickly to the appointment reminders for my annual physical and yearly teeth cleaning. Pretty soon, all that was left in the inbox were a to-do list from Denise, a letter detailing all the meetings that would be required of me the first week of classes at MacEwan, and seven responses marked "U of A English reunion" as the subject.

As I went to open the first on the list, another identically titled email pinged into my inbox. I looked at the sender. G. Larmour.

I stared at the email, leery of opening it. Even though the response had been sent to an anonymous-sounding Alumni Association address and then forwarded to me, I felt as if somehow Guy would know to whom he was writing.

I clicked open his email.

Guy.larmour@rosetownu.edu
U of A English Reunion

I was quite frankly delighted to get the invitation in the mail last week, but haven't had a spare moment to respond till now. I am just getting back from a sabbatical year, and everything I used to manage by rote now seems an ordeal.

I would love to come to the U of A Homecoming. So hard to believe it has been twenty years. I want to do everything except the football game (of course) and I must get one of those famous Tuck Shop/CAB cinnamon buns.

And I do hope there will be time set aside to connect with old friends.

Yours in anticipation,
Guy

I read it through a second and a third time. I couldn't tell whether he knew it was me he was writing to or not. Maybe he hadn't kept close tabs on me after all. This sounded just like him being charming in the abstract. That line about connecting with old friends, though, that might be aimed at me. I wasn't sure how many friends Guy Larmour still had in Edmonton.

How could he even think about coming back to where I was, having gutted my thesis for his own use? Who had that much gall? Mind you, he might be thinking he was in the clear since I hadn't challenged him in the decade he had been waltzing around as the Ahlers expert based on my research.

Maybe he had figured I had decided not to stir anything up, given the whole sense that my work had driven Quinn to take her own life. There was some truth to that. It probably had something to do with why I had never tried to turn any part of my thesis into a publishable article. If I hadn't been so insistent on digging for the truth, she might still be scaring grad students with her icy efficiency, just ready to retire into emeritus status about now. Or she might have risen up the ranks to become Dean of Arts. She might have even invented another writer or two, and given the world another couple of great works of literature.

Because, when it came down to it, that was Quinn's real legacy. As much as she had wanted to be an academic, it was her creative lens on the world she had delivered in the four books she'd written as Margaret Ahlers that were the true gift to the world.

If I could have written even one of those books, I could have died a happy woman. I wonder if Quinn had died a happy woman.

In fact, I wondered if Quinn was really dead, at all. Maybe it was the dream I'd had still hovering, but her suicide being so quickly dealt with combined with the thought of a new Ahlers manuscript being discovered, added to my penchant for conspiracy theories—well, it had all the markings of a Byzantine plot.

Maybe Quinn, on her own or with the help of her trusty acolyte Guy, had managed to lure someone who looked enough like her to double for her dead into the office, and blew the stranger's face off to avoid questions.

Dressing the corpse in her clothing after the fact would be gruesome, but not impossible. Maybe she had offered the woman a new outfit and a shared trip to wherever she was headed. They just needed to stop off in Quinn's office on the way, where she was planning to leave a couple of things, like a shotgun tucked into an equipment bag? I could imagine it all too well. Who would believe a well-dressed, educated woman was planning to do you harm?

The hard part would be leaving everything that pertained to the old life: car, house, credit cards, clothing, and mementos. In this scenario, Quinn would have needed an alternate bank account and persona at the ready, so that she could just step off the earth as Hilary Quinn and show up somewhere else as a what? Roving academic? Freelance writer? Journalist?

I wondered if there was still a file on the apparent suicide of a professor, some twenty years after the fact. If the case were open and shut, would the paperwork even still exist? Would there have been tests done? Would Quinn's fingerprints have been on file for any reason? Who fingerprinted professors? CSIS? Were routine DNA tests done back then?

I had a lot of questions that were going to be tough to ask without arousing a whole lot of suspicion. Thank goodness for Steve. If I had to break my silence about the works of Margaret Ahlers to one person, I was glad it had been him. If there was one person in the universe I could trust, it was Steve Browning.

Resolved, I worked my way through the rest of the RSVPs and sent off a note to Sherry Brownlee to see if she wanted to meet for lunch in the next couple of days. By the time I was through populating Denise's chart for yeses and nos, I had an enthusiastic response from Sherry and a lunch date for the next day.

I tidied up the apartment and had a quick shower before dressing for my date with Steve. It was still warm enough eat on outdoor patios for another month, but cinemas were notorious for being icily air-conditioned, and I would shiver through whatever show it was Steve had his heart set on if I didn't plan appropriately.

I was just braiding my hair back when I heard the knocking at the door.

"It's open," I called from the bedroom door, and Steve let himself in, ready to launch into one of his diatribes about me and locks. "I just unlocked it this minute," I fibbed, "because I was going to have my hands full of braid and didn't want you waiting. I'll be ready in a minute." I went back into my bathroom for an elastic and last look.

I'd do. I was dressed in a peach and blue cotton blouse tucked into freshly washed blue jeans, the kind without holes or bling or bizarre lines of fading. I had laid out a peach cardigan, which I grabbed off the bed on my way back out into the living room.

Steve hadn't bothered to take off his boots, and was standing at ease in the doorway corner of the room. I tilted up for a kiss and he obliged. I closed my eyes for a moment and drank in the warm, clean, safe smell of my man. Things would be all right. I would find a way to lay out all my fears and possibilities, and Steve would find a way to disprove the worst of them and help me through the rest.

"Shall we head right to the cinema and eat at the pub beside it?" he suggested.

"Sounds good to me," I smiled, and after locking the several locks that made him happy, we left out the back door where his unlocked car was waiting.

I cocked my head, and he smiled ruefully at me.

"Do as I say, and not as I do?"

"Right."

In no time at all, we were circling our way up in the City Centre parkade. While pricier than some, it was conveniently located right beside the downtown mall with the cinemas on the third floor. Also located on the third floor was a mock Irish pub called Fionn MacCool's, a franchise that served Guinness on tap and waitresses in microkilts. We ate here quite regularly when heading to the movies, and I already knew what I wanted to order.

"Shepherd's pie with the house salad, and a pint of whatever your summer ale is," I told the waitress who was at our table with large tumblers of iced water almost as soon as we'd been seated. She laughed and asked if I was sure I didn't want to hear the specials.

"I'll hear the special," Steve allowed, "but don't get between Randy and her favourites, I'm just warning you." The waitress rattled off a fish dish, the soup, and a sandwich platter, and then Steve calmly ordered the steak and kidney pie and a Big Rock Traditional, as he always did. She wrote down our orders dutifully and raced away.

"You make me sound like a stick in the mud, but you always order that, too," I complained. He laughed.

"You have to let people do their job, Randy. It's her job to upsell the specials, and it's our job to listen."

Just then our server returned with our pints and cutlery

rolled tight in dark cloth napkins. Steve took a long swig of his beer and sighed.

"Now that hits the spot. What a tiresome day."

"Want to talk about it?"

"Not really. The bits I could talk about are tedious, and I would just rather shake them off. What about you? How was your day?"

I told him about having a nightmare and then heading back to bed for a morning nap. He looked mildly concerned. I knew why. It certainly wasn't my normal way of conducting a day. I rarely napped, and almost never had nightmares. In fact, I could rarely even recall a dream. This nightmare still was so vivid that I could describe the sensations as well as the timing of every moment to Steve.

"Spooky. So what do you think brought that on? Something to do with this fellow stealing your research? Or were you eating pepperoni before bedtime?"

I told him about Guy's email, stating he'd be coming to Homecoming.

"And you think he was part of the hoax that Quinn had perpetrated?"

"That's what I can't be sure of. He certainly doesn't intimate anything of the kind in his book, and now that he's set out his shingle as an Ahlers scholar, he has a vested interest in not revealing the secret, if he knows it."

We ordered another round of drinks, but decided against dessert. Popcorn would be enough. I checked my watch against the movie times I could read from our vantage across the atrium from the cinema. We had time. I took a deep breath and hoped I didn't sound too stupid to the man I loved.

"So it occurred to me that Quinn might have faked her death, by killing someone else who fit her basic body description. Would that be possible?"

Steve frowned. "It would be hard to determine one way or another after twenty years, but I would say it would be difficult on a variety of levels."

"But not impossible?"

"Nothing is impossible, I guess. Hard to prove, though. Think about it. She would have to find someone, within twenty-four hours of talking to you, who matched her general build, and had no one especially looking for her. She had to lure her up to her office on some pretext, pull a shotgun out and shoot her, and then strip her and dress her, all without messing with the blood spatter and shifting residue. Then she would have to disappear effectively."

"I know. It sounds like a Liam Neeson film—almost doable, but doubtful."

Steve laughed. "Well, it would answer the question of who has penned the new Ahlers book, so we have to consider it a possibility."

"I wish we could get our hands on a copy of that book," I mused.

"When is it coming out?"

"Supposedly for Christmas, so by book standards, that means October."

"Is there any way you could write to the publishers as a

potential reviewer? Don't they send out review copies willy-nilly to anyone with a blog these days?"

I looked at Steve with admiration. "That's not a bad idea, at all. I will try to get a copy, and we can compare it to the previous books. It's obviously close enough to the original books to fool her publisher, but would they have read them so deeply as someone researching them for an academic response?"

Steve nodded. "You check that out first, and then we will figure out if we need to be pulling cold cases out of storage. And in the meantime, I will pay up here and we can just make the movie, if you're still in a mood to sit in the dark with a man who loves you?"

"Well, since you put it that way, I just have one question. Can I pour M & Ms into the popcorn?"

32.

It was surprisingly easy to get a copy of *Seven Bird Saga*. I had logged into a free blogging site and crafted a book review blog, tossing a few recent reads up there, before sending in my request. I got a return acknowledgment almost immediately, with an offer to package two others of their new releases into the parcel. On the principle that free books are free books, I agreed.

Meanwhile, my lunch with Sherry Brownlee of the Alumni Association had been very pleasant. She had taken me to the Faculty Club, a place I loved. Their food was the best in town, and you could eat either casually at the buffet downstairs, in the patio during the summer, or upstairs in a more refined and sumptuous manner. I had attended several weddings there, and been invited to a couple of open meetings of the Canadian Federation of University Women, who met to fund bursaries for young women graduate students and to continue to enhance their own learning through a program of fascinating guest speakers.

"You should consider becoming an Associate Member of the Faculty Club, Randy," urged Sherry. "The monthly dues are really nominal, and the benefits are pretty luxe."

"No one is going to look askance at a lowly sessional from another institution coming to drink or dine?" I wondered.

"Pah! You have a graduate degree from here, you have taught here in the past and possibly will again—why wouldn't they want you as a member? Remind me to get you an application on the way out. I will sign the sponsor line, if you like."

It wasn't as if it were a hard sell. It would be nice to have a place I could take Steve without him fighting to pay the tab once in a while, too. I nodded and took another mouthful of the amazing salmon on my plate.

Sherry had wanted to talk logistics of our event in the context of the larger Homecoming itinerary. I was pretty sure Denise had fobbed this off on me because her style of organizing and Sherry's didn't meet in the middle. I didn't mind at all. Sherry was a listmaker, and that was all it took to sell me.

We went through the all-invite general events first. In return for putting us into the programming, and setting aside room for our meet and greet wine and cheese in the Old Arts building rotunda, we were obliged to steer our attendees to the various events Sherry and her small but mighty crew had set up. I didn't think too many of our bunch were going to take in a football game at the Saville field, but I could be wrong. Who knew what happened to people over the course of twenty years? Maybe some English major had moved to Alabama and married into a "Roll Tide" sort of family. Stranger things had happened.

I dutifully wrote down the football game times, and agreed to stuff our "delegate pouches" with information on campus tours, talks from two Olympians, the *Animal Planet* bat guy and a nuclear physicist, the times when the Tuck Shop tent would be open selling their famous cinnamon buns and tickets to the LGBTQ poetry reading at Alumni House.

That would likely be of interest to our gang, I figured, both as a literary evening, and as an indication of how far the university had come in inclusiveness over the years. We were still dealing with overt misogyny when I'd been enrolled. I had no concept of how marginalized students had managed prior to the embracing of Queer Studies. Twenty years ago, Hilary Quinn had still been able to fend off interest in her activities by pretending to be a lesbian at the lake. Maybe we really had come a long way, baby.

True to her word, Sherry stopped us by the manager's office on the way out of the Faculty Club to pick up and sign her sponsorship of my becoming an Associate Member. I was assured that my various cards and paperwork would arrive in the mail, but that I was to consider myself a member immediately. With old-world charm, the manager shook my hand solemnly and welcomed me to the Club.

As we walked out into the late summer afternoon, Sherry giggled.

"It feels like you should be heading to your courses in academic robes after that, doesn't it? Well, there is something to be said for upholding traditions." I walked with her back through the winding road toward Assiniboia Hall, the first of the three original buildings along the west quad. Athabasca Hall, in the middle, was where Alumni Services was housed. Pembina Hall, the closest to the Students Union Building, had been a female residence hall, and in fact had been where my mother and her friend Gloria had roomed when they had been U of A Juanitas.

Sherry waved me off, and I set out across the quad to wend my way through the alleyways between Cameron Library and the Power Plant, around Rutherford Library and HUB and across the residential blocks toward my own wee apartment building. It was a fair hike, and I found myself wondering just how many calories I could burn off by walking to and from the Faculty Club for dinner once a week. There was no way I'd be able to afford more than that. Still, it would make a nice way to treat Steve and occasionally Denise, who had never felt the need to become a member.

My apartment looked rather uninviting, with its piles of paper on both my coffee table and desk. I grabbed some files from the bottom drawer of my desk, and set to trying to bring order to the reunion papers before they got lost amid my class notes for the fall term.

It was five o'clock before I knew it, and all I had to show for it were two piles of filing folders, neatly labelled. Paperwork is so underrated as labour. I pushed myself away from my desk, and set the reunion files into a clear dish tub, my travelling filing system. The class notes could stay on my desk.

Steve would be here soon, and I wanted to get a fresh perspective on the whole Ahlers situation. Having not revealed all to Denise, it felt even more imperative to talk with Steve, who knew everything. Well, everything except how deep my relationship with Guy had felt. And knowing Steve, he had probably intuited most of that.

I changed out of my buttoned-down look and pulled a Ralph Lauren peasant blouse over my head, one of my great Value Village finds. Steve was going to be wanting to eat somewhere a little more upmarket than Swiss Chalet, given he'd been talking steak for the last three messages. Luckily, there were very few places in Edmonton that required you to dress as fancy as an Arcade Fire concert to eat. They didn't call the full denim look the Alberta Tuxedo for nothing.

Steve and I drove out west to the Sawmill, one of the last of the great steak and salad bar restaurant chains in Edmonton. I opted for the prime rib and busied myself with the salad bar, while Steve reveled in the "baked potato with everything" lazy Susan.

"This is the sort of meal I used to have when my parents would take us out for dinner. Everyone used to bring out the sour cream and chives and bacon bits. Somewhere there is a whole mountain of these swivel servers." I laughed, thinking of them lying somewhere with a Smaug-like dragon guarding them, though it would more likely be a junkyard dog.

"Everything is shifting and changing, that's for sure."

Steve looked at me quizzically. Maybe I'd let more anxiety out in my voice than I'd realized. "Something happen today?"

I shrugged. "I went to see the coordinator for the Homecoming weekend. She was rattling off things for our alumni to attend, and it got me thinking just how much campus has changed since we were all there. How much the world has changed, really. You know, things would have turned out so much differently, if all that had happened today."

"Like how?" Steve was working on his steak, steadily cutting bite-sized pieces and swirling them in the juice on the plate before popping them in his mouth.

"Well, if Dr. Quinn had owned a laser printer, it wouldn't have taken me forever to print the last manuscript. Maybe I wouldn't have been so overtired when I wrote my last chapter, and she wouldn't have caught me out."

"Well, if she hadn't been using carbon paper, you wouldn't even have known there was a fourth book. Heck, if she'd had better windows installed in her cabin, you wouldn't even know she wasn't two people."

I leaned forward, careful not to get the tassels at the neck of my shirt into my Yorkshire pudding. "Do you think it was my fault? I do. That's why I have kept her secret till now, as some sort of penance. I didn't even tell Guy what she confessed to me at the end. As far as he knew, she killed herself because she'd been caught out for killing her novelist lover, and the only reason we didn't trumpet that fact was that we'd have had to admit to breaking and entering."

"But you think she killed herself because her life was no longer worth living once she had admitted her fraud to her graduate student."

"Well, yes. Although spoken out loud like that, it does sound sort of small."

"And you've been beating yourself up about this for twenty years?"

I shrugged again. "Give or take. It's not like I think about it all the time. Every once in a while I have a nightmare."

"That is why Guy figured he could get away with stealing your research, and probably how he did. You have avoided discussing your thesis, or talking about Margaret Ahlers because it is too painful to think about Quinn's death and your part in it."

"Thank you, Mr. Amateur Psychologist. It could also be that I have backed away from my thesis work because of the whole lack of support for remaining in academe. Maybe it's one of those 'you can't reject me if I reject you first' sorts of things?"

"You think you are being rejected from academe?"

"Ejected, more like. I got assigned more classes twelve years ago than I get now, when I actually know more about both theory and teaching. In fact, there is a stricture against giving sessionals more than a certain number of classes, so there is really no way to earn a living wage teaching anymore, unless you can patchwork together a term from more than one institution. This may indeed be my last year butting my head against the ivory tower."

"Really? What will you do instead?"

I pushed Yorkshire pudding around my plate, swirling it in the gravy. "I don't know. Maybe I could get a government job."

Steve raised his eyebrows, Groucho-style. "Wow, that would be a change."

"I need to feel as if I am doing something that is valued," I said slowly, hearing my thoughts clearly as I spoke. "It's not enough to keep shoring myself up with the thoughts that delivering an understanding and appreciation of literature and the means to critically speak of ideas are useful gifts to society. I go in front of recalcitrant youth who are all staring at email on their laptops rather than taking notes, or hauling up crappy notes and facts off their smartphones to toss at me in the form of arguments. At a staff meeting, it was suggested we walk behind the students, to keep them on the straight and narrow, but I don't have the heart to do that. Besides, I like to write things on the white board up front. I can't be policing them at the same time as I am supposedly feeding their souls."

Steve looked sympathetic, which was all it took to open the floodgates.

"If the institution took me seriously, well, all sessionals, but I'm talking from a personal focus here, then maybe it would bolster me up to go in there day after day. But we are just cannon fodder, covering the compulsory courses that all the students have to take. We are a dime a dozen, and completely replaceable with any other MA or PhD who didn't land a tenure-track job. English departments survive on the required courses that other programs make their students take, and yet the people hired to teach the very courses that keep them relevant are treated like drones."

"You are sounding burned out."

I nodded. "I really think I am. The whole time I was landing other jobs, like the contract work for researching and writing the websites, or the short stint teaching for the summer camp, I was pining for the classroom. But this last year back in the classroom has changed me. I am really not looking forward to starting classes next month."

"It's sooner than that, you know. August is into its second half now."

I sighed. "I know. You don't need to remind me. Denise is so annoyed that we are not hearing back from reunion people already. I could have predicted that English majors would leave it all to the last minute, though."

"Have you heard back from anyone?"

"Comparatively, I would say loads."

"What does that mean in real people numbers?"

"Eight."

Steve laughed so loudly that several other tables of people looked over at us. "Eight people are coming?"

"No. Eight people have responded. Three of them are actually coming."

He laughed again. "And how many people were invited?"

"About one hundred and seven. You have to realize, we pulled it down severely as we went, to people who would have met and known each other in the halls. So we have everyone who graduated with a PhD, MA or BA Honours in English that year. There are all sorts of other folks who were around, but at a different point in their program."

"And of those hundred and seven, eight have responded and three of them will come. That leaves you with ninety-nine yet to hear from in the next month?"

"I think the Alumni office wants people registered by the end of August, to be able to send out name tags and such, but Denise has told me she'll hang on till the week before Alumni Weekend, before putting in final orders to the caterer."

I thought it was utterly brilliant that Denise had managed to snag the old Graduate Lounge for our mixer soirée. People were allowed to spill out into the lobby area. The general office would be closed, as would most of the offices and classrooms in the Humanities Building, but with a liquor licence and dispensation from the Dean of Arts, we were going to serve beer, wine, and canapés at our mix and mingle event on the Thursday evening.

"Who has responded?"

"Leo Durochers, whom you met, come to think of it. He was still around while I was teaching and had my office in the House."

"Leo, the flamboyant fellow with the blond tips and Gatsby scarves?"

I smiled. "That's the one!"

"He seemed solid," Steve nodded. "Who else?"

"Lyle Weis, who is now a kids' author and living in the south end of the province. I think he might still have some family up here, so that makes it more of a draw for him. And someone named Bill Rankin, who I cannot remember at all, though Denise says she does."

"Maybe reconnecting with all these folks will re-inspire you in terms of teaching?"

"More likely I will see that they're all tenured professors or went on to become lawyers or writers, and I've been spinning my wheels this whole time."

"Randy, don't be so hard on yourself. Reunions are bad for that sort of thing—you start tensing up to compare yourself to everyone you weren't even thinking about for years, as if their consideration of you will make or break your own stature in the world."

"Well, in the grand scheme of things, I have not cured cancer or written the great Canadian novel," I said, feeling worse.

Steve smiled. "But you have taught diligently, and worked to your max on every project you signed on for, and kept up with your rent and paid your taxes and sustained some great friendships and read some fantastic books and watched some exciting movies and played and listened to some fabulous music. On the whole, aside from refining cold fusion, what else could you want?"

I smiled at him. "When you put it that way, where the heck is my Order of Canada?"

"Are we staying for dessert?" asked Steve.

"Not with this reunion looming. No sirree, I am moving into diet mode starting tomorrow. If I am not going to be the most successful, I will settle for the most recognizable."

"That's the spirit," laughed Steve. "By the way, am I invited to this reunion? Can significant others attend?"

"Do you want to? I would love to parade you around on my arm. That would ease the lack of published articles and security completely."

"Get me a name tag, and I am yours."

"I love you, Steve Browning."

"Mutual, I'm sure."

Steve drove us to his condo overlooking the river valley and we proved it to each other. There is nothing better than feeding a steak to a red-blooded Canadian man. I am just saying.

I spent a lazy morning drinking coffee on his balcony before finally hauling myself back down Saskatchewan Drive and into my little apartment. The sun was making everything sparkle, including the dust motes. I did a quick whip around with a damp cloth, and then changed into shorts and a tank top so that I could wash the clothes I'd been wearing for a second day along with my bedding and towels.

Clean sheets, fresh scents, and open windows made me feel as if I could once again tackle the chores that had seemed too much the day before. I sat down with a glass of iced tea to check my email.

"Coming to the Reunion" was the subject line I was hoping for, and there were ten of them. I copied and pasted their names into the database Sherry Brownlee had provided. Things were beginning to look promising.

As I looked at the list, the majority of names dimmed and one stood out in harsh, strong print. Guy Larmour. My mouth went dry. This was not going to be a cakewalk.

He really was coming, and there was nothing I could do about it.

33.

The weeks that followed were a blur of activity and stress. School began, with all the kerfuffle of room changes due to class size expansion, and the ensuing need to run off more copies of the syllabus, order more books in a rush at the bookstore, and discover that there was very little chance of making it to my second class on Tuesday/Thursdays on time unless I deked out the side door in building five, and ran outside to building eight. That was going to be fun in January.

Denise, who was also starting classes across the river, had got very demanding about the reunion, wanting updates every evening on whether anyone else had responded to our invitation. We had to get thirty to qualify for a timeslot in the alumni tent on the quad, or some such, and she was apparently trying to will the last few people to RSVP with the power of her mind.

My review copy of *Seven Bird Saga* had arrived in the mail, which was just as well, since my having started a bogus book blog in order to get it was getting on my nerves. People were suddenly linking to it, commenting on the few reviews I had put up, arguing with each other, and I'd received a variety of come-ons to link to a series of other blogs, join a consortium of book sites, and nominate my site for a Webby award.

On the plus side, I lost eight pounds without trying.

Steve was busy, too, with changes being made to the roadways and bike lanes and bar closures in Old Strathcona, so we didn't see all that much of each other through the week. I already had marking the second weekend of classes, and was considering letting it stretch out, but we were planning to take in the Edmonton Expo the following Saturday, so I dutifully stayed home, when I so much would rather have been biking the river valley trails.

It was a crime in Edmonton to squander good weather, especially as we moved toward our long, cold winter season. Once the leaves began to turn, every nice day felt like a gift. I compromised by pulling on capris instead of jeans and opening all the windows in the apartment.

By 5:30 p.m. on Sunday I had graded three piles of introductory essays, sorted and flagged notes for my lectures for the entire week ahead, packed my satchel for hauling to class, checked my email for reunion responses, sent off two more welcome packages, and updated Denise's list to twenty-eight.

I made myself a plate of nibblies rather than a big meal: olives, crunchy baby dills, cherry tomatoes, pretzel Goldfish crackers, and little squares of Swiss cheese. Setting it on the coffee table, I allowed myself to curl up on the loveseat with the newly discovered Ahlers book.

I'd already pored over the cover notes and preface to the book. There was nothing that really spoke to the discovery of the manuscript. Someone was being coy, but I couldn't tell from parsing the language whether it was the publishing house or not. Maybe they didn't have the answers either. All they were saying was that the new manuscript had been discovered and while it was impossible to ascertain where in the oeuvre of the late writer's work it should sit, scholars had determined tentatively that it was a later work, rather than an early, unpublished manuscript assigned to a bottom drawer.

I was wondering how they could tell such a thing, and just who those scholars were. It had never occurred to me that it might be an early attempt. Maybe Quinn had not found a publisher for her first try, and shelved this one. Or maybe it was on another floppy disc I hadn't found when going through her office that fateful time. Maybe Guy had nabbed it, even before inviting me to check out the place. Or maybe he or someone else in the know had forged this manuscript, hoping to cash in on the nostalgia wave that was sweeping Canadian literature. New editions of Morley Callaghan, Farley Mowat, and Mavis Gallant were showing up in Chapters, on a chirpy "homegrown" table. That could have been the impulse to retool Margaret Ahlers for a new generation.

Or maybe it was really a lost work by a dead Canadian writer who had been used and killed by Hilary Quinn, my former thesis advisor. Maybe Quinn had bamboozled me, to keep me from fingering her for murder. At this stage of the game, I was willing to believe anything. None of it made sense to me.

If I had the wit and talent to write the four novels I'd cherished and enshrined in my thesis, I would have stood proudly and owned up to them. Quinn's admission to me that it had been an exercise entirely created to give her fodder for scholarship was just too hard to understand, and if I, who aspired to be part of the world of academe couldn't buy it, then how could I expect the rest of the world—who celebrated and celebritized writers and artists—to believe me?

I stared at the cover, featuring a photo of seven magpies strutting in a sunny glade. The focus was on the birds, and the green of the leaves on the tree above them shaded out into a blur on the white cover. Only the faintest hint of iridescence could be seen in their black feathers, and the title and author name were the same black, printed above and below the photo. I wonder what it said about the publisher's hopes for the book that the title went above the image, and Margaret Ahlers was in decidedly smaller print below. Added to the fact that the newly discovered work by a Canadian icon was being brought out in trade paperback rather than hardcover, it made me worry about the Canadian publishing industry as a whole. Well, the publishing industry for fiction. There were probably more than enough readers for self-help and investment, leadership, or organizational principles tomes. And e-books were hot, too, unless everyone I saw were watching movies on their phones and tablets on the bus. Maybe soon no one would be published first in hardcover ever again.

Whatever the case, the book was in my hands, and the moment had come. I smoothed back the crease of the first flyleaf page and noted the publication information. There was something exciting about reading a book a month before the publication date listed, as if you're on the A-list of invites, rather than being part of the catering staff.

The dedication page was next. In italics, it said: *To H, for everything I am.* Whoever was responsible knew of the ties to Quinn, obviously. Unless someone was trying to make out that Ahlers was a heroin addict. I chuckled, in spite of myself. I was making way too much out of this. I turned the next two pages, one of which was blank and the next had a huge Roman numeral I on it, and suddenly I was face to face with the words. Words from a dead woman? An imposter? A copycat imposter?

We would see.

34.

Around 8:30, I had to stand up to turn on a lamp and draw the blinds. I took the time to go to the bathroom and make a pot of tea, but I didn't put the book down for either of those chores.

By 11 p.m., I was finished.

I put the book down on the table in front of me, next to the plate of crumbs of cheese and pickle juice. I wasn't sure whether I was happy or sad or in some parallel universe. Maybe I wasn't completely out of the world of the book yet.

It sure felt like an Ahlers story, whoever had written it.

There were differences from the first four books. For one thing, there was no solid female protagonist in this one, let alone one with a first name beginning with a vowel. The story revolved around a view from a window, and it wasn't completely clear whether it was the same window at different times, with different people sitting at the desk, or whether it was the same time, and view, but from different vantage points in the same building. Each of the seven sections of the book began with the same paragraph, describing the magpies on the lawn, but in the first section a man named Martin gazed out at the scene without taking it in, worried as he was about his wife's pre-eclampsia and hospitalization. The next section had Tomas observing the birds and wondering whether they were picking at something that had died, and musing on the scavenger nature of magpies before taking a phone call that changed his life for the better.

Walt saw the birds, but his attention was drawn to the woman jogging along the path beyond. He was trying to come to terms with the fact that his daughter was about to marry a jerk. Interestingly, the jerk sounded a lot like Terry, who was the character in the next section. He was looking at porn on his phone, so that it wouldn't be flagged on the company mainframe, and not noticing the birds at all.

Fran was a cleaner, or maybe she was packing the office. It was not clear which, because her section involved a long memory triggered by the birds of finding the dead body of a cow in the back forty with her brothers. They had tossed stones at the bloated corpse, hoping to see it explode. Instead, they had dislodged a swarm of crows who flew at them like a murderous thundercloud.

Sam was logging the movements of the birds, and apparently had banded the legs of a bunch of magpies the year before. His work was being called into question and he was hoping for results that would astound his committee. It wasn't clear whether he was an MA or PhD student, or whether his work was in zoology or some sort of computer synthetic gaming work.

The final section, devoted to a boy called Simon, was almost dizzying in its lists. He seemed to be autistic or some sort of odd savant. The view outside the window went from the now-familiar bird paragraph into a detailing of every tree, horizon, car, and jogger. The vision moved to the inner walls of the office where he had been placed to wait for his mother, and each was clinically listed, until he returned to the window, having rotated on the office chair 90 degrees each time.

It was a disquieting novel, if one could even call it a novel. The dissonance of thought, as shown by the seven different interpretations of the natural scene outside the window, was a strong theme. Of course, it was hard to tell whether they were all seeing the same birds, or whether it was meant to be a continuum of thought, with each new generation or iteration of people unable to build on what had come before.

I wasn't certain what to make of it. It didn't pull me in the way the other books had. If this had been my first exposure to Margaret Ahlers, I wasn't sure I'd have been so ready to devote two years of my life to the study of her works.

Did that mean it wasn't Ahlers? Or was it early Ahlers? Or late, disillusioned Ahlers? Or was it my vision that had changed over the years? Was I still the naïve reader who had been besotted by the stories of young women setting out to conquer their worlds? Did novels have to feature women for me to treasure them, clearly mirroring my life in some way back to me? I hoped I wasn't going to be turning into some reverse snob in my dotage.

It was late and I had a headache from the concerted reading I'd been doing. I picked up my dirty plate and took it to the sink before padding off to bed. I needed to be lively enough to engage first-year students in the art of the short story the next morning. The puzzle of the new Ahlers could wait.

My dreams were muddled and confusing, and all I remembered from them as I showered the next morning was that they had been monotonously work-oriented. As a result, I felt tired from the effort. What a great way to start a new week. I splashed toner on my face before my moisturizer, to try to tingle me awake.

I had time for a proper breakfast, thanks to my marginal work schedule. I had only one class on Mondays, Wednesdays, and Fridays, which didn't start till 11 a.m. I had scheduled my office hours for the hour after that, which supposedly worked for my Tuesday/Thursday students, as well. Them I saw from 11-12:20 and then from 12:30-1:50.

Taking advantage of my morning at home, I made toast and eggs, brewed half a pot of coffee and read a couple of news sites on my laptop. I then washed up, and got ready to leave the house. At the last minute, I stuck the Ahlers into my satchel.

I had planned to walk each day to Grant MacEwan University, across the High Level Bridge and down 109th Street to the corner of 104th Avenue, where the compact university stretched along the former CN railway yards corridor. It seemed, though, like just too much effort for that morning, so I instead popped across the street to catch a downtown bus. The rush hour had abated, and I managed to sit all the way to City Centre Mall. I got off there and zigzagged the few blocks west to the east end of the pedway-connected college.

Construction on the arena and the myriad tentacles that seemed to stretch in every direction had pretty much made 104th Avenue impassable, and as a result, the traffic both on wheels and on foot along 103rd was more than the narrow sidewalks could bear. Buildings laid claim to land right where the sidewalk ended, and if you were passing someone using up too much space, you risked scraping your arm on the bricks beside you.

Panhandlers chased from Jasper Avenue by vigilant peace officers leaned out of doorways, and some were a little bit crazier or more aggressive than I was comfortable with. I tended to skirt the very edge of the sidewalk as I headed to the college, willing to risk a dash into a busy street if necessary.

As a result of my brisk avoidance striding, I made it to the college ten minutes earlier than I'd estimated. I stopped in the cafeteria area to line up for a cup of coffee. There was a coffee pot made in the English Department staff room, an all-purpose storage and photocopying room behind the secretary's desk, but you had to pay in five dollars a month to be part of the coffee crowd, and I had never had the ready cash at the right time for things like that. I had to forage for myself for coffee and lottery tickets. Not that I had ever been anywhere where a group of lottery players had struck it big. That reminded me that I had a 6/49 ticket stuck to my bulletin board at home from my parents' birthday card. One of these days, I had to check those numbers.

Coffee in hand, I took the stairs to the English offices on the second floor. The glass elevators scared me, mostly because I thought the only thing worse than being stuck in a box would be to be stuck in a box where people could see you panicked and stuck in a box. The stairs, polished granite and open, wound their way around the elevator. They were harder to climb now that I had progressive lenses to deal with, and my focus would waver between the stair and the space beyond.

I'd gone back to see Myra McCorquodale several months after she'd first prescribed me glasses, and at her suggestion I'd opted for invisible trifocals. I rather liked wearing them, since grit from the roads no longer blew into my eyes on windy days, and I fancied my mock-turtle frames made me look dashing and artistic like some female Raymond Chandler. I couldn't carry off bigger-statement glasses like Sophia Loren or Nana Mouskouri, and there didn't seem to be any other female glasses-wearing icons to emulate. The journalist Alan Kellogg had already cornered the James Joyce look here in town, so I had to be content with an ex-pat thriller writer.

My office was moderately close to the main department office, and closer to a washroom, suiting me perfectly. Fulltime staff had the furthest offices, as if they were older and more dependable and didn't need watching over. They also had offices to themselves. We sessional folks had to share office space and time. There were three of us in this space, which also held two small desks, a large bookcase, four chairs, one telephone, two garbage containers, one blue box for recycling, a huge rhododendron on the windowsill, and two desktop computers.

I had yet to meet the third member of the office, Peter Snaring, who apparently taught one evening and one Saturday morning class. Wendy Parrot, who owned the rhododendron, taught Tuesday/Thursdays at 8 a.m. and 12:30 and Monday evenings. She had her office hours during my 9:30 class times and whirled in to drop her notes off at about the same time I was finished teaching my 12:30 class. I never saw her on Mondays, Wednesdays, or Fridays, though I sometimes had to shoo away students looking for her on those days.

I hung my jacket and straightened myself up, looking in a mirror someone had kindly glued to the back of our office door. It didn't do much for morale if you showed up in class with parsley between your teeth or bird poop on your shoulder. I pushed stray hair out of my face and pasted on a trial smile. I would do.

This year's schedule was better than last year's, where I had taught 8 a.m. and evening classes, picking up the timetable dregs no one else wanted, but it was still taking a while to get back into the groove. I longed for the sort of panache with which Valerie Bock strode through the halls, her laptop ready to connect to the AV in any room, offering her notes and slides for every lecture.

She was really the model of the job I had envisioned for myself, back when I'd been lured by Margaret Ahlers' first book into doing my MA. I saw myself teaching freshman English, turning reluctant students into lifelong readers and making critical thinking and the formulation of elegant arguments the accepted mode of discourse. That, of course, hadn't been the path.

I wondered what would have happened if I'd published my understanding of the Ahlers/Quinn hoax. Would that have secured me the sort of academic career I'd been seeking? I stood in the middle of the office, and then shook myself. That sort of "what if" thinking was the route to madness. Every choice had been the right one at the time, and there was little except the lack of security that I would trade about my life as it was. Even that was becoming less of an issue, with the way the governments were playing with old-age pensions. More people than just I were finding they would have to start considering working till they died as a retirement option. My grasshopper lifestyle wasn't looking quite so headstrong and silly anymore.

I gathered my books: the class anthology, a file of notes, the plastic folder containing the class information, and my coffee, and made my way back down the stairs to a classroom on the main floor. The tiers of tables with their locked in place seats were half-filled as I got there, and students streamed in while I busied myself getting ready for the class.

We were supposed to be discussing *The Yellow Wallpaper*, the most consistently anthologized story I'd ever known. Charlotte Perkins Gilman, the author, was lauded as an early feminist, and her story of a postpartum depressed young woman being misdiagnosed and driven mad by the choices of her physician husband was both accessible and tantalizing for students to play with. I liked, as well, to point out the ways that fiction was developing in terms of the reader being able to suspend disbelief. The story was written in journal or diary style, which was an accepted form of writing. Although fictionalized, one could believe in the possibility of finding a person's diary and reading it, making it easier for a reader to buy into the reality of the fictional world. For a long time, when published, the story had people shocked by Gilman's seeming candour of her own bouts of madness.

I spoke to the class of the anecdotal accounts of people overseas worrying about a serial killer in Vancouver when the book *Headhunter* came out in the early '80s.

"Since the Canadian fiction market was mostly high culture and mainstream fiction, people ascribed a true-crime sensibility to the novel, and Vancouverites formerly from England with relatives back home were getting letters worried about them, with that madman running about."

Some students laughed, but others looked a little bemused. They had probably never thought of books having an impact on real life. This was my cause, on the whole—to make them understand the value of fiction, poetry, and essays in the world they inhabited. If I managed, over the course of the next few months, to get them to see how the publication of a controversial piece of writing could change the course of how people behaved, I would have achieved my goals. Being able to construct a solid three-point essay was bonus.

The class went well, and those who had bothered to read the story engaged in a good discussion over whether she was mad to begin with, or made mad by the confinement in the room. Several people made mention of the ways in which the room sounded like a torture chamber rather than a former nursery, which gave me hope for more close reading in the weeks to come. I reminded them about the upcoming essay and my office hours before dismissing them, and turned to erase the white board.

Two or three students stuck around to talk to me outside

in the hall, one of them still stuck on his interpretation of the story and the other two wondering whether citations in MLA were all that different from APA. By the time I shook them off to their satisfaction, it was 12:15 and my stomach was grumbling audibly. I took my notes to my office, checked my email, listened to two phone messages from students who were too ill to come to class, and then grabbed my coat and left campus.

There was no way I was going to make it all the way home without expiring of hunger, or at least that was how I was feeling. I checked my phone to discover a message from Denise. She was downtown, having had a dentist appointment, and was I interested in meeting for lunch? I texted back immediately, and we agreed to meet for what Denise and I referred to as "crack chicken," because it was so amazingly good.

Chicken for Lunch, a mainstay of downtown lunchtime dining, was located in a basement food court of Scotia Place, one of the shinier office buildings in the city core. Run by Amy Quon, whose family had owned the fancy Lingnan Restaurant for as long as I could recall, it was testament to both her personality and her cooking that lineups often wound round the entire food court to get a Styrofoam box of rice, vegetables, three types of chicken, and a spring roll on top.

Denise was three-quarters of the way down the line when I got there. Like the rest of the business-suit-clad crew, we visited in line.

"I wonder how these other food kiosk people feel, getting one or two people while this line taunts them every day?" Denise mused.

"Right. How do you compete with this sort of success?"

"They must make enough from people who just can't take the time for the line, I guess. But on the whole, it moves quickly enough."

"Quickly enough for what you're going to get," I agreed.

We were settled soon enough with our steaming hot chicken, chopsticks and cans of Fresca. I had chosen curried chicken, hot and dry chicken, and chicken with mushrooms, my very favourite. Denise stuck to the ginger chicken and hot and dry, which she said was the only food she actually dreamed about.

"Did you have a toothache?" I asked.

"No, it was the annual checkup and cleaning," Denise said, dabbing her lips with her folded paper napkin as if it was thick damask. "My mother would be so proud of me. I've gone three years without a single cavity, and the hygienist was impressed with my flossing technique."

I smiled. Of course, Denise would ace a dental checkup. Denise aced all her tests.

We chatted about our class compositions, and schedules. Denise had a Shakespeare, a grad seminar in Elizabethan women writers, and one freshman class. Normally she taught two classes per term, but was aiming for a half-year sabbatical, so had frontloaded her academic year to make it feasible.

"I really haven't taught first-year students in about six years, and it's amazing how different they seem than kids that have been around campus for two or three or more years."

"How do you mean?"

"Well, I'm so used to third- and fourth-year students, most of whom have self-selected an English degree, right? So few people take Shakespeare for an elective, although I find the ones who do rather refreshing. But anyhow, the students seem to have created their own personae by the time they get to senior-level courses. What I guess I mean to say is, I can tell them apart."

I laughed. "I know exactly what you mean. I had three girls with long blond hair who sat in the back row of one of my classes last year, and I couldn't ever get their names straight. They were sort of interchangeable in my mind, because they all had the same coat, and wore the same look."

"Right! They haven't moved out of the high school herd mentality yet."

"Is that what it is? Oh good. I thought it was me getting too old to absorb that many new names in one go."

"Nope. It's never our fault, Randy. There is always a sociological explanation for problems that beset us. That is the great joy of the rational world: rationalization." Denise laughed, and I swear seven men in business suits turned as if a mermaid was singing.

"So," she segued abruptly, "how are things with you and Guy going to work?"

"I don't really know," I confessed. It had been eating away at me, and it was sort of a relief to confront it and discuss it in the middle of a busy food court. "I am not sure how I am going to react when I see him, or what I should do."

Denise wrinkled her brow, he mouth set in a grimace. “You should be reporting him to the authorities.”

“What authorities? The graduate student association? The provost? Who handles plagiarism and theft of intellectual property at that level? And besides that, even if I found the right window to complain to, what sort of argument do I have, being ignorant of the theft for so many years? It speaks to my intellectual rigour, or lack thereof, that he has stolen my thesis out from under my nose.”

“There have been cases of work from another language being stolen. I’ve heard of a dissertation being translated into German and passed off as one’s own, and the reverse from Norwegian to English,” Denise nodded, “but I hear you. To have someone you know take your material and publish in the same language on the same continent does raise the question of how much you were keeping up with your topic.”

I bristled in spite of knowing I’d opened the door to this discussion. Who was Denise, in her tenured position, to lecture me on keeping up with my academic stakehold? I’d been spending the last dozen years doing anything and everything to keep kale on the table, without the luxury of time to read every literary journal and attend conferences. Guy could have published the complete works of Lucy Maud Montgomery under his own name, and I wouldn’t have noticed.

Speaking of Lucy Maud, I wondered if Guy would use the Colleen McCullough argument if I confronted him with his transgressions. He might say that having spent time with me in his grad school days, he’d inadvertently absorbed the arguments of my thesis without recalling having read them in his youth. That, as I recalled, was her argument for recreating a Montgomery story as her *Ladies of Missalonghi*. It was a similar argument to George Harrison's apologia for "My Sweet Lord," the inadvertent remake of "He's So Fine" by the Chiffons.

And speaking of Guy, I wondered when he was going to be showing up in town. Actual Alumni Weekend events didn't begin till the Thursday of the third week after classes began, and since they'd started late this year, that would be the last full week of September. If Guy were teaching, he'd be needing to watch his timing rather carefully, one would think. Of course, he might be on sabbatical, or taking course relief to do research, or wherever he was teaching might be on the tutorial concept, where he could slate his students for fortnightly sessions and be relatively free every second week.

I didn't want him sneaking up on me. If there was going to be one good thing about helping out with the organizing of this clambake, it should be having an inside eye on everyone else's timetables.

Denise had popped on the LRT from campus to come downtown, so I agreed to travel back with her. We were lucky to find seats on the train heading toward Century Park, which was the direction for the university. Once term began again, the entire city seemed to teem with students, especially on transportation corridors. School zones made traffic denser, and backpacks doubled the size of passengers headed for the university, NAIT, Grant MacEwan and several high schools to be found near the tracks. There was a lot to be said for living close enough to walk to most of the places I frequented.

Denise and I calved off at the HUB egress from the LRT. She headed north to the Humanities Building where her office was, and I wandered past the Fine Arts building and turned east to head through the residence buildings on 88th Avenue, then down the back alley toward my apartment. It was a warm autumn sun on my back, and even the skiff of early leaves in the lane didn't bother me. If we could make it through September without me digging out my plush-lined tights and boots, I was considering it a victory.

I turned on my laptop on my way to put on the kettle. From the kitchen I heard the pinging of email announcements, which startled me into splashing water on myself as I swished out my teapot. I popped a couple of peppermint teabags in the pot, and went to check my mail.

There were two emails from Leo, the first thanking me profusely in his Leo-nine way for the offer of my sleeping bag and air mattress, and the second reminding me that he was lactose-intolerant, and could I see my way to having some specially formulated skim milk on hand? Another email had come from Sherry Brownlee letting me know that as we now had sixty-five registrants identifying themselves as English Grads Twenty, the name Denise and she had concocted for our subset, we were entitled to an hour of specialty time in the quad Homecoming tent.

There was also a promotion from the Bay, four Groupon offers, a letter from my Aunt Muriel, and a Call Me from Steve, one of his subject-line-only messages.

I could hear the kettle singing from the kitchen. I headed for it, wondering briefly whether that noise pissed off my upstairs neighbour as much as her acrobicizing on Saturday mornings annoyed me. I was extra careful with the boiling water, and soon had settled myself into my small sofa in the living room to read the email from my aunt. Her chatty letter calmed me down for the moment, but I was going to have to do something about my nerves over this whole reunion and plagiarizing situation.

I had to admit, I was worried about receiving more messages from Guy. I had no idea how I was going to react to seeing him again. It bothered me that he might even know my email address. The invites had gone out with the alumni association address, not mine, but still. Had he been keeping tabs on me? And if so, for how long? Till he stole my thesis and then there was no need? And moreover, why the hell was he coming back to this shindig? What did he have to do with the new Margaret Ahlers novel? And would his hair be grey, or would he still have any hair? Would he still be good-looking?

That thought made me feel uncomfortably disloyal to Steve. Thinking of Steve reminded me I was supposed to call him. He had likely tried to reach me on my cellphone, too. I scrabbled for it in my purse, which was near the foot of the loveseat, where I'd dumped it when I came in. I really had to stop putting my ringer on silent all the time. Maybe I could find a ringtone that approximated noises people didn't associate with the rudeness of a cellphone, like a whiny child or a yapping dog, and not be constantly worried I was infringing on other people's noise barriers.

I called into my voice mail to hear Steve's message. It was

always easier for him to leave a voice message than type in a text, because he was usually on the road or in transit somehow.

"Hey Randy," his voice sounded warm in my ear, "I wanted to know if you're okay for eggs. Robin's sister-in-law brought in some farm eggs before heading to her stall at Mother's Market, and there are a dozen going begging here. I could bring them over after my shift—around 5:30? Let me know."

The voice-mail voice told me the message had been left about an hour earlier, when I had been on my way home. I quickly texted him to say I would love the eggs and to see him, and could have some supper ready for us both, if he liked.

I got back a smiley face, which I took to mean he would be at my door in about another hour.

The apartment was in pretty good condition, considering I hadn't been in all day, or perhaps because of that. I put away the dishes in the draining rack, set the kettle on, and cleared off the unnecessary mail on the kitchen table.

Steve was true to his timing and emoticon. He looked very happy to see me, and maybe my guilt at receiving a message from an old boyfriend made me a bit more effusive in my kiss at the door. He broke away, still hugging me, and cocked his head for a moment, and then came back in for another kiss.

"I like it," he announced, as I pulled back from our embrace. "That is the kiss a true hunter receives."

"A hunter? What have you been hunting? And what have you caught?"

"You would be amazed."

"Would I?" I had no idea what Steve was talking about, but

he was in such a good mood, it didn't bother me. "These must be some great eggs."

He laughed, and handed me a cardboard container. I peeked in at beautifully brown eggs, a couple of which had chicken dung still clinging to the side. Farm fresh came with its own issues.

"I didn't mean the eggs, but yeah, they're pretty wonderful." He followed me into the kitchen, where I put the eggs in the fridge. "What would you give, though, to have a look at this which I am holding in my hand?"

I turned to see him waving a file folder at me. He must have pulled it out of his satchel. It was faded and official-looking with large numbers across the tab and a large stamp on the front that reminded me of an old library stamp sheet, probably because I could see signatures and dates written into the boxes on the stamp.

Steve looked at me trying to process it, and grinned.

"Oh, it's official all right. This is Hilary Quinn's incident and autopsy file. I figured it might be of interest."

35.

He figured correctly.

We sat side-by-side at the kitchen table as he walked me through the notes and forms in the twenty-odd-year-old file. When the kettle sang, he got up to fill the teapot as I worked my way through the scribbled notes in the margins of poorly typed statements.

I found my statement in the bunch, as well. It looked as if they had interviewed everyone she had been teaching, as well as the professors who had offices along the same hallway and two of the secretaries. There was one name missing from the interviews, though. Guy Larmour had no statement recorded. I wondered if it was missing, after all these years, or an oversight of the original officers. Surely someone would have told them he had a key to her office.

But what was Guy's involvement with Quinn, anyhow? He had told me she was his third reader, but that normally was not much of a connection in academe. A third reader read and made comments on finished work, not work in progress. The commitment to a student was almost peripheral, except for a week or two of intense connection during the last two weeks.

I reached for my own notepad and scribbled a "where was Guy?" on it, and turned the last statement over to find the typed autopsy report, transcribed from a recording made by the Chief Medical Examiner for the Province of Alberta. The typing bounced up several levels of competency.

There was a lot of medical and anatomical verbiage I didn't quite understand on first reading, though checking for Latin roots helped me guess at a few terms. I skimmed through the first section, and slowed down at the summary.

The shotgun had taken away the structure of her jaw and upper sinuses, making dental identification impossible. She also had quite a bit of alcohol in her system at the time of death, which was understandable. Dutch courage, possibly. There was something else in there about her liver, which was how I presumed they understood her alcohol levels. Her lungs were discussed, as well, but I wasn't entirely clear on that. From what I could gather, it seemed that Hilary Quinn was a pack-a-day smoker, which surprised me. I hadn't pegged her as a smoker, and that was back in the day before "no smoking" signs in the buildings. Although we hadn't been allowed to smoke in our offices, there had been a smoking room on the main level of the Humanities Building and ashtrays in every bar. I hadn't really been aware of her habits, though. After all, it wasn't as if she and I were going for drinks at the Faculty Club together all the time.

Steve coughed and I looked up. He had been watching me, and smiled as I focused on him.

"Interesting reading?"

"*Muy interesante,* yes. How did you manage to get hold of this?"

"I requested it. It takes a while, but our archives can usually get their hands on anything that has passed through the squad. The question is, does it suggest anything to you?"

"Well, the first thing that surprises me is that Guy isn't mentioned in here anywhere. He was the one who told me about it, and I thought he had found her. I must have got that wrong."

"Why did you think he found her?"

"He had a key to her office, or at least he did while she was away. Maybe he'd had to give that back when she got back into town." I looked back down at the papers. "Does it say here who did find her?"

Steve pulled the file back across the table, and straightened it out, turning back to the initial report, which was pinned to the left of the file.

"A man named Anton Moritius called the police at 6:37 a.m., having gone into Dr. Quinn's office to clear the trash can. He and a Professor McConnaghie were waiting for the police outside her office. Apparently, McConnaghie had the office next door, said he had heard nothing, but had not been near his office for a week prior due to the flu."

"I remember Professor McConnaghie. He used to wear academic robes to lecture, and had model airplanes all over his office. Right, he would have been right next to Quinn. So, Guy must have just glossed all of that and called me after he'd found out about things. I wonder if he even saw her in her office."

"Do you remember what he said to you? Did he describe the crime scene in any detail?"

"Crime scene?"

Steve shrugged. "Suicide was on the books as a crime till 1972, and old habits die hard. The officers there would have been treating it as a suspicious death, until suicide was confirmed."

"Confirmed how?"

"Probably with their finding this," he said, handing me a photocopy of a typed note. A square at the top showed the photocopy image of a paperclip, and a scribble saying *Found in typewriter on desk*. The note was a straightforward declaration that she was taking her life, that she was passing her role of literary executor over to the department chair, with the executor's stipend to go toward the writer-in-residence program, and the rest of her will could be found in her safety deposit box.

"That is the coldest suicide note I've ever seen," Steve said.

"Sounds just like everything of hers I've ever read, though. I can't imagine her not dotting her I's and crossing her T's right down to the last second."

"What about Guy, do you recall what else he said to you?"

"You know, I can't remember what he said, and everything I have learned about him recently, with his stealing my work and all, has really coloured my thinking about him, anyhow."

"Jot down anything that comes to you. It's a red flag to me that he's not mentioned here, for sure."

"You bet. Maybe we shouldn't tell him what it is you do when

I introduce you two at Denise's reunion party, and you can pump him for information under the guise of polite conversation."

Steve laughed. "First of all, entrapment is still on the books as a crime, and second of all, there is no way that a police interrogation would ever pass for polite conversation."

"But what if he cuts and runs when he finds out you're a policeman?"

"Then we'll be pretty sure he is guilty of something."

"But what, you mean?" I nodded. "Yes, I see. He could think he was going to be arrested for plagiarism. It wouldn't have to be murder."

"Murder? You think Guy Larmour killed Hilary Quinn?"

"I am not sure what I am thinking, anymore."

"Why did you decide to cover up the hoax, Randy? I mean, it would have been a hell of a thesis."

I shook my head. "I just loved those books. I was so worried that no one would read them anymore, if they turned out to be just evidence of a hoax, and no one would take them seriously as important entries to the Canadian canon. I figured, since Guy didn't know all of the things Quinn had told me, if I never spoke of it, we could go along, revering Ahlers as a writer cut down in her prime."

I wiped away a rogue tear. "It never occurred to me that Guy would try to pass off another manuscript as a new Ahlers."

"Are you sure it is Guy doing it?"

"Who else could it be?"

"Honestly, I have no idea, but we aren't getting any closer to knowing now. Let's go for dinner and shake this off for a bit."

The minute he said "dinner" my stomach gurgled so loudly that he heard it as well as I did. We both laughed and I went to get my purse. Steve put the file back in order and slid it into his briefcase. As we got into his car, he locked his briefcase into a box in the trunk.

"Can't be too careful. Julia in records would have my guts for garters if I lost a file."

The records person was a woman. I wondered idly if Guy had managed to get into the police station and talk his way past her, to eliminate himself from the file. That seemed too preposterous to consider, but Guy was so far from whom I'd thought him to be that I was ascribing super-villain powers to him in my mind.

We drove out to Tasty Noodle for some dim sum à la carte. Buoyed by the waitress's comment of "you sure can eat a lot," we scarfed down sticky rice, har gow, shu mai, curried squid, shrimp cakes, cocktail buns, and loads of hot tea. Part of my theorizing dimmed as I ate, making me suspicious that conspiracy theorists might all just need a bit more nourishment.

"So, what do you think will come of this reunion?" Steve asked, spearing another pork dumpling.

"Probably most of us will expand our Christmas card list and Facebook friends for a while, but aside from that, I am not sure. I'm bound to spend a year in therapy working out my sense of failure when I get a load of all the amazing things other people have done with their lives."

"You in therapy? I don't see it."

"No? Watch me. I wallow in self-pity whenever I think about Denise's pension plan. Just multiply that by one hundred." He laughed, which he was supposed to do. I wasn't necessarily joking, though. I had grave reservations about what this whole reunion exercise was going to do to my psyche.

"I would say you had a pretty nice life carved out for yourself, Randy Craig."

"I'm not complaining. Most of the time. But the whole lack of security does grind me down from time to time."

"You do know there is a way out of that, right?"

"What do you mean? Are you going to want that last cocktail bun?"

"Go for it." Steve cleared his throat. "I've been meaning to say this for a while, and I have thought it for a lot longer than that." I bit into the lovely coconut warmth of the sweet bun as he reached for what I presumed was a handkerchief in his pocket.

He pushed a small blue velvet box at me and reached for the hand not full of cocktail bun.

"Miranda Craig. I love you. Would you marry me?"

36.

So there I was, proposed to in the Tasty Noodle on the Calgary Trail, at 7 p.m. with the autumn sun streaming through the lattices of the blinds and the tanks of fish and crabs bubbling behind us. It could have been worse in terms of romantic surroundings, I suppose. I knew a couple who proposed to each other in an A&W.

The ring, which Steve told me had belonged to his grandmother, was a series of small diamonds circling a larger stone. It was nestled in the small box in a sea of pale blue satin, though the material was a bit worn and frayed where the tight hinge sat at the back of the box.

Some jewellery just sits there looking either bland or ostentatious. This ornate little ring fairly glowed with love. I stretched out my left hand, which maybe women are all just programmed genetically to do, and Steve slid the ring onto my finger. It fit beautifully. And felt like it belonged.

It also felt tremendously scary.

I looked up at Steve, who was beaming like he'd just won a marathon, and laughed. He looked a bit startled, and then he began to laugh, too. One of the older waitresses ran over to us to ask if everything was all right. Steve smiled at her, bringing her into our complicit circle and said, "Everything is great. We're engaged!" He waved my hand at her, and she began to clap.

There was a flurry of activity, and we were soon having our photo taken with the owner and several of the waitresses, who all seemed to think this was an event worth sharing widely. Finally, Steve threw enough money down on the table so we didn't have to wait for change, and we fled the cheering and waving.

"We'll be up on the wall next to his photo of shaking hands with Ralph Klein, just you wait." Steve opened my door magnanimously and ushered me into the car. I sat and admired my hand, which somehow now looked entirely different, lying on my lap. The diamonds were cut for brilliance, because the sun hit myriad angles and refracted all over the glove compartment in front of me. For an old ring, it gave off a great deal of opulence.

"What's the story on your grandmother?" I asked Steve as he settled in behind the steering wheel. "I've not heard you talk about her much."

"There's not that much to tell that doesn't sound like a lot of grandmothers here. She was the daughter of a wealthy family out east, but they sent her west after the Great War to take care of her brother, because her fiancé had died in the war. She met my grandfather out here, and he asked her if she wanted a diamond ring or a fancy new stove, because he couldn't afford both right away. She told him she'd had enough of diamonds, and would take the stove. I never saw her wear this ring, but it was in an envelope marked for me, the eldest grandchild. It must have been given to her from the boy who died in World War I."

That was both the most romantic story I had ever heard, and a great relief. The ring hadn't been pulled off a dying old woman to hand to me. It had been waiting in a dresser drawer all these years, to commemorate another great—and hopefully this time, not doomed—love.

"It's beautiful and I love it, and you." I smiled over at Steve, who leaned over to kiss me.

"I love you, too, Randy. And don't worry, I'm not going to rush you into anything at all," he smiled. I looked at him in wonder. The man really could read my mind. "We can just keep going on the way we are for now, forever if you want. I needed to make a grand gesture at this point, I suppose. Maybe it's all these people from your past returning or maybe it's my birthday looming, but I wanted to declare to the world that we're a partnership."

"We certainly are," I nodded. "And thank you for doing this before the reunion, too. It will take some of the heat off of not doing much else since any of them saw me last." Steve roared with laughter.

"The old reunion one-upper," he pulled out his Maxwell Smart impression as he turned out of the parking lot onto Gateway Boulevard, heading back to the heart of the city.

"You bet. Engagement to your true love trumps tenure, any day!"

"Well, I was thinking, if you were to write up and publish

your knowledge of the Margaret Ahlers/Hilary Quinn conspiracy, and in doing so find a way to defang Guy the Plagiarist, you might just manage to get yourself a regular gig teaching in a university, no?"

"Oh gosh, I think I might get excommunicated by the Alumni Association! Academe doesn't mind controversy, as long as it isn't within its hallowed walls. Besides, I am starting to think there really are no jobs in academe left for the likes of me. There are too many PhDs who need to land somewhere, and more lining up at the gate. I got three courses this year across the river, but I'm not sure I'll even be on the lists for Grant MacEwan next year, when they can take their pick from specialists who can pinch-hit senior-level courses, too." I smiled. "Of course, writing up the conspiracy would mean I went out with a bang. And I might even get invited to speak at things like LitFest."

"There you go. So go for it! It could even make the novels more popular, you know."

"Just as long as they don't become merely curiosity pieces. Like the J.K. Rowling mystery she first published under the assumed name of Robert Galbraith, you know? *The Cuckoo's Calling* is a damned fine mystery novel, and I've read the others in the series since, but no one reviewed it or commented on its merits. The only story was that it was her branching out incognito, and how many more books were sold once her identity was leaked. The poor book got lost in the shuffle."

"As I recall, that book then sold millions," Steve commented.

"Well, yes, I see your point. Some of those people must have liked it. But it has lost its own stance, somehow."

"Okay, so I sort of get your point, but it hasn't done any good to the memory of Margaret Ahlers if someone else is profiting off of writing another one. Have you read it? Is it any good?"

"It's different from the earlier books, for sure," I said.

"You're sounding uncertain. Is it a long-lost manuscript that Guy or the executors stumbled across? Or is it someone else pretending?"

"It is a very different format from the other novels. It is seven linked short stories. But it has a similar ambiance in terms of location and sensibility. I am not sure, to tell you the truth."

"Can you send it through a concordance program to check it for usage?"

"That's a possibility, but I think they are awfully expensive. I wonder if my web specialists the Black Widows could run that sort of thing for me. They are so on top of tech stuff, they must have some sort of scanning capabilities."

We were by my apartment, and with his usual luck, Steve pulled up into a vacant space right in front of the doors.

"Is it too unromantic to say I can't come in tonight?"

I laughed. "We should be past the point of worrying about things seeming romantic or not, shouldn't we?" His grandmother's ring danced in the streetlight's beam, as I reached up to pat his face. "Don't worry about me. As long as I can parade you around the reunion, I don't mind sharing you with Edmonton's Finest for now."

He leaned in and we kissed. It was the sort of kiss I remembered from when we were first seeing each other, long, searching and dizzying. I pulled back, finally, and drew a breath.

"Maybe there is something to be said for grand gestures, after all!"

Steve laughed, a bit shakily. He had felt it, too. "Maybe, eh?" I got out and he drove off, leaving me to admire my hand opening the door, checking the mailbox and turning my keys in the locks on my apartment door. It glinted at me, as if to say, "Take care of my boy's heart."

"I will," I whispered. "I will do my best."

37.

Denise was the first person I told about the engagement, and she squealed with all the delight of a young co-ed in the early minutes of a horror movie. It was gratifying to have a friend to reflect and amplify the feelings one should have at turning point moments in one's life.

I was still a little bemused and shell-shocked by the whole concept. I wasn't positive about my motives in accepting the proposal, though I trusted Steve's in proposing. We loved each other and he wanted us to seal that pact officially. I hoped I wasn't jumping into security for the sake of security. He deserved so much more than that. I hope we didn't move too fast.

The best part of the whole situation from my point of view was that I could stop having to call him my "boyfriend." That had to be the stupidest word for anyone over the age of thirty, and it was what we had been stuck with for more than a decade. Come to think of it, moving fast had not been one of our problems to date.

My work at MacEwan and at home had taken on a strange rhythm of feeling totally normal for as long as it took for my left hand to move somewhere within my peripheral vision, and then segueing into an odd sensation of getting distracted, slightly hot behind the ears, and forgetting for a moment what I was saying. I am not positive my students even noticed, but Valerie spotted the ring a day after it had taken possession of my hand, and was suitably congratulatory.

"Oh Randy, that's wonderful! Have you set a date yet?" We were standing in the third-floor hallway toward the English main office, where students didn't go until papers were due.

"No, I think just taking this step has been a bit surprising for both of us. We just want to play it by ear for a while." I wasn't sure of that sentiment on Steve's side, but we hadn't actually talked about anything concrete since the engagement. Mostly we had played back and forth with calling each other fiancé. Steve's big joke was trying to make the extra "e" audible.

It was going to make all those awkward meetings between people I hadn't cared enough to keep up with for twenty years a whole lot easier. I too would have something to share with them as an accomplishment or marker.

Valerie's enthusiasm for my engagement made me a bit cautious about flashing my ring around, and I took to shoving my hands into my jacket pockets as I strolled about, giving me what I hoped was a distracted, thoughtful sensibility, but likely looked as if I were planning to rob a convenience store.

The week before everyone was due to descend on us, Denise invited herself over to make table favours for our Homecoming soirée, along with two glue guns, glue sticks, a stack of shiny and matte papers, a slew of scrapbooking edging scissors and a package of googly eyes, which apparently she couldn't resist. She promised she had not purchased any glitter, which someone had once dubbed the herpes of crafting, so I let her into my apartment.

The plan was to make memory signs. Denise had found pictures of professors who had since retired or died, and was mixing them with catchphrases from television shows and advertisements, and old photos of HUB and the rest of campus, together with photos sent to her by people who had signed up to attend. A dark green piece of construction paper went on to stiffer cardstock, and then some gold accents were added. The googly eyes were a nice touch of whimsy, pulling your eye to a lovely variety of reminiscences.

"I think we should stick some back-stands on to some of them, and tape the rest up on the walls, don't you? We can set them on the serving table, and the two coffee tables, and even along the counter of the department general office across the way. Their roll-down gate will be down, but the counter could be a good place to put up the drinks station."

"Have you invited any of the profs we knew?" I asked.

Denise sat still for a moment. "There honestly aren't that many around anymore, but I did send an invitation to some. For instance," she held up the memory card with a picture of Ted Bishop on it, "Ted said he would be there, but then he got invited to read at Toronto's Word on the Street. Bella Spanner might be here, though she snowbirds down to Scottsdale, Arizona and is usually gone by late September. Dale Wilkie will be here and so will Marion Markham. Gary Watson said reunions were appalling things, and Juliet McMaster will be out of town."

"This is going to be so strange," I mused, looking at the photos of Leo, Shannon Murray, and Alan Knight bobbing for apples at a Halloween party. "If it weren't for social media, I don't think I'd even remember most of these people's names, and I am certain they'd have forgotten mine."

"You never know how important reaching back to a touchstone time can be for people, especially after twenty or thirty years," Denise said, with a little too much certainty for my liking. "For instance, the entire Honours English class who graduated that year have all accepted. I am not sure I will recognize even one of them, but they sound eager to reconnect."

"Are there a lot of undergrads coming?"

"Enough to make us a viable class for the Alumni Association, that's for sure. There are more women than men returning, which must say something about the draw of reunions on the sexes, since we seem to be one of the oddly equal departments on campus. Quite a few of those are coming with husbands, but not all."

"Are you going to be bringing anyone to the events as a date?" I asked. "I have to say I am relieved that Steve has agreed to come. People can spend all their energy trying to figure out our relationship and they may forget to ask about my career trajectory."

Denise laughed. "I wouldn't be so sure of that; these are trained researcher/readers, don't forget. I was thinking of inviting someone, but then decided it was more trouble than it would be worth to think about someone outside the crew at the same time as maintaining order. So no, I'll be lone Wolff-ing it."

I applauded her pun, and finished glue-gunning the last pair of googly eyes to the sign in front of me.

"I wonder who will be the first to arrive," I said.

That was probably not what I should have been wondering. I should have been thinking about who might be arriving with more than reminiscing on their minds.

38.

Leo called me from the airport, wanting to know how to get to my place. I persuaded him to find the 747 airport shuttle, which would take him to the LRT, and promised to be waiting at the top of the escalator at the east end of the University Station. If he was too cheap to get a hotel room, he was definitely too cheap for a fifty-dollar taxi ride.

I timed my arrival just right. Within minutes, Leo appeared, rolling a carry-on sized suitcase and hauling a bulging satchel. I offered to take one or the other, and he gratefully handed over the satchel, pausing to give me a bear hug first.

"Randy, you look great! I had visions of you all dolled up in some Chanel suit like Jackie Kennedy, I have no idea why, but I am glad you're not. A pillbox hat would just not suit you. Look at your hair! It's still brown! Tell me you colour it, please. Mine went absolutely grey the minute I stepped away from this campus, I swear. I've been colouring it ever since, thank god for the rise of the metrosexual or I'd just look like a desperate old queen." He gave me another hug. "Oh, it is so good to see you!"

"It's good to see you, too, Leo," I said, and meant it. There was no way you couldn't enjoy Leo once you were in his orbit. It was the exhaustion that set in later that made one leery of his company. For now, though, it was good to have an ally. And Leo was that. He might be flighty and flamboyant, but there were few people truer and more dependable on the planet. Something told me I was going to need all the allies I could take.

We hauled Leo's possessions back to my place, sticking to sidewalks so his rollers could work, with Leo nattering the entire way about the flight he'd been on, the layout of his apartment in St. John's which overlooked the Atlantic, a recent article about a post-theist church in Toronto he'd read, and his success teaching Douglas Coupland's *Hey Nostradamus* to his first-year students. I was glad I lived so close to campus.

After I had settled him in, and made tea, we picked up again. Leo was as good a listener as a declaimer, and soon he had winkled out of me the entire history of my relationship with Steve. At heart, Leo was a romantic, and he was holding his hand to his clavicle in a manner befitting a Southern belle and beaming at me by the time I'd finished.

"I am so happy for you, Randy. Finding a soulmate in this world is not a given, you know."

I stopped pouring tea to absorb what he'd said. Was Steve my soulmate? He was certainly the most constant element in my life, and with all the swirling memories of grad school happening, he compared most favourably to every man I'd ever known, especially since Leo played for the other side.

I looked at the warm diamonds glistening on my left hand. Soulmate was such a strong word, but it landed comfortably into my mind.

I smiled back at Leo, and topped up his cup of black currant tea. "Yes, I am really lucky."

We sorted out Leo's air mattress and sleeping bag, which we agreed could slide in on edge beside my bed during the day and be set up in the living room each evening. He had a list of things he wanted to see, including two or three old professors and a former landlady, and promised not to be underfoot the whole week. I gave him a set of keys and explained that if he came in after I'd gone to bed, he'd have to creep through my tiny bedroom to the bathroom. He agreed not to stay out past ten and I agreed to stay up till eleven. For the most part, we'd be at the same events for three or four of the days he'd be staying, so it would all work out.

I was clearing away our tea things when Steve called. I invited him over to meet Leo and he said he'd be over in half an hour and wondered if he could take us both for dinner.

Leo opted for the Highlevel Diner, so Steve told us he'd park in the Diner's lot and text me when he had arrived. We walked out the back door of my building, and through the alleyway to meet up with Steve. Leo moved in past Steve's proffered hand and gave him a hug.

"I knew the minute I met you all those years ago that you and Randy were meant for each other. Besides, anyone who is smart enough to see Randy for the gem she is has got to be simpatico," Leo trilled. I laughed out loud at Steve's slightly shocked look, which amounted to one raised eyebrow, and then grimaced myself at Leo's purported compliment which made it sound like I was some weird acquired taste, like the anchovy of women.

There was no lineup in the restaurant, a good thing since they didn't take reservations, and we were shown to a table overlooking the hedge of trees masking the bridge for which the restaurant was named.

"When I was a lad, this was a ski shop called the Abominable Snowman," said Leo, who had been born in Edmonton. "I remember the door to the shop was at an angle on the corner of the shop, which I found fascinating. For the longest time, I wanted to be an architect, someone who had the power to move the ordinary forty-five degrees, just because of that door. Of course, by the time I got to university age, this restaurant was opening, and now, of course, it's the institution and no one recalls the layer before. Just like no one going into that trendy coffee shop down the street will recall Pharos Pizza," he gestured elegantly in a southerly direction. "I suppose this entire weekend is going to be filled with this sort of stop-and-start memory dump."

Steve nodded. "That's what reunions are all about, eh?"

"I am hoping people don't find the lack of their old haunts to ruin their homecoming. There is a lot of the university that has changed, but there are bits that still look as if we just walked past them yesterday."

"But you have just walked past them yesterday, Randy, so

how do you know what people will make of it all? In the short walk from the train station to your apartment, I passed only three buildings I knew from before. That new theatre building, the fancy Telus Centre, all the student housing, some of the new condos along the street; even HUB looked like it had received a facelift. And how about the underground train station itself? That wasn't even being talked about when I was here, at least not to the likes of me."

Leo was right. A lot had changed in the twenty years since we'd been students. Maybe Denise had been right all along in determining this was an important exercise for us. Memory was such an elastic thing. Our collective sense of time would shift and sort the past into something manageable for us all. Or else it would drive us all to drink in requiem to our lost youth.

We ordered, and just as the waiter left, my cellphone rang. The number said Telus Public Phone, and it occurred to me that Denise had asked me to leave my number on the reunion materials in case people needed to connect with us. I excused myself, and took the call, walking back outside the restaurant to be polite.

"Randy? Randy Craig?"

Guy's style had always been that of a distracted rock star: seemingly casually thrown together, but calculated to turn heads. His voice was the same, laconic but resonant. My breath felt as if it was suspended in my body, while my intestines were turning to water.

"Guy? You're in town?"

"Yes, just booked into the Garneau Hotel, this shiny new

boutique place where I think there was a flea market the last time I was in town. I had thought it would have more of a campus vibe than the Chateau Lacombe. Seems there are quite a few alums wandering the halls. I couldn't wait to connect with you, though. How are you?"

He had been away a long time, and had no inkling of how the university flavour had spread across the river, overtaking the old Hudson's Bay building with the Faculty of Extension and some of the Business division. Grant MacEwan had moved its full resources downtown, as well, and was a bustling university itself now. He'd have actually felt more at home in the Matrix on 106th than he was going to feel in Old Strathcona. Not that I cared whether he felt at home or not.

"Just fine, Guy. You're here for the reunion?"

"Yes, you are coming to it, aren't you?"

Was he toying with me, or did he not know I was helping to organize it? Maybe he wasn't keeping tabs on me, after all.

"Yes, Denise Wolff is the Class Organizer and I'm helping her, so I will be there for sure."

"Well, I was wondering if there was going to be some time for you and me to get together to talk old times?"

He was fishing, trying to see if I knew about his unattributed use of my work. I was having a hard time trying to keep emotion out of my voice. Letting him know my feelings would give him even more the upper hand. I took a deep breath.

"You know, Guy—" I began, but he cut me off, sounding distracted.

"Randy, let me get back to you." The line went dead.

I growled my frustration, startling a cyclist going by, and headed back into the Diner. Steve looked up at me with only slight curiosity, and I just shook my head that it was nothing. I could share the conversation, for what it was worth, with him later. Leo noticed nothing, and was still prattling on about things he was recalling and missing about Edmonton.

The food was great as usual, though Leo threatened to cause a scene because he couldn't find curried chicken on the menu.

"Don't they realize I dream about that curried chicken?" he wailed.

"So do I, Leo, but I think they just got tired of cooking it."

Leo sniffed, but from the way he was slathering housemade relish on his burger, I had no worries about him enjoying his meal.

Once we had satisfied our initial hunger, we settled in to discuss the upcoming weekend.

"Am I the first to arrive?" Leo asked.

I nodded. "Most of the events begin on Friday, and I think people are either coming in tomorrow night or Friday morning. There are some general campus tours and a couple of guest lectures that you could attend tomorrow, in between your visits and pilgrimages." Leo laughed.

"That is what it is, isn't it? A pilgrimage to our collective youth. You know, I just might take one of those tours."

"The campus, especially out to the west end where all the new science and engineering buildings are, has really changed," Steve said. "A tour of the nanoLAB and such might be kind of interesting."

"Would you have time to join me, Steve? I know Randy has to teach, but we could do a tour and then have lunch on campus." Leo turned to me. "Is there still decent food in the basement of CAB?"

I shrugged. "Not really. Why don't you pick a tour that leaves you done by 12:30 and I can tootle over and take the two of you to the Faculty Club for lunch? I am a member now, doncha know?"

Leo whistled and Steve looked a little surprised. I had forgotten to mention it to him, in all the craziness that had been happening.

"Sounds like a divine plan, darling!" Leo pulled out his cellphone to get Steve's number, and send him a connecting text. Steve reciprocated by pulling out his own phone, which buzzed with Leo's text, and then again.

Steve looked sombre as he read the second text in. He grimaced and made his apologies.

"Can you settle up, and I'll pay you back, Randy? I have to head out right away. We have an incident on Whyte."

"An incident? How intriguing!" said Leo.

"I wouldn't say that, Leo. Homicide is a lot of things, but never intriguing." With that, he bunched his napkin by his plate, rose to leave, taking a quick moment to give me a kiss on the cheek. "I'll call you later."

Leo waited only seconds after Steve had left the building to speak. "Isn't he just scrumptious?" he remarked. "And I don't care what he said. Murder is obviously fascinating, at least from a vantage point of being completely removed from it personally. How else do you explain the popularity of detective fiction?"

I smiled and nodded. "I hear you. But I agree with Steve. Having been a bit too close to it from time to time, it's not something I'd want to ever be involved with."

"It doesn't mean you don't watch *Masterpiece Mystery*, does it? Alan Cumming is so dishy, I watch it religiously, just for the introductions." Leo was moving into archness, a little of which went a long way as I recalled.

I suggested we get the bill and head home for an aperitif. I had some brandy left over from the previous Christmas, and a decent bottle of wine. Leo agreed with alacrity, and soon we were back at my place, sipping wine and reminiscing about life during dissertation and thesis writing.

"So who all is coming to this bun fight, and will I know them all?" asked Leo.

"You probably will know everyone across all the faculties, if I know you. As for our crew, there are approximately thirty-five coming with an additional thirty or so Honours students, though the Alumni Association office warned us to be ready for at least ten more per event, because apparently last-minute decisions get made about going to reunions. I think there is probably an element of talking a partner or spouse into joining you as an ally in running the gauntlet."

Leo laughed. "You're really not selling this all that heartily. I take it Denise was the push behind the plan?"

"You got that right. I just helped send out emails and count up responses. Denise has been the one to organize the Friday party, and coordinate the Sunday brunch and liaise with the hotels where people could get reunion rates."

"Which I for one am so glad I ignored and invited myself to stay with you, Randy. This is so much more fun than sitting on my own in an anonymous hotel room." Leo looked admiringly around my living room. "You have become quite minimalist in your middle age, haven't you?"

This comment led to me explaining about some of the not-so-salubrious adventures I'd had over the years, one of which had been the ransacking of my apartment. Leo was gloriously aghast and kept pressing me for more details, but I didn't like to dwell on the past.

"That really isn't the best attitude to take on the cusp of a reunion weekend," Leo tapped his finger to the side of his nose, in the manner of Paul Newman in *The Sting,* but ended up looking more like an inebriated Lady Bracknell. "Rummaging around in the past is what it's all about."

"Yes, but I hardly knew anyone back then. No one is going to say to me, 'Gee Randy, you have fewer bookcases than before.' I don't know that I ever let anyone except you, Denise, and Guy into my apartment. Oh, Candy and Lynn might have dropped over for tea once, way back then. But if you are dusting off your memories of way back then, you probably will recall that I wasn't surrounded by an entourage during grad school."

"I tell you what I remember the most, was the evening you'd broken your ankle and you sang show tunes to keep the pain from getting to you."

I was touched that Leo recalled that much detail about our shared past. Of course, having that memory of me at my worst be his touchstone wasn't all that flattering. I shook my head, trying to physically remove the memory from my own personal slide show, the way you dissolved the effects of an Etch-a-Sketch when you were ready to move onto another picture.

"Well, anyhow, I am pretty sure that most people will be connecting with one or two other folks, rather than all linking elbows and starting a line dance. We weren't a hugely collective group, as I recall."

"You're right," sighed Leo, obviously relishing the line dance image. "I'm betting we recognize everyone, but I would be hard pressed to put names to them all." He looked momentarily frightened. "We will all have name tags, won't we?"

"Oh don't worry about that. We have name tags with a huge font, so you can check them at a distance before moving in to pretend you remember people. And they are attached to lanyards, making them easier to wear and not lose."

"Oh goodie. Then when I get home I can hang it with my collection of plastic-names-on-lanyards. Wouldn't you like to be the person who invented the lanyard? We have one at work, to wear at all times now. As if anyone would come onto campus and try to fake their way through a lecture on Boswell's biography of Dr. Johnson."

"We have them at MacEwan, too. All the doors are swipe-locked now."

"It's the dystopian future of *Brazil* already happening," Leo wiggled his fingers at me with spooky menace. "Your movements are being recorded and your thoughts monitored."

"Ha, I don't think it's quite that bad," I laughed. "It more like the whole visual recognition element, like school uniforms letting people know where you belong and that you belong where you are supposed to be."

"Oh, speaking of school uniforms, you'll die when you see what I found in my bottom drawer. I just had to bring it." Leo reached over to the left of the loveseat where his satchel and carry-on were tucked, and pulled out a dark green tee shirt. On it was a growling Golden Bear waving a pennant. "Isn't this just too 'Twenty-three skidoo' for words? I intend to wear it to the football game."

"You're going to the football game?"

"Of course I am! I used to go to all the games when I was a student here."

"I had no idea you liked football."

"I like football uniforms, Randy. The game is a bonus."

I offered to make us a pot of tea, but Leo was beginning to wane. It had been a long day for him, what with travelling across the country and not being able to order curried chicken, so I obligingly hauled out the air mattress and sleeping bag, along with pillows and an extra blanket. Leo went to use the bath room while I made up his bed, and I cleared away the glasses off the coffee table, which I wanted to push to the wall so he didn't inadvertently hit his head on it in the night. It was going to be a tight fit in the living room with the air mattress set up, but doable.

Leo came out of the bathroom looking a bit more vulnerable without his glasses. He was also wearing plaid sleep pants and a Mickey Mouse sweatshirt.

"I really do appreciate this, Randy. It's more than just saving the hotel fees. I think coming back to a reunion without a partner to help buoy you up is just the scariest thing. It really helps to be connected."

"I'm glad you're here, Leo." And I was. Catching up and visiting with Leo had kept me from fretting about Guy for almost twelve hours, which had to be a record. Since I had discovered he'd plagiarized my work, I doubt an hour had gone by without me fixating on what was going to happen when we met up at the reunion. I realized I hadn't yet told Steve about Guy's having called me.

As I took my turn washing up and crawling into bed, something Steve had said popped up to the top of my mind. He was off to an incident on Whyte Avenue. I wondered how close that incident was bringing him to the Garneau Hotel, where Denise had booked most of our reunion class.

I hoped his serious incident wasn't connected to our reunion and his body wasn't going to end up being one of our English alums. I hoped Steve wasn't right at the moment running into Guy Larmour somewhere in his investigation. I hoped that my newly minted fiancé was going to be okay to be paraded about as part of the reunion weekend.

I lay under the covers, and turned my ring clockwise, like a worry bead. With any luck, the serious incident would have nothing to do with us, Homecoming would slide by in a breeze, Guy would apologize and rework his research to acknowledge my work, I would get such great student evaluations that MacEwan would move heaven and earth to hire me full-time, Steve and I would get married and grow tomatoes, and life would be merry and bright.

I fell asleep while accepting the Order of Canada. If only dreams could last longer than a night.

39.

Steve called at 5:30 a.m., beating my alarm by thirteen minutes. I had brought my cellphone into the bedroom with me, so as not to disturb Leo, and it was just as well. I fumbled for it, and answered in a croak. "Hello?" At that time of the morning, you don't have to pretend you are awake.

"Randy, I need you to get dressed and ready to come over to the station to make a statement. There has been an incident connected to your reunion. A man registered as Guy Larmour has been murdered in his hotel room. When I was called in, and the identity was made known, I was obligated to divulge the information I had."

I must have made some sort of indistinguishable groan, because Steve hurried up the pacing of his words. "There is no reason to worry. From what I can tell, according to the preliminary time of death, I can give you an alibi for your whereabouts. It is just that we need to fill in some of the background about the reunion, and about his plagiarizing your thesis. If he did that to you, there is precedent that he may have stolen intellectual property from someone else at the U of A. Anyhow, we need to move quickly on this. The hotel is antsy and so is the university."

Steve's thought that I might be worried about being a suspect was slightly jarring, but we had been down that path before, so I suppose it was reasonable of him to assume I'd be reacting to that. I wasn't sure what I was feeling. Something was affecting me about news of Guy's death, of course. I could feel it in my stomach. I didn't want to explore too closely and discover it might be relief.

Like all English majors turned humanists, I tried to live by the whole John Donne anti-island concept of "each man's death diminishing me" but in tourist brochures, islands were linked to paradise. I shook myself mentally, realizing I was still connected to Steve, who was waiting for a response from me.

"Right, I will get there as quick as I can. Do you know how long it will take? I may have to call in and cancel my morning class at MacEwan."

"Call them from here. I will call Denise and see if she can come down, too. Take a cab and get a receipt." He rang off without a closing goodbye, so I knew he had to be in a busy area.

I pushed back the covers and stood up. I had to work quickly, and that always meant forgetting something if I didn't watch out. I headed to the bathroom with a fresh set of underwear in my hand. A fast shower later, with a slather of moisturizer on my face, I was back in the bedroom pulling on a pair of black jeans and a lightly felted pink and black shirt I'd picked up the year before in the Army & Navy. If worse came to worse,

I could teach in this outfit, though normally I went for something slightly more formal, as my way of signalling respect for the students whose task it would be to stay awake staring at me for an hour.

It would be chilly out now and warm later. Edmonton weather was a challenge to dress for in spring and autumn. A cardigan would be warm enough to wear to the police station, which I could then stash in my satchel if need be. I made sure I had my class folder in my bag, in case this meeting went longer than Steve imagined and I had to boot it to class straight from the police station.

I had left a quick note for Leo on the kitchen table, since he was still zonked out on the air mattress as I tiptoed through the living room. The sun was just starting to make the eastern sky pink as I left the building. Once I was out on the street, and walking toward 109th Street, I pulled out my phone and called a cab. I had made it to the vegan restaurant a couple of blocks south by the time a yellow taxi pulled up, and I climbed in.

The south side police station on 51st Avenue was in dire need of a makeover, but I doubted it would ever happen. Who thinks making an alleged criminal's first impressions with the legal system a pleasant one is vital at tax or election time? People would rather get snow removed, potholes fixed, and the scare of Jesus put into petty thieves.

I identified myself at the desk, letting them know Steve Browning had called me in, and didn't have to spend long on the moulded plastic chair bolted to the floor where I had been pointed. Steve came out of the back area and buzzed me through. We wended our way through the desks till we arrived at his. Iain McCorquodale's desk was piled high with paper, but Steve had a different system, with a line of binders across the back of his desk, creating a fence between him and Iain. They had been partners for a long time, but their methods were complementary, rather than identical. Obviously, their hours weren't identical either, as Iain was nowhere in sight.

Steve noticed my glance, and nodded. "Iain went home about an hour ago. He was the first on site and helped document the scene. Now it's up to me to pull in statements from the initial list."

"And I'm on the top of that initial list," I grimaced.

"Afraid so," smiled Steve. "On the plus side, having told me as much as you have already, I think we can make the interview go fairly painlessly, unless you'd rather just make a statement."

"No, we might as well do an interview. I am not sure exactly what you'd want in a statement, so it would probably take me longer." Steve nodded and stood up.

"In that case, let's go into the interview room and get it over with. I might be able to get you on your way in time for your class." I checked my watch. It was 6:30 a.m. I didn't have to teach till ten. I sure hoped we'd be done by then.

Steve spoke into the machine, stating the date, the time, his name, and mine. He also listed a number with a couple of letters in it, which I presumed must be the way they identified the case relevant to the interview.

"Can you tell me how you knew Guy Larmour?"

"We were at graduate school together."

"And why would he be back in Edmonton now?"

"There is a reunion planned for our group, twenty years since grad school in the English Department. About sixty-five people are coming for Homecoming Alumni Weekend."

"And did you know where Mr. Larmour would be staying?"

"No, but if I'd been asked to guess, I would have said the Garneau. Most of the people coming had chosen to stay there."

"Were you in touch with Mr. Larmour since graduate school?"

"Not really, not until this past week. He called me last night."

"He did?"

"Yes, that was the call I had to take when we were at dinner."

"And did he mention during that call where he was staying, or ask you to meet with him prior to the reunion?"

"Yes, he was wondering if we could meet up but just as I was trying to tell him I had no spare time, he cut me off, as if he suddenly had to deal with something else." I looked at Steve quizzically, wondering if he was going to ask about the more incriminating stuff. I needn't have worried.

"Were you aware that Mr. Larmour had published a book recently about Margaret Ahlers, the Canadian novelist?"

"Yes, I just took it out of the library a week ago."

"And why did you do that?"

"Well, I wrote my thesis on Margaret Ahlers, and as far as I knew, Guy had no interest in that line of research. He was doing his dissertation on godgames and metafiction when I knew him."

"And Ahlers didn't write metafiction?"

"Not as such. She was playful in her style, but nothing like the Latin Americans."

"Was Larmour's book familiar territory to you?"

"You might say that. Three or four chapters of it were lifted straight out of my thesis."

"Your thesis on place and voice in the work of Margaret Ahlers?"

"Yes."

"And was there any conversation between you and Mr. Larmour about the use of your material in his book?"

"No, it wasn't until the new Ahlers book was published that I even knew he had published on the subject."

"This new Ahlers book is unusual?"

"Yes, it's a posthumous publication, and when I was studying her work, there was no sign of it, so it coming out after all this time is very unusual."

"Your advisor for your thesis was Dr. Hilary Quinn, is that right?"

So, Steve was planning to get everything down on tape.

"That's right." I pointed at the machine and then ran my finger across my neck. Steve stopped the machine after announcing he was stopping for a moment, and the time. "Do we have to get into all this now?"

"Randy, I think it's your best bet to make as clean a statement as you can. Something very ugly is bubbling up, ugly enough to get somebody killed. Keeping secrets at a time like this just makes you vulnerable."

He had a point, and I knew that whatever was happening,

Steve would always have my best interests at heart. Under the table, I twisted his grandmother's ring, already my go-to way to keep calm and steady.

"Okay."

He started the recorder once more, stating the time, and picked up where we left off.

"Dr. Quinn was a specialist on Ahlers and was personally acquainted with the writer?"

"That is what brought me to the U of A in the first place, yes."

"How close was Quinn to Ahlers?"

"Well, you might say inseparable. They were the same person."

"You are saying that Quinn wrote the works under the assumed name of Margaret Ahlers? What proof do you have of that?"

"Dr. Quinn admitted it to me before she took her own life."

"And did you tell anyone else of this confession?"

"Not at the time. About a week ago, I told you."

"And your reasons for keeping this secret?"

I sighed audibly. Let the transcriber make of that what he would. "My reasons were complicated and sort of stupidly romantic, I guess. I didn't want the power of the books themselves to be diminished by the story of the hoax. Quinn was dead. There was nothing to be gained by exposing her as the author, and mucking up the provenance of the works. And I figured I owed it to her. She had worked so hard to keep it a secret, and staked her academic reputation on writing about the books—who was I to take that all away without her around to defend her actions?"

"So you told no one else of the secret?"

"No."

"Not Guy Larmour?"

"No one."

"Do you think Quinn told anyone else?"

"Not that I know of, or it would have come out by now, right? What is it that they say—a secret between two people is only a secret if one of them is dead."

"And Dr. Quinn took her own life while you were in graduate school."

"Yes."

"Did you identify the body?"

"No. I believe the professor in the next office did that. Dr. Quinn had no immediate family left, as far as I knew." I thought about Dot up north, who was likely long gone herself by now.

"Was Guy Larmour a student of Dr. Quinn's?"

"She was the third internal reader on his committee, I think. I am not sure how much he had to do with her, but he told me she had loaned him her office over the break, in return for him taking in her mail and forwarding whatever was important." I wasn't about to tell the police that I had stolen a look at the last manuscript because of that connection, no matter what Steve said about clean sweeps.

At that point, Steve read another file name into the recorder, identifying it as the inquiry into the death of Hilary Quinn.

"All right. To capsulize this, you believe you are the only person to whom Dr. Quinn revealed she had written the books of Margaret Ahlers. Guy Larmour published a book of criticism about the works of Ahlers, using your work without attribution. A new Margaret Ahlers has recently been published, meaning that either Dr. Quinn had written another book which was just recently discovered or that someone else discovered the secret and has penned an "Ahlers" of their own. And Guy Larmour, arriving in Edmonton for a twenty-year reunion, has been killed in his hotel room, shortly after having called you. Where were you between the hours of noon and 7 p.m. yesterday?"

"I was in the company of my friend Leo Durochers, who has come in for the reunion and is staying with me, from about 11 a.m. onward. I met him at the LRT station, and brought him to my apartment. We then went for dinner with you, until you were called away."

"Right. So this concludes the interview with Miranda Craig on the 21st day of September, at 7:15 a.m." Steve turned off the recorder. "I can get you a copy of this to sign later today, if you want to head out now."

"That would be great. It means I can head back home to sort myself out and make my class in plenty of time. Thanks. By the way," I was trying for casual conversation mode, "how did Guy die?"

"I can't discuss anything at the moment, Randy, you know that."

Steve walked me out to the front lobby, where two grimy-looking young men were looking sullenly at the desk sergeant. "I can get an officer to drop you off at home, if you like."

"Don't worry. There will be a bus along pretty quick, and I

can transfer at Southgate to the 9. I'll be home within the hour." I hated the smell of police cars, and it did nothing for one's reputation to be brought home in one.

Steve knew what I was thinking. "Unmarked car, no vomit. I promise." He pulled out his cellphone and hit a contact number. "Carl? Are you near the station? … Yeah, I would appreciate it if you could give someone a ride home? … No, it's Randy. She was in giving a statement.… Right, well, Keller will just have to deal with it.… Right, thanks." He signed off and smiled.

"Carl is three blocks away in a green sedan, and would be happy to drop you off home. I don't want you having to risk cancelling a class because of me." He leaned forward and kissed the tip of my nose. "I have to get back to work. Take care of yourself, and say hi to Leo for me. Thanks for coming in."

"Are you going to be questioning Denise?"

"Yes, she's coming in at 11; she had a 9 a.m. class to get around."

"Good, she'll have more of the ins and outs of the hotel particulars."

"Right."

"Will we be able to continue with the reunion, you think?"

"I hope so. As far as I can tell, that will be our best pool of persons of interest."

"Oh, I see. Well, unless there is someone else here whom Guy robbed. Let me see what I can find about his other publications for you."

"Not a bad idea. Thanks."

"I am sorry I forgot to tell you about the phone call. I just didn't want to dredge up anything in front of Leo, and then it slipped my mind."

Just then a dark green sedan pulled up, and a man waved to Steve and me. Steve waved back and I hurried out to meet my driver.

Carl was a man of few words, but pleasant enough. We mostly listened to the police scanner as he cruised down 51st Avenue and turned onto 111th Street. He took the curve to 109th Street with the arrogant ease of someone who normally drives with lights on the roof of his car, and I figured Officer Carl hadn't been out of uniform long. I suggested he could let me off in front of Remedy, across the street, and he complied. I popped into the store to get a couple of Kashmiri chais to take home to Leo.

Leo met my offering with delight. "What a wonderful drink! Are you ready for teaching?"

I shook my head as I sipped the pistachio chai goodness. Leo continued, unabated.

"No? I'll give you ten minutes to change into your lecture drag, and then you have to tell me everything. In fact, how would it be if I came with you to MacEwan? You only have the one class today, right? We could pop over to Audreys Books after, and go for lunch downtown."

I agreed to his plan, shut the bedroom door in his face, and quickly changed into a pair of black trousers, a black-and-white chiffon top and a black jersey-knit blazer. I pulled my classier black walkers out of the closet, and shoved my running shoes back under the bed. A dash of mascara, silver and lava drop earrings, and a clip to hold back my hair, and I was ready.

"Woohoo, Professor Craig! How many chili peppers do you get on the rating sites?"

"None, I hope. I try not to go on those places. It makes me feel too self-conscious to think about people discussing me and the manner in which I teach. I barely feel comfortable turning my back on them to write on the whiteboard as it is."

"Oh, I know. I feel like sneaking on and rating myself from time to time, with lines like 'Professor Durochers' sartorial splendour adds a cachet of piquancy to the study of the subject' and see what they'd make of that."

"I can see people booking into your classes in droves for that sort of promise."

"Of course you can. But we can't all teach the Jazz Age by living it, now can we?"

By this time, we were off the bus and walking cross-country through the downtown streets, in order to miss the traffic and construction connected to the new arena. Leo was properly in awe of the changes wrought in the last couple of decades, which made it fun to stroll along. He was especially delighted with MacEwan University.

"My goodness, it's all grown up!"

"It's rebranded itself at least four times since you were here last. At one point it tried to go all lowercase, but people were mispronouncing it and thinking 'ma-ce-wan' was a Cree word of some sort."

I left Leo browsing in the bookstore, with a promise to meet me at the clock in the library at 11:15. That would give him enough time to stroll about and see the whole campus, and me enough time to deal with students after the lecture, pick up mail in the office and do my due diligence in watering the plants by my desk.

It was odd to be standing there discussing the concept of place in the Alice Walker story "Use." Many of my lecture points were drawn directly from my own research into Margaret Ahlers' sense of place in her work. Yet, in twenty years of off-and-on lecturing, this was probably the first time I'd made that connection. The past was hopping up and hitting me in the face all over the place these days. That is what you have to thank reunions for, connecting dots you've not aligned.

Does it make people happier to find tidy patterns in their lives? Is it more satisfying to know there is an underlying reason for why you veer left here, or choose that item on the menu there, or long to wear your hair in a pixie cut even though you know it would never suit your bone structure? It seems to me that life as a glorious jumble of a mystery is a far easier path to navigate.

A good discussion took place between students who were firmly aligned on either side of the argument in the story: whether to use the quilts that had been handed down through the family, or treat them as artifacts and hang them on the wall as art. One particularly discerning student noted that Walker was having her cake and eating it too by writing the story about the incident. "By writing about the quilts, even though she gives them to the daughter who will use them as blankets, she is preserving them as art." I nodded and smiled. Being able to read passionately with a foot in criticism is a fine art, and to see it in first-year students always gives me hope.

I tidied things away, cleared the whiteboard and exchanged pleasantries with the Anthropology sessional coming in to take the room as I left. Soon, I was waiting behind the huge glass-and-polished-chrome clock for Leo to show up. He was three minutes behind time, but that's what you get for meeting at a clock. We decided to head up the road we could see from the window, which was now being called Capitol Boulevard.

"Why don't I treat you to lunch here at the Parlour? I love Italian food."

"That sounds great. I have heard good things about it, but I've not been here."

We pushed the door open and the yeasty smell of bread and the scent of garlic and oregano made both our stomachs grumble. Soon we were seated in a cozy table, with hot bread and cappuccinos, waiting for spaghetti dishes I couldn't pronounce.

"So tell me everything about this morning. What have you heard and what do you know?"

"All I know is that Guy was killed and Steve wanted a statement from me because he knew I had just discovered that Guy had stolen some of my research for this latest book he wrote on Margaret Ahlers."

"The nerve! So you are a suspect?"

"I would be what they refer to as a 'person of interest,' Leo. I am off the hook because it turns out that Steve was with us during the time they think Guy was killed."

"So I am off the hook, too."

"Yeah, I suppose you are. Though, come to think of it, I wonder where everyone else from our reunion class was during that time."

Leo's eyes danced. "This is going to be the yummiest reunion. It's as if we all went to grad school with Jessica Fletcher!"

I laughed. "Yes, it got so I wondered why anyone ever asked her to a party. Someone always died when she'd showed up. You'd think they'd start putting two and two together."

"You are my personal Nancy Drew, Randy. The only two police investigations I've ever been connected to have had you right in the middle of them."

"I swear I am not in the middle of this one, Leo." I laughed, a bit shrilly, and took another piece of bread, buttering it defiantly with more butter than I should.

But deep down, I wasn't sure I wasn't sitting right at the epicentre.

40.

By the time Leo and I got back to my place, Denise had been in to give her statement and had come straight over after the fact.

She and Leo spent half an hour hugging and catching up before we all sat down and dealt with the issue at hand, the death of Guy Larmour.

"Had he called you when he got in?" Denise asked. I shook my head.

"Nope. I checked my phone for ring-throughs, too, because sometimes I miss calls because I've turned the sound off. But there was nothing. Leo and I connected, we met Steve for dinner, and then Steve was called away to the hotel."

"From what I understand, Guy was shot at close range in his hotel room. There was a pillow used as a silencer, but people in the room below heard something, and that was how he was discovered so soon."

"Who did you hear that from?" Steve had been so

close-mouthed with me, and here was Denise knowing everything about the case.

"Myrna Danyluk was being interviewed after me. She came in on the same flight from Toronto as Guy, and they'd been talking in the airport. She was going to offer to share a cab with him, but he disappeared, so she took the shuttle to the hotel. Apparently, she spotted him in the lobby of the hotel later, checking in and talking to someone. She couldn't really say if they were together or had just connected."

"How many people from our group are here already?"

"Well, if you count those of us who still live here, there should have been fifteen already on the ground yesterday, with another twenty-five or so who came in this morning. A few stragglers will be here later on this evening, in time for the events on Friday, and the rest will be here by Saturday morning."

"And Steve is interviewing all fifteen?"

Denise shrugged. "I'm not sure. Leo, have you been called in?"

Leo shook his head sorrowfully. Denise laughed. "You wouldn't like it so much if you were. There is something so unnerving about being questioned by the police, even when you are squeaky-clean innocent." She turned her attention back to me and her earlier train of thought. "I know he is interviewing everyone at the hotel. He probably isn't going to be interviewing the list of professors emeriti who live here still and are invited. You and I were in the mix because of the organizing, I think."

"And the fact that Guy plagiarized my thesis."

Denise nodded. "Right. Although as motives go, that is rather mild, right? I mean, who kills to avenge being plagiarized?"

Leo chimed in. "Oh, but to the police, we're probably all rife with petty jealousies and harbouring vast grudges against each other. Those of us with tenure will be targets of malignancy to those who haven't landed a fulltime job. Sorry, Randy, present company excepted." He went on, gesturing grandly. "Those of us who have books out will be the envy of those who are under the gun to publish or perish. It stands to reason that anyone who has stolen intellectual property amid a crowd of intellectuals would be a likely target for all sorts of people."

"Well, then, thank goodness you are my alibi, Leo."

"Mutual, I'm sure, darling."

"This isn't getting us anywhere, though," Denise said. "We have a party tomorrow night, where walking among us there may be a murderer. How's that for a reunion highlight?"

"Oh sweetheart, it just doesn't get better than that!" Leo gushed. Startled, Denise laughed, and we joined in, the stress of the day fuelling our mild hysteria.

"I think this calls for a pot of tea." Leo got up to fuss with the kettle and tea pot, leaving Denise and me to go over the plans to decorate and haul the drinks up from her car around 3 p.m. the next day. The alumni and professors were supposed to arrive around 5:30, but we were pretty sure some would be early, since the last tour of the campus ended at 5.

"Dr. Spanner has called me twice about the event just this last week, and wanted to know who all was coming for the reunion, and what the plans were," Denise said, sounding rather awed.

The former chair of the department had been retired for several years, but she cast a long shadow still, especially when it came to anything about the writer-in-residence program which had been her baby till Denise took it over.

"So I take it she is turning up for the mixer?"

"I guess so! Wacky, eh? I heard she had declined to attend some fancy centennial celebration of the department a few years back, but she's decided to turn up to our little party."

"Maybe one of her pets from her supervising days is one of the folks coming back?"

Denise nodded. "That's probably it. Anyhow, I am considering it a feather in our caps that so many of the professors emeriti have accepted the invitation. We must have been a good crop, all in all. Now I just hope it goes smoothly."

"I'll come over right from class," I offered, but Denise reminded me I was supposed to be dressed up for the event. "Okay, I'll stop here, get into my glad rags and get there by 3. I can wait out by the loading dock doors for you. Leo?" I called into the kitchen. "When were you planning on getting to the Humanities building tomorrow?"

Leo appeared with mugs dangling from his fingers and my teapot in his other hand. "I can be there any time you want. I have the football game this evening, a tour and a lecture tomorrow morning, and was thinking of hanging around the tent in the quad after that to see if I recognized anyone else. I can be wherever you want me whenever."

"And you don't have to come back here to change?"

"No, I was thinking of dressing a bit more splashy tomorrow

and just going with it all day. By the way, has Dr. Leahy confirmed he was attending? He was my advisor."

Denise pulled her list back out of her briefcase.

"We have Babchuk, Cormoran, Daniel, Davies, Leahy, Markham, McGivern, Samson, Spanner, Tretheran, Wilkie, and Zyp. So yes, your advisor will be there. Does he know you will be?"

"No, we only exchange Christmas cards anymore, but I don't suppose seeing me at a reunion will give him a heart attack."

Denise slid the list back into her bag and dusted off her hands, as if she'd been doing heavy manual labour. "So, the three of us at the loading dock doors tomorrow at 3, and we should manage to get everything up there in two loads." Denise looked pleased. I figured she had been more worried than she'd let on about Guy's death throwing a wrench into all the plans that were underway for the reunion.

Though I still couldn't believe it, Leo trotted off to catch the LRT to snag a good seat for the football game. He was armed with directions to the Saville Field, which was adjacent to the South Campus LRT stop. In his days on campus, that would have been the middle of the University Farm, where a herd of placid Holsteins used to graze. He promised to retrace his steps after the game and be home around 10.

"If not, I will call, don't worry." He waved happily and marched off up the road toward campus. I went back to the apartment, where Denise was pouring herself another cup of tea and once again sorting through her lists.

She smiled with a tired wrinkle on either side of her mouth.

"If they don't call us back to the police station umpteen times, I think everything will go off without a hitch." The stress of the term's beginning coupled with pulling this off was making her look weary, the look we wore at the end of term, not the beginning. Once more, I questioned the wisdom of organizing this reunion.

Denise waved it off.

"This is just fretting about the police. What if it turns out Steve can't be part of things because he has to work the case?"

That had occurred to me. It would be awful to be waving around a sparkly left hand without a fiancé to point to. People might think I was making it all up. Denise wasn't through with her prognostications, though.

"Or they may decide to pin it all on you, even though you seem to have an airtight alibi. Maybe they will decide you and Leo did it together, and are alibi-ing each other."

I looked at her in horror. The last thing I wanted was to get dragged into another murder case. It was bad enough dealing with the whole secret of Margaret Ahlers, without having to fight for one's own freedom. I wondered if it would be a good idea to spill the beans about Ahlers to Denise, right then and there, but I took another look at her pile of lists and decided to spare her, at least for now.

Once Alumni Weekend was over, I would sit her down and tell her everything. When she had less on her plate—that would be the best time. After all, I'd kept it a secret twenty years; four more days wouldn't matter.

41.

Steve came over an hour or so after Denise had left. I had gone through the opening paragraphs I'd taken in from my students, bleeding green ink all over them in the hopes of stirring them into stronger arguments and stances. "Death to the wishy-washy first-year essay" was my motto this year. My satchel was sitting near the door, ready for my lectures on Monday. I had arranged for my Friday classes to see a movie of "The Lamp at Noon," a Sinclair Ross short story we were tackling. I could use the downtime while the film was playing to gather my thoughts and prepare myself for the onslaught of humanity.

Put me in front of a class, or an amphitheatre, and if I know my topic, I will speak with pleasure and little in the way of nerves. Set me, however, in a dinner party situation where I know very few people and I will remain quiet and shy till I've either had a good conversation with one new person or two glasses of wine.

This whole idea of partying with people who were virtually strangers with the added horror of their having known something about me when I was younger and stupider was giving me hives to just think about. Sipping tea in a dark classroom, thinking about prairie angst, would be just the thing to calm me down prior to the party that evening.

So I was quite pleased with myself and my own organizing around Denise's shindig. I explained it all to Steve, who was looking a bit drawn. Although I didn't really want to sound curious about cases he couldn't actually talk about, I had to ask.

"How did it go today?"

He shrugged. "I helped with getting statements, but once Keller saw your and Denise's names on the statement list, I was officially off the case. I'm assigned to my desk for the next week and a half."

I knew that deskwork wasn't his favourite, but this sounded like good news to me. "Does that mean you are still okay to go to the reunion stuff with me?"

He laughed. "Yep, you're stuck with me."

I leaned over and draped my arms over his shoulders, leaning my forehead against his. "You don't know what a relief that is to me. I mean, I am sorry you are on desk duty, but I was so worried you'd be enmeshed in all that stuff and we'd not be able to talk and it would all get awkward and tense, and besides that, I would look so weird with this fabulous ring and no man to go with it."

Steve laughed and hugged me back. "Not in a million years. You are going to introduce me to everyone at that party as the man who finally pinned you down."

We were interrupted from our nuzzling by a key in the door.

Leo was back from the football game, carrying a pennant and sporting a green and yellow scarf he hadn't been wearing when he left.

"We won!" he announced, waving his pennant merrily and ignoring the fact that we were tidying ourselves up for a prime-time audience.

"Would you like a cup of tea, Leo?"

"As long as it's not caffeinated. I'll be up all night if I touch caffeine after 10 a.m."

"It's peppermint."

"That would be lovely. Don't get up, I will go get myself a cup." He returned in a flurry of scarves with a cup and I poured, touching up Steve's cup at the same time. Leo sat down and proceeded to ask Steve all the things I had tried not to.

"How is the investigation into Guy's murder going? Do you have any leads?"

Steve shrugged. "I'm off the case, but from what I can tell, they are going through numbers on his cellphone to determine who he'd been in contact with, and trying to pin down his movements from the time he landed at the airport. An officer is going through the CCTV from the hotel lobby and hallways, to see if there is any correlation, but that's the needle-in-the-haystack sort of search. They're usually set on a five- or ten-second stills shot, so you get jerky motion at best, and people wearing hoods and hats and not looking up. Someone else is going through Denise's list of attendees, and matching them to people signed in at the hotel. Aside from that, I couldn't tell you what lines of inquiry they're following, nor should I."

"Are they going to want to speak to me?" Leo was obviously hoping so.

"I doubt it, Leo," Steve deflated his hopes as gently as possible. "You hadn't seen him at the airport, and Randy can alibi your overlapping time in town. Unless your phone number is on the list they are checking, I don't think you'll be getting called in."

Leo was pretty sanguine, on the whole. "I suppose it would put a cramp in the festivities, if I was, so perhaps it's a relief. I do hope they catch whoever did it before the weekend's over, though. It would be terrible to have to go home without knowing how it all ended."

"Spoken like a true English major," I laughed. "We are so smitten with plot and closure and endings. Even when we talk theory and characterization and motifs, we are all about the plot."

"I'm all about the plot, about the plot, no theory," sang Leo, to the tune of an earworm song from a season or two earlier. Steve and I laughed, and on the whole it struck me that although I might once have, no one in the room was mourning the passing of Guy Larmour.

I wondered if anyone was, anywhere.

Steve left a little while later, promising to shine up nicely and meet me at the Humanities Building at seven. Leo and I got out the air mattress from my room, and soon he and I were ensconced in our separate beds, conducting a conversation à la *The Waltons*.

"Do you think they will catch whoever did it?"

"There is bound to be all sorts of forensic evidence in that hotel room."

"Do you think it was a robbery gone wrong? Or one of us?"

"Leo, I don't know. Maybe Guy had a whole backstory in Edmonton we didn't know about. He could have been connected to something bad when he was here in grad school."

"Maybe you're not the only person he plagiarized."

"Right."

"I hope you're not. Because otherwise, you're suspect number one, right?"

"Goodnight, Leo."

"Goodnight, Randy."

42.

Classes went according to plan on Friday, and I left my satchel in my desk drawer, all ready for Monday. No matter how much partying I did with my classmates of yore, I could be ready to roll come the new week.

I caught the 9 home, jumped into a pair of velvety black trousers I usually reserved for Christmas parties and a black-and-gold pullover. I hooked gold hoops into my ears, dusted a bit of sparkly bronzer over my cheeks and dabbed on a bit more mascara. I was ready.

At 3 p.m., I was waiting under a sign that said, "Turn off your ignition. There is an air intake here." Denise was ten minutes late. Still, she managed to beat Leo, who came loping along from the direction of the Arts Court.

Denise's small car was filled to capacity with bottles of wine and cases of beer. Three bags of cheese and crackers were in the trunk.

"Maybe we could wedge this door open and unload it all in one go?"

"Is there a dolly or a trolly we could use?" asked Leo.

"Let me go check." I said. There was no sign of a maintenance person, who could probably have helped us out in a minute, unlocking some magical cupboard full of rolling stock. I took the elevator up to the third floor, where the secretary of the English department showed me to a dolly they kept for moving boxes of paper in the photocopying room. Promising to get it right back to her, I pushed it back to the elevator and back on to the loading dock, where Denise and Leo had stacked the crates.

Leaving Leo to stand guard over the rest of the hooch, Denise and I wheeled up most of the beer, me doing the manoeuvring of the dolly, and she carrying the nibblies and pushing the elevator buttons.

Another load, this time with Leo along, got all the wine upstairs. Denise left us there to set up the bar, while she moved her car back to her parking area. I found the fun-fact sheets and proceeded to tape them to the walls, as Denise and I had envisioned. Leo was festooning the tables with the plastic tablecloths, and setting them all along the west window. The plates of crackers and cheeses, as yet still wrapped, he placed in groupings of three at either end, with the fruit and pickles in the middle.

Denise clapped her hands, happily. "This is perfect. Leo, was there another tablecloth in that bag? I was figuring we could cover the wee table outside the room, giving people the hint that the party could spill out into the hallway. And once the office closes in," she checked her watch, "another thirty minutes, we can set up the bar on the counter, in front of the grill they'll be pulling down."

"This is great, Denise," Leo smiled. "It's just classy enough to show us we've come along, and still makeshift enough to feel grad-studentish."

"That's exactly what I was going for," Denise burbled. "I wanted us to reminisce about the paper plates and stubby beer bottles of our student days, without it looking tacky and cheap."

Leo gave Denise a shoulder hug. "It's great, and if they don't appreciate it, they're boors who need to turn in their symbol-reading expert status cards!"

I looked around the room. It was perfect. All Denise's planning had paid off. A few streamers, with an Alumni Weekend official sign, were at the south end of the room, blocking what was a non-view of the parking lot, anyhow. The yellow and green tablecloths caught the colours of the banner, and the rest of the room had changed so little in the intervening years that the memory factor was on overload. I could practically see Guy lounging on one of the settees at the end of the room. I shook my head to clear my thoughts.

Steve would be here at six. Some folks would be showing up by 5:30. That left us just under two hours to set up the bar and wait. Denise had put me in charge of registration, so I set up a station on the outside of the doorway, with my box of name tags, and list of names.

We had put everyone's tickets into their name tags, which were on lanyards. It occurred to me that it would be far less embarrassing to just set out all the name tags for people to pick up themselves, instead of risking not recognizing people as they approached the table.

I set them out alphabetically, with the lanyard tucked in behind the name tag. I popped my own lanyard on, as a positive example, and set Denise's and Leo's to one side to give to them. Halfway through my task, I came upon Guy's name tag, bringing me up short once more. This weekend was going to be a minefield of emotions, or as my students said, this would be a time of "all the feels."

Setting his name tag back into the box, which I placed at my feet beside the chair, I took a few deep, cleansing breaths to bring myself into the equilibrium I was going to need for the evening.

"Hi Randy, Denise said to come see you for a name tag." A voice brought me back to reality. It was Dr. Samson, who had just retired the year before, but shared the emeriti office down the hall. He had taught most of us one way or other, since as well as Romantic Poets and the History of Theory course he also had taught the Teaching and Pedagogy course, helping us all to be better teaching assistants and eventual lecturers.

Denise and I had worked out a system to cover the professors we'd invited as a matter of form. We didn't think many of them besides the ones who had officially confirmed would turn up, but we wanted them all to feel welcomed. We had printed up name tags for everyone, but only purchased twenty extra lanyards. I flipped through the alphabetized prof pile, and deftly slipped Dr. Samson's tag into a lanyard. He smiled at me, and popped it over his head. "This is a real walk down memory lane for me. Two of my favourite students are planning to come back this weekend. We keep in touch through Christmas cards, of course, but it will be lovely to see Shannon and Gerald. Do you still keep in touch with your advisor? Who was that again?"

I grimaced. "No, I'm afraid not. I studied with Dr. Quinn, before she died."

Dr. Samson looked flustered, and I made a mental note to figure out how to get around mentioning death to elderly people this weekend. He smiled at me distractedly, and I pointed to the bar, which Leo had set up across the rotunda, to where he gratefully escaped.

While we had been talking, three or four other people had appeared in the area, and were lining up for name tags. I smiled as they found their names and we pretended to remember each other. I surreptitiously checked my watch. It was 5:15. It would be still two hours till Steve arrived and another three hours before I could even think of the party running its course. We had to be out of the building before 11, but at this point, that seemed a lifetime away.

Shannon and Gerald, Dr. Samson's former students, showed up together, which was a good thing, since they were apparently still happily married to each other. I did remember Shannon, but mostly because she and I were connected on social media. She reached out to hug me, which, being Shannon, seemed totally natural, so I hugged her back. I caught sight of Leo watching me and laughing to himself. He had probably already figured out there was going to be more hugging than I was used to involved in this weekend.

More fool I.

The people were streaming in by now, and it made my job a

bit easier. I pointed at name tags, created another three or four professor tags for staff and former staff, and smiled and nodded at people who looked a whole lot older than I felt.

Denise was flitting about, ushering people into the grad lounge, heading over to the bar with one or another alumnus to introduce them to Leo and top up their red plastic cups. She headed over to my table, where there were only three or four tags left out.

"I got a message from Eleanor that she won't be able to come, so we can pull that one, and David and his family get in too late for this event. That leaves Steve, who should be here any minute. I'm going to get Dr. Spanner a drink and then I think things can pretty much take care of themselves, don't you?"

I looked over where Denise was gesturing and spotted the former chair. She had held up remarkably well, and still looked chic and and modern in what had to be vintage Chanel. Her bobbed hair was now completely white, and it suited her complexion of creamy skin and rosy cheeks. It was funny how some women aged into looking like grandmothers and others turned into Anna Wintour.

Denise was still talking. "I am impressed with how many Honours students decided to attend, as well. It makes us look like quite the impressive crowd, don't you think?"

We couldn't see everywhere from our vantage point, but the conversational buzz was strong from inside the lounge, and several groups were creating circles in the open area between us and the makeshift bar.

"Are we sure we know any of these people? I think I only recognize about seven."

"Well, you should mingle and find out."

"As soon as Steve gets here, I promise."

"Why don't you scoop up his name tag, put the rest away for tomorrow at the tent in the quad and come get yourself a drink? Then you can mingle and have fun."

It sounded like an order. I must have been letting the horror show on my face a little too much for her vision of how the evening should progress. I dutifully put away the lanyards into the shoebox and stowed it behind the door to the grad lounge. As I was heading over to get a beer from Leo, Steve came out of the stairwell, and I felt the tension leach from my body.

He hugged me, and shook Leo's hand while receiving his lanyard from me. He took a beer, as well, and soon we were walking into the bedazzled grad lounge, ready to take on the shared reminiscences of people I had never been all that close to in the first place.

"So, is this limbo, purgatory, or hell?" I muttered to Steve, who had done almost a minor's worth of religious philosophy during his Sociology degree.

He laughed. "Nothing close, although introverts would liken it to one of Dante's inner circles of hell, I suppose. I am not sure why you don't like this sort of thing. You can get up in front of classrooms and talk, what is the difference?"

"I'm no extrovert, though. I do it because it has to be done, and because in those situations I am the one with the most knowledge to impart and the means to offer it up. I think I am what they're calling an 'ambivert' these days. I can be in crowd or spotlight situations, but it doesn't feed me like it would an extrovert."

"That makes sense. So, do you think Denise is an ambivert, too?"

"Nope, she is classic extrovert. Look at that glow. Put her in the centre of things and she becomes even more adept, more on point, more adroit. She will be high as a kite for three hours after this party ends, too, whereas I will be ready for an eight-hour nap to get me rested enough to go to bed."

Steve laughed. I steered him over to the wall where some of the memory posters were hanging. He pointed to a photo of the House, the North Garneau home that had been bought up by the university and turned into sessional offices. It was where Steve and I had first met. Like much of what had personal history for me, they had knocked it down a couple of years ago. It was a good thing I'd worked for a while at Rutherford House; it was a designated historic site, so they couldn't pull it down.

We were so focused on the photos that we didn't hear the woman come up behind us.

"You're Randy Craig," she stated, as if she was saying "you're on fire" or something equally abhorrent. As I was turning and nodding my agreement that indeed I was, her hand came up toward me quickly, blurring in its speed and proximity.

"You killed Guy!" she screamed in my face. I noted spittle in the corners of her mouth, and how one of her front teeth was slightly yellower than its twin. She was way too close for my comfort, and as if to agree with me, my collarbone began to throb in violent discomfort.

43.

I heard someone scream, and Steve was somehow wrestling the woman with the bad teeth to the ground. I saw Denise running toward me, but before she could reach me, Shannon Murray was clamping a wad of paper napkins to my neck, telling me to sit down. She was pushing on my neck, right where it curved down into my shoulder, which seemed to pinch a bit, but I felt too distracted by everything to ask her to stop. She was looking stern and telling Gerald to call Emergency. He was suggesting that he might not have the roaming capabilities to reach the local 911, so Dr. Samson pulled out his smartphone and dialled quickly.

Steve had the woman trussed, and was asking a couple of the beefier alumni to keep an eye on her. She had a defiant Squeaky Fromme sort of look to her, and was saying nothing. When I looked at her, she spat at me. I looked back to Shannon, who was holding her compress to my neck, but beginning to look a bit pink along her sleeve. I realized it was blood. My blood.

Dr. Spanner was looking fraught, and saying something about being asked to point me out, and not being aware of the reason, but my focus was pulled back to the fact that I was bleeding out of the side of my neck.

The thought of that was suddenly making me feel a bit faint, but just then, a couple of paramedics stormed into the room with a gurney and a big black gym bag. They came right toward me, which was in itself a bit scary. In that whole room, knowing that you are the one the medical professionals zone in on immediately has to mean something.

Denise leaned into my line of sight and held my purse up, and then pointed to Leo. I tried to nod but that set off waves of pain. Steve squeezed my hand, and then backed out of the way to let the medics take over. I was soon strapped on the gurney, with a tighter bandage on, and an oxygen mask over my mouth and nose. As they wheeled me out, I had a fleeting hope that Denise would find the rest of the name tags behind the door, and then giggled a hiccough, thinking that those three or four people who hadn't made it to the opening reception were really going to be annoyed having missed all this action. This was the sort of special event Sherry Brownlee had been suggesting would make the alumni weekend something to remember for all who attended, and something to regret missing for all those who didn't. Too bad I couldn't personally take the credit for it.

My giggle must have worried the paramedic near my head, because he reached over and patted my hand. "Don't worry, we're going to get you to the hospital right away. My partner has radioed ahead and they're waiting for us."

Instead of reassuring me, this actually made my heart start beating a little more frantically. Why would the hospital need to be on call for me? What had happened? I thought back to the strange woman's angry face, and what she had shouted at me. What had she shouted at me? Where was Steve?

I must have passed out in the elevator, because I have no recollection of the ambulance ride. It couldn't have been all that long a ride, anyhow, since we were only a few blocks from the hospital.

I do recall pushing through the automatic glass doors, and the universal noise of the emergency room, which is two parts moaning, one part baby crying, and a pinch of muttered cursing, mixed in with intercom voices and the constant swoosh of shower curtains being drawn back and forth.

The paramedics handed me off to an emergency nurse and two interns who took my vitals while waiting for the doctor to arrive. She didn't take long, which again was a worrisome thing. It meant I was triaged up to urgent, which is really something you never want to be, in your heart of hearts, even if it means you get through the emergency procedures first.

"Hi there, Miranda," she said, "I understand you were stabbed at a party?"

"Was I?" I croaked. She looked at me as if I might have a concussion, as well. I tried to elaborate. "It all happened so quickly. She just screamed at me, and then my shoulder hurt."

"Yes, well you have a plastic picnic knife thing lodged over your clavicle and piercing your supraspinatus muscle at the very least. It may have nicked a ligament, as well. You are exceedingly lucky that she didn't manage to connect with your subclavian artery or get an inch or two over and hit your jugular. You are also lucky that your friends knew enough not to pull it out. As it is, you've lost a lot of blood and we are going to give you an infusion after we patch you up. How does that sound?"

"Scary."

"Yes, well, maybe you should rethink the kinds of parties you attend, right?"

She left the cubicle, and the nurse patted my hand. "I'm going to have to cut away this top, to get you ready for the surgery." I nodded. My reputation was already in shreds, why shouldn't my clothing follow? Leo could bring me something to wear home, I figured.

Since everyone around me seemed to have it all in hand, and I had been demoted to being a girl who puts herself in danger by going to wild parties, my brain decided to opt out of the process. Any time they went near my shoulder, the pain radiated all the way down to my fingertips and up to my eyebrows, but the nurse kept murmuring to me that they couldn't give me anything for the pain since I'd be under anaesthesia soon. I moaned a little, and then I must have passed out again, because the next thing I knew I was being patted on the right hand, and a voice was calling, "Miranda, Miranda."

I fought to open my eyes. A woman in green scrubs was standing beside me.

"It's time to wake up. You're in the recovery room. You've had plastic taken out of your shoulder muscles and been stitched up, and you've had a pint of blood top-up. You're going to feel pretty weak and woozy for the next few days. We're going to keep you here in the hospital over the weekend, and then the doctor will decide what to do with you, okay?"

I was indeed pretty woozy. I tried to nod, but movement from my head pulled against whatever they had done to my left shoulder, and it felt like a deep burn somewhere. I wiggled my fingers, and they seemed fine, so I decided to take what the nurse was saying at face value.

"The doctor will be in to see you in a while. Meanwhile, there is a fellow outside named Steve Browning who says you will want to see him. Would you like me to show him in?"

I nodded again, and it was worth the burn to see Steve loom up into view a few minutes later.

"Jesus, Randy, you had me worried. How are you feeling?"

He sat beside my bed, and held my right hand. I started to cry. Now that the danger was gone and the emergency was over, my eyes welled up with tears. That's me, always at the ready at the wrong damn moment.

"What happened, Steve? It's all mixed up in my head."

"It's all mixed up in everyone's heads still," Steve grimaced. "The woman who attacked you is named Natalie Dussault. Does that ring a bell?"

"Nope. I swear, I never laid eyes on her before."

"No? Well, she according to her, she had a relationship with Guy Larmour off and on since his grad school days, though it sounds more as if she was stalking him these past few years. She was his student in one of her first-year courses and went into the Honours program to be close to him. When she got to the hotel for the reunion—which she wasn't officially registered for, but had heard about through the Alumni Association newsletter, and was attending with the hopes of running into Guy—she heard about his death, and someone told her that you were involved."

"Who would say that?"

"She won't say, she only admits that she asked someone to point you out at the party. It makes me wonder if there isn't someone manipulating a lot of this behind the scenes. I can't do much more than relay information to Iain and the rest of them at the station, since I am officially not on the case. I was interviewed last night, along with Denise and Leo, who by the way is coming in to see you as soon as visiting hours are open."

"What time is it?"

"Right now? It's just after nine in the morning. They operated on you around 4:30. I guess the emerg was hopping last night, and that was the soonest they could get into the theatre. Still, be glad you weren't taken downtown. A plastic knife in the shoulder would probably still be waiting to be seen at the Royal Alex, while they dealt with the steel blades."

I must have looked as bleary as I felt, because Steve called over to a nurse passing by. She consulted my chart, and told us that I was going to be moved upstairs in about ten minutes, but she would go get me a warm blanket from the autoclave to make me a bit more comfortable.

Pretty soon I was cocooned in warmth, with Steve sitting beside me as I faded in and out. It was almost half an hour before the moving men came to take me upstairs, and they turned out to be one small nurse who refused aid from Steve. She manoeuvred my bed adeptly through several sets of double doors, down two or three corridors, into an elevator and up over a bridge walk high in the atrium-covered hospital. Soon I was settled into a room for four, with two of the other beds occupied. I wasn't in any mood or position to make introductions, so I decided a nap was the better part of valour.

Steve pulled the privacy curtain obligingly, kissed me on the forehead and told me he would be back in a few hours. I smiled a weary smile and watched him move down the length of my bed and beyond the curtains marking my space. The anaesthetic was just beginning to wear off and a dull pain was creeping up the side of my neck and settling in around my elbow. I was just looking for the nurse's button when she appeared, pushing a blue box on a pole with an IV bag hanging from it along ahead of her.

"For the next day or so, you are going to get pain relief when and how you want it. I am just going to attach this drip to your hand." She talked brightly as she swabbed my hand with mercurochrome, found a vein and taped the tube to my hand to avoid it ripping out accidentally. She then pressed a few buttons on the blue box, handed me a control and showed me the button to press.

"However much you want to control the pain, which is going to be pretty impressive as the anesthetic wears off. I find most women tend to underdose, but there is no badge at the end for being a brave little cowboy. If you're in pain, press that button."

I smiled. It was a good speech, and worked as intended. I pressed the button and pretty soon the morphine slid into effect.

44.

The next time I woke up, it was Leo sitting beside my bed.

"Oh my god, girl, you had me so scared! And now look at you, all Joan Crawford gorgeous, hooked up to god knows what. How are you feeling? Would you like a piece of candied ginger? My grandmother always insisted that was what one brought to a sickbed, and do you know how damn hard it is to find candied ginger in this town? If you need any more, it's at Planet Organic, but really, the lengths to which I had to go."

"Water?" I croaked.

Leo busied himself pouring water from the blue plastic carafe into the glass, and pop the bendy straw toward my mouth. He held the glass carefully, and watched to see the moment my lips unlocked from the straw.

"Better?" he nodded, and sat the glass onto the rolling table over my bed. I smiled my agreement, and surreptitiously pressed my button for another jolt of pain reduction.

"How are things going with the reunion?" I asked.

Leo laughed. "That's what you're wondering about? Denise really does have you trained well." He sat back and rearranged what I realized were three scarves around his neck. "Well, last night was a bit of a shemozzle after you left with the paramedics. Steve had Alan Knight and Gerald almost sitting on that Natalie Dussault character till the troops arrived to haul her out of there. She was spitting and cussing, and acting as if she was the wounded party, so Denise had to make a couple of announcements after she was gone to bring everyone else up to speed about things that had been happening. Turned out most of the people there had already heard about Guy's death, so that wasn't all that much of a shock."

"How?"

"Oh, they're all staying at that Garneau Hotel, it turns out. Denise managed to get the best deal in town for alumni, so half of the medical class of '81 is there, too. The whole place was buzzing with the murder and then the Golden Bears beat the UBC Thunderbirds, so that became the topic of discussion. I was over there for breakfast this morning, to meet up with Alan Knight, and Shannon and Gerald joined us. For someone who doesn't say much, Gerald certainly knows what is happening all around him. For instance, did you know that Dr. Spanner was Guy's PhD advisor? Neither did I. Gerald thinks the police should be examining her connection to Natalie Dussault, as well."

I smiled. It amazed me to think Gerald Wandio would even get a word in edgewise with Leo around. And his theories did sound worth pursuing. But it didn't surprise me at all to hear that Denise had worked miracles with the hotel bookings. I was sorry that I'd been the cause of problems for her alumni weekend. For the amount of effort she put into things, it should have come off without a hitch.

Leo must have been able to read my mind, or perhaps it was because of the same old "don't play poker" face that Steve teased me about.

"Don't worry about messing things up, Randy. For one thing, you can't help it if a homicidal fangirl goes on the attack, and for another thing, you have been instrumental in making this a homecoming weekend no one is ever going to forget. You should have seen those doctors this morning looking longingly at our table. I am just hoping their organizer doesn't off one of them just to match us."

I laughed, and far from being the best medicine, it caused a seismic wave of pain radiating from my collarbone, making even my intestines wince. Leo winced too, in sympathy. "Oh Randy, I am sorry. I will try to be less entertaining and diverting. Don't laugh. Let us pray."

I smirked. Leo was going to make me use up a day's worth of morphine if I didn't watch it.

"Did you talk to the police?"

"Oh my, yes. I spoke with Steve's partner, who, let me tell you, is not your greatest fan. I think that most of that is because Steve is officially not on the case, due to being part of the *mise en scène,* and that means more work for Officer Iain." Leo flicked one of his scarves. "They had us all processed and interviewed and in and out before 11, because the university security folks were hovering and wanting to lock up the building. I tell you, there is just something about a man in a uniform, and they were milling about everywhere last night!"

"What is happening today, then?"

"Denise was hoping to get by to see you after she has done her shift in the homecoming tent in the Quad. There didn't seem to be a way out of that, because that is the price you pay to the Alumni Association for having your events publicized in their online newsletters and in the *New Trails* summer issue."

"That publicity is what got me here, though, right?"

"I don't think they're focusing on that."

"Are you going over there?"

"Yes, I thought I would join her for a bit, and then get myself a Tuck Shop cinnamon bun and do a campus tour. The dinner at the Faculty Club has already been prepaid, so I wasn't planning to miss that, either. But I could come back here after dinner?"

I shook my head slowly. I probably didn't need Leo pouting about missing anything, and I figured Steve would be back to see me later, anyhow. The thing that worried me was getting keys back from Leo when he had to leave on Sunday night. We sorted out the fact that since Steve had a key to my apartment, Leo could just leave the keys on the table and pull the door closed with only the doorknob lock. All this, of course, was contingent on me still being in the hospital, which I wouldn't really know about until I saw the doctor.

I waved Leo off and drowsed a bit more.

45.

Around 3 p.m., the surgeon who had patched up my shoulder appeared. She seemed awfully young to have been tinkering with my trapezius, but I was too tired to worry about it. She explained the various bits she had patched up, but I had a hard time following what would dissolve naturally as the muscle knitted back together and what I would have to come back to the outpatient area to have removed and seen to in a few weeks.

Her determination, after poking around under the huge white bandaging on my left shoulder, was that I would likely be a guest of the University Hospital for another couple of days, but after that I should be able to pick up my life as usual, with only a few modifications. As she left, I tried to sort out in my mind what I would have to do. If Steve could call the English Department on Monday, or pick up my laptop and bring it over to help me write an email, I could have my Monday and Tuesday classes cancelled. This early in the term, it would be no hardship to the students, who would probably give me higher points on Rate

My Professor as a result. I could cut one short story from the syllabus and still manage a good cross-section.

I would have to apologize to Denise for copping out of helping her with the tent event, but the rest I decided to forget about. Since I still couldn't even place the woman who had stabbed me with plastic cutlery, what help was I going to be at a reunion?

I surrendered myself to the rhythms of the hospital, and was pleasantly surprised to see Steve standing beside my bed the next time I woke up.

He reached over to squeeze my hand on the unbandaged side of my body, but even so I must have winced, because he just patted it and sat down next to my bed.

"Does the name Natalie Dussault mean anything to you now?"

"No. I've been trying to place her and I'm still getting nothing."

"Don't worry about it. No one at the reunion seems to be any the wiser, either. She apparently was doing a BA in English around the time you were doing your MA and Guy Larmour had been her TA for English 100. It's pretty clear from her statement that she figures they had a closer relationship than just student and TA. According to her, she was going to be meeting him this weekend to rekindle their love."

"And she stabbed me because she thinks I was the one who killed him?"

"Supposedly. At any rate, she has associated you with his death, so I think we need to pay attention to the angle that Guy was killed by someone associated with the whole Margaret

Ahlers/Hilary Quinn situation. The woman is clearly insane, but sometimes people like that have an uncanny instinct for an actual truth."

"Leo was saying something about Gerald thinking something useful."

"Yes?"

I tried to pull back the conversation I'd had with Leo, but my thoughts were blunted and fuzzy, no doubt due to the little button close by my hand. "It was something about Guy," was all I could manage.

"Don't worry about it. I am sure Iain and his crew will be on top of things. I've briefed him on all the nuances, so he'll be aware of what to be looking for."

"How can I help you?"

"You can help me by resting up and getting mended and out of here. I'm not on the case, remember? Even more so, now that you are perceived as another victim, rather than just a person of interest in the original murder."

"If it was the original murder," I said.

"What do you mean?"

"Well, with Guy's death and this Natalie's focus, I am leaning more and more to the possibility that Hilary Quinn was murdered, and didn't actually commit suicide. There is someone else moving around in this. But who else benefits? Guy gets a book deal. The writer-in-residence trust gets the executor's stipend. Ahlers' heirs get whatever royalties roll in. You have to follow the money, Steve."

"I think Iain and the crew are way ahead of you on that one, Randy."

"I should have said something then, shouldn't I? If I had come forward about Quinn's hoax, maybe none of this would have happened. She might even still be alive."

"You can't readjust the lens like that. You have no idea how events would have played out."

"Actions have consequences, and inaction does too."

"And sometimes fate takes a hand. If Hilary Quinn was willing to move outside the way things are done, taking what seemed to her to be a shortcut to success, then she was probably prepared for the consequences of those choices."

"Do you think people are ever prepared to be murdered?"

"Once you move to the dark side, you are subconsciously prepared for anything. Your sense of morality skews to believing that everyone has the same wonky compass as you do, and therefore you are more likely to expect bad from others rather than good."

"That make sense, but it makes my head hurt to think about it." I tried to smile, but reached for the morphine button instead. Steve took that as a hint, and leaned over to kiss me.

"I'll be back in the morning, sweetheart. You get some rest."

Who am I to go against police orders?

46.

I slept, for how long I wasn't sure. The next thing I knew it was dark, the room lit only by the spill of light from the corridor and the buttons and numbers on the blue machine at my bedside. As I looked on drowsily, one of the numbers went out. No, only half of it went out.

My sleepy brain computed that a hand was moving across the machine, obscuring the number from my vision. I must have made a little grunt of comprehension, because the hand stopped, and my eyes took in the complete shadow of the person beside my bed.

There was something familiar about the outline, but I couldn't put a name to the face, which I had a hard time making out in the dim light, anyhow. It was a woman, wearing scrubs, with a long sleeved shirt underneath. She seemed older, maybe something to do with the slope of her shoulders, or the prominence of her knuckles on the hand that was still frozen by my morphine machine.

It wasn't Siti, my nurse, that I could tell. Aside from the thirty more years on the clock, this person didn't have any of the aura of a competent, nurturing caregiver. There was something off about everything.

I searched my foggy brain for an old woman to slot into the mix. Dale Wilkie, whom I'd spoken with at the reunion party wasn't old enough, nor could I imagine her sneaking into my room in the middle of the night.

Dr. Bella Spanner, former chair of the department, and the person who had identified me to my would-be assassin, swam into my brain. That's when I recalled what I had been meaning to tell Steve. Dr. Spanner had been Guy's PhD advisor. And she would have been the connection to the literary executorship of Ahler's will when Dr. Quinn was killed.

Was Dr. Spanner the killer? Was she here to confess? Or kill again?

I reached for the call button, but it wasn't where I remembered it being. I tried to turn my head to find it, but everything was getting much foggier than I'd felt earlier in the night. I wondered if I'd pressed the morphine button by accident in my sleep.

"So you're awake? That is better," the figure whispered to me. Even in my groggy state, I knew that whisper was not the voice of the woman whom I had recently heard giving a five-part *Ideas* series on the CBC about Thomas Pynchon and the eccentricity of creativity. Dr. Spanner wasn't the mystery woman.

But I knew that voice. Cold and distant and acerbic, even after all these years. And all at once I knew who was in my hospital room in the middle of the night.

Hilary Quinn wasn't a corpse for Iain McCorquodale to exhume. She was still alive, slightly altered. Maybe she had received some plastic surgery, maybe she had just got old. I was betting it was the former.

I felt a bit guilty assuming a scholar like Dr. Spanner was also a cold-hearted killer. Quinn hadn't been murdered, nor had she taken her own life. Here she was in my hospital room, making me decidedly uneasy.

So if she had orchestrated her own disappearance all those years ago, that meant she had killed someone to take her place that night in her office, probably much as I had imagined at some point. That sort of act took planning and cool reserve.

And she had probably killed Guy, too, if he had worked it all out, or she had run into him somewhere in his plagiarizing adventures. Maybe he had worked it all out and was trying to blackmail her to keep quiet. Or maybe I was just hallucinating all of this.

"You're finally putting the pieces together, Miranda? Frankly, I was surprised you hadn't done so earlier, but then you just walked away from the whole story, didn't you? Defended your paltry little thesis and let sleeping dogs lie."

"Seven for a story never told," I whispered. It was hard to speak, and I realized that Quinn's hand had been monkeying with my morphine drip. I was getting too big a dose. Her hand wrapped around the button dispenser and pressed again.

"Yes, well, times being what they are, a lost manuscript can bring a little ready money into the estate. I might as well fill you in, as you head into the arms of Morpheus."

This wasn't a morphine nightmare. My former advisor, whom I had thought dead for twenty years, was totally alive and in my hospital room, about to kill me. Of course, as soon my emotional brain put it that way, my logical overlay determined it had to be a morphine dream.

"I didn't expect your silence about the novels. My plan had been to create the suicide scenario to leave you with everything tied up in a bow. Penitent ghostwriter of books of a fictional author, sacrifices herself for the sake of propriety and art, sales skyrocket, ghost of ghostwriter slinks away to spend the rest of her days beachcombing in Belize." Her fingers busied themselves with something on the blue box on the morphine stand, but it was as if I was mesmerized, a loagy rabbit watching an oncoming snake in slow-motion horror.

"But no, instead, you do nothing! You defend your thesis, and do nothing with it. You don't go to a conference, you don't give a paper, you don't even try to get it published. My death is a nine-days' wonder, and it isn't until Larmour decides to cash in on lesser-known studies from back home that Margaret Ahlers surfaces at all."

"Guy found you out?"

She laughed. "No, while he was writing the book he cribbed from your thesis, he tackled Bella about the proprieties of the estate, who wrote to Ahlers' 'cousin' who lived in the Caribbean. McKendricks sent the royalty cheques to the university where Bella carved off the executor's fee before shipping the rest to Ahlers' heir apparent. With the reunion happening, he wrote to her again and she got in touch once more. I suppose she thought he was sniffing around ready to possibly kill the gravy train, as meager as it was, so she was more than willing to forward a new manuscript to the publishers that the cousin had 'discovered' in my papers."

"*Seven Bird Saga*," I muttered.

"It was something I'd been tinkering with for a while. It's not as if I had all that much choice. Even though it's cheap to live in the tropics, one still has to pay one's bills. I had to do something because the royalties were drying up; no one was teaching Ahlers in their classrooms anymore, the first book was going out of print. And it's not as if I could teach. It's one thing to fake a passport and driver's licence—I just kept up my late cousin's paperwork and shifted into becoming her. It's quite another to produce a fictional CV. So I figured I'd give in and write another book.

"Don't even get me started on trying to get a first book published by an unknown writer. Besides, what else is there to do when you're hidden away in paradise? Joseph Conrad wasn't creating a metaphor after all, you know. Idleness in a tropical stupor can drive you crazy."

"You weren't working together with Guy way back when?" My voice sounded slurry and as if I was speaking from down a deep well. I hoped Lassie was off getting help.

"While you were nosing around? No. He was a convenient distraction for you, that is all. Having a grad student trying to do research into Ahlers while I was trying to keep her background fuzzy was not an easy thing, you know." Quinn sounded as if she were chastising me for interfering with her plans. "I was frankly as surprised as you that he turned out to be a thief. He swiped a bunch of work on Frederick Philip Grove from a foreign student who submitted the year before you did, too, by the way. If the academic police come digging, they're going to find more to cavil about in Guy Larmour's closet than in mine, that is certain."

"You killed people."

"Well, besides that. I am speaking of academic and creative matters. The others were necessary evils of the path I'd chosen."

"You killed Guy."

"I was doing academe a favour, believe me. And he was getting a little too nosy for my liking."

"And Natalie Dussault?"

"Oh that was just kismet. She was crying in the hotel restaurant, at a table right beside mine. A couple of well-placed hints and a bit of innuendo turned her into a superb weapon. If only she'd gone for a cheese knife instead of a spork."

She stood at the end of my bed, and I could sense she was smiling that same tight little smile that would follow one of our uncomfortable graduate sessions.

"There is very little left to say. You won't be waking from the nap you're about to take, not with the amount of morphine in you I have given you. And don't bother looking for the call bell."

"I'll scream," I croaked. Quinn laughed.

"We've been chatting away quite a while and neither of your neighbours here have noticed. I think they're drugged, you know. Besides, vocal cords are so temperamental when narcotics are concerned. It's as if they are the first to shut down. I'll just leave you, shall I?"

"But you haven't explained it all," I wheezed.

"I've noticed that people who spend their getaway time explaining things to their victims tend to get caught more often than not. I have spent too much time living in the shadows for the last couple of decades to want to get nabbed now. It was foolish pride that kept me here to talk to you at all. Goodbye, Randy Craig."

She was gone, disappearing into a hospital filled with tired-looking workers in scrubs. She could get away on the LRT with no one looking at her the wiser.

I reached for where the call bell was pinned to the sheet of my bed. It was gone. She had also pushed my table out of the way, making it impossible for me to reach anything to throw on the floor and make a sound.

I tried to call out to the sleeping people on the other side of the curtain. My voice barely sounded like a sigh. I was going to fall asleep and die here in a hospital bed on the fifth floor of the University Hospital, where I would become just another sad statistic. And Hilary Quinn would disappear again.

Well, if I couldn't throw a thing on the floor, maybe I could throw myself. I took a breath, which felt ragged, and pushed myself over onto the bad shoulder. The sharp pain cut through the morphine cloud for a moment, making me gasp. This was not going to be pretty, but the alternative would be much, much worse.

I pitched myself off the bed, bringing the morphine tower crashing down beside me, and a heartening beeping alarm began to sound from the overturned equipment. Before I passed out from the pain and the drugs, I thought I heard the sound of running feet.

47.

It took two days for my system to clear itself of the narcotics. Thank goodness the fall had pulled open the repairwork in my shoulder—necessitating a return to the OR, instead of just tucking me back into bed—or they might not have noticed the incipient overdose. As it was, the anesthetist took one look at the colour of my skin, tested my blood pressure, and connected the dots. They got me on naloxone, the antidote to a morphine overdose, right away, but it was several hours before I was in a state to be sedated properly for repairs.

It was apparently also touch-and-go for a while with my respiratory system, so I wasn't the one giving Steve the earliest news about Quinn. She was long gone and still at large, but Iain had managed to get a semi-coherent statement out of Natalie Dussault, my cutlery-wielding attempted murderer.

An older woman at the hotel had told her about my involvement with her longtime dream date, Guy Larmour. They had managed a composite drawing of Quinn from Natalie, which ended up looking a lot more like the Quinn of my memory rather than the present-day shadowy Quinn of my hospital room.

Quinn had apparently decided to use the crazed younger woman as a weapon against me, offering her a buffer between her actions and desires. What she hadn't counted on was Natalie not having enough of an anatomical aim for the jugular or the sense to use a proper weapon, and the Canadian police force not killing Natalie before she could divulge her incriminating babblings.

I wondered if my recollections of Quinn's looks changing in the hospital had been due to the morphine. Steve wasn't so sure, and sent the police artist to me for a second sketch. This one ended up looking like Quinn with a slightly more pronounced jaw, wider nose, and eyes slightly tilted. Whatever plastic surgeon she had used must have wondered at the choices that made her less attractive and distinctive.

Steve took the new sketch to the airport, to pass around among the security agents and ticket folk who worked the tropical flights. She looked familiar to two or three people, one of whom had fixated why someone who actually lived in the tropics would ever want to holiday in Edmonton. Everyone's a critic.

While Iain and Steve were researching extradition agreements between Canada and various Central American countries, I was recuperating at home. Denise had taken Leo off to the airport, but before he left he had rearranged my spice rack, dusted the shelves in the front room and bought a huge bouquet of freesias for the kitchen table. It was a salve to the fact that I had lost the classes I was teaching at MacEwan to a replacement sessional. Oh well, it wasn't as if the students had had time to imprint on me, like orphaned ducklings following the farm's red setter about.

Of course, I also had a wedding to plan, which ought to keep me busy for a year, if the emails I'd been getting from my mother were anything to go by. I had no idea she'd be this excited with our news, and it made me feel a tiny bit guilty that I'd not managed to bring her this sort of gift earlier. She and my father were thrilled I was marrying Steve, and I had a sense they were secretly more in love with him than I was, if that was possible. He had made a great impression on them the first time they had visited me, and they had been including him on the Christmas gift roster ever since.

I was answering the third email of the day from her just as a strange email address popped up on my screen. It was from Goldwin's, a respectable publishing house. Thinking it had to be a come on for some sort of purchase, I waited till I had finished Mom's letter, in which she was extolling the value of creating registry lists in a country-wide chain department store, to aid everyone in purchasing wedding presents.

The letter from Goldwin's was written personally to me by the chief editor, Marissa Dayn. She had heard about my involvement in the works of Margaret Ahlers and understood there was a story regarding creativity, fraud, murder, and mayhem in Canadian academe that they would be interested in publishing, and I might be interested in writing. Would I be interested in taking a meeting by Skype in the next day or two to discuss her idea?

Would I ever. If Hilary Quinn and Guy Larmour could profit from deception and blood, why shouldn't I? It was a story I was perfectly equipped to tell. And who knows, after I got through all the research and the rewrites, if academe didn't want me, maybe I could make my name as a crime writer.

Stranger things had happened.

ACKNOWLEDGMENTS

This has been a strange voyage, jumping back in time to an earlier book and grafting it into a whole new story. There were people then whom I thanked who are gone from this world, and a few who would be decidedly off a present list. At the same time as this story took me back into Randy Craig's world, I had to revisit pockets of my past I'd sewn shut so the coat would hang better. This really wasn't the easiest of projects, but I am so much happier with this way of serving up the genesis story than with people digging up old copies of that first slender novel and judging me. Besides, it won't fit on the same shelf with all your other pretty volumes.

I'd like to thank the folks at Turnstone for allowing me to find a way to bring a lost story back into circulation—Jamis Paulson had a quizzical look in his eye when I proposed it, but he let me try. Sharon Caseburg, my editor, juggled the established norms of the previously crafted work with the story arc that had grown in the meantime, and kept me sane. And Michelle Palansky has championed this strange hybrid of a book to everyone who would stand still to listen. What's more, between them, they have crafted another gorgeous book to hold, to keep, to sit in pride of place as number six, as well as number seven or perhaps number one (it's a mystery!).

My friends and family continue to be supportive, interesting and fun to be with. You are all intelligent and attractive. Thanks especially to Marianne Copithorne and Martina Purdon for cheering me on; Conni Massing for tackling university with me in the first place, as well as recent reminiscences about the beauty of youth; Susie Moloney and Suzanne North for commiserating on the process; Sandra Gangel and Wayne Arthurson for sharing the genre road; Candas Jane Dorsey, Timothy Anderson and Cora Taylor for being there with laughter; Dale Wilkie, Jim DeFelice and Tom Peacocke for championing me; Kate Orrell, Kelly Hewson, Alan Penty, Brad Bucknell and Marni Stanley for living it with me; Gudrun Hansen for being outside the door the day I defended my MA with a cup of coffee and a rose; Michael Rose for the hospitality whenever we blow into town; Sabra Kassongo for graciously sharing her baby for hugs and giggles; Dianna Wilk, Angela Pappas, Var Passi and Arif Kassam for keeping me centered during the workaday world; Mary Montgomery, Valerie Bock, Cheryl Fuller, Morgana Creeley, Karen Hanson, Kristie Helms, Kathryn Nettles, Jo Howard, Andrea Lobel, Howard Rheingold, Richard Lee, and Iain McCorquodale for being the best imaginary friends; Jossie and Maddy Mant for delighting me always; and the wonderful and virile Randy Williams for loving, cherishing and promoting me.

To the Alumni Association of the University of Alberta, I wish you a very happy centennial. To Sherry Brownlee, I appreciate your support for the Freewill Shakespeare Festival. To Steven Sandor, Axel Howerton, and Jason Lee Norman, thank you for recently letting me show the world some facets beyond Randy Craig. To Sharon and Steve Budnarchuk, Kelly Alanna, Barry Hammond and Michael Hare, bless you for hand-selling the whole series. To Angie and Linda and Matthew, blessings on your heads for reading it with blurbing in mind. To Kim at the Highlevel Diner, thank you for the bread pudding and the hug whenever I come in.

And thank you to the stalwart readers of this series. You are amazing: you have taken a heroine who is not quite young, not quite invincible, not quite hardened and yet definitely not cozy, into your collective hearts. By dint of your loyalty and your no doubt annoying insistence to your friends that they read an obscure mystery novel set in Edmonton, Alberta, you have turned Randy Craig into a household name. Well, a condo-sized household.

On the whole, this one's for you.

Sticks & Stones

by Janice MacDonald

How dangerous can words be? The University of Alberta's English Department is caught up in a maelstrom of poison-pen letters, graffiti and misogyny. Part-time sessional lecturer Miranda Craig seems to be both target and investigator, wreaking havoc on her new-found relationship with one of Edmonton's Finest.

One of Randy's star students, a divorced mother of two, has her threatening letter published in the newspaper and is found soon after, victim of a brutal murder followed to the gory letter of the published note. Randy must delve into Gwen's life and preserve her own to solve this mystery.

Sticks & Stones / $14.95
ISBN: 9780888012562
Ravenstone

The Monitor

by Janice MacDonald

You're being watched. Randy Craig is now working part-time at Edmonton's Grant MacEwan College and struggling to make ends meet. That is, until she takes an evening job monitoring a chat room called Babel for an employer she knows only as Chatgod. Soon, Randy realizes that a killer is brokering hits through Babel and may be operating in Edmonton. Randy doesn't know whom she can trust, but the killer is on to her, and now she must figure out where the psychopath is, all the while staying one IP address ahead of becoming the next victim.

The Monitor / $10.99
ISBN: 9780888012845
Ravenstone

Hang Down Your Head

by Janice MacDonald

Some folks have a talent for finding trouble, no matter how good they try to be, especially Randy Craig. Maybe she shouldn't date a cop. Maybe she should have turned down the job at the Folkways Collection library—a job that became a nightmare when a rich benefactor's belligerent heir turned up dead.

Randy tried to be good—honest!—but now she's a prime suspect with a motive and no alibi in sight.

Hang Down Your Head / $16.00
ISBN: 9780888013866
Ravenstone

Condemned to Repeat

by Janice MacDonald

For anyone other than Randy Craig, a contract to do archival research and web development for Alberta's famed Rutherford House should have been a quiet gig. But when she discovers an unsolved mystery linked to Rutherford House in the Alberta Archives and the bodies begin to pile up, Randy can't help but wonder if her modern-day troubles are linked to the intrigues of the past.

Condemned to Repeat / $16.00
ISBN: 9780888014153
Ravenstone

The Roar of the Crowd
by Janice MacDonald

Wherever Randy Craig goes, trouble seems to follow. With the help of her friend Denise, Randy has landed a summer job with a high school theatre program linked to the FreeWill Shakespeare Festival. But when a local actor shows up dead and Denise is the prime suspect, Randy has to find to a way to solve the mystery while surrounded with suspects who have no trouble lying to her face.

The Roar of the Crowd / $16.95
ISBN: 9780888014702
Ravenstone

Janice MacDonald is the author of eleven books, including novels, non-fiction titles, and a children's book. She has been widely anthologized, and her popular Randy Craig novels were the first mystery series set in Edmonton. Janice has taught English literature, communications, and creative writing at both the University of Alberta and Grant MacEwan College. She currently works for the the Government of Alberta. Born in Banff, Alberta, Janice lives and writes in Edmonton. You can visit her online at www.janicemacdonald.net.